A great story!

Judith

PinChiNg
ZWieBaCK

Pinching Zwieback

Made-up Stories from the *Darp*

MITCHELL TOEWS

AT BAY
press

WINNIPEG

Pinching Zwieback

Copyright © 2023 Mitchell Toews.

Design and layout by Matthew Stevens and M. C. Joudrey.

Published by At Bay Press October 2023.

Some of the selections in this collection have previously appeared in various forms in periodicals: *Groota Peeta* in *River Poets*, *Nothing to Lose* in *Fiction on the Web*, *Fast and Steep* in *The Moon*, *Died Rich* in *Fabula Argentea*, *The Raspberry Code* in *Voices*, *Fall from Grace* in *Fiction on the Web*, *The Peacemongers* in *The Moon*, *A Vile Insinuation* in *CommuterLit*, *Sunshine Girl* in *Cowboy Jamboree*, *Mango Chiffon* in *Agnes and True*, *Breezy* in *Literally*, *A Heckuva Thing* in *WordCity*, *Worth of Sparrows* in *CommuterLit*, *Narrowing* in *Scarlet Leaf*, *In the Dim Light Beyond the Fence* in *Riverbabble*.

Library and Archives Canada cataloguing in publication is available upon request.

ISBN 978-1-998779-05-5

Printed and bound in Canada.

This book is printed on acid free paper that is 100% recycled ancient forest friendly (100% post-consumer recycled).

First Edition

10 9 8 7 6 5 4 3 2 1

atbaypress.com

I went to the window
saw sheets and pillowcases flapping

the wind   in march
was cornflower blue

—Patrick Friesen

Title

"Zwieback" is the High German name for a double bun. Also *"Tweeback,"* in Low German, this iconic staple dates back to sixteenth-century Netherlands and may be found today wherever American or Canadian Mennonites break bread.

Pinching *Zwieback* is the traditional process of slinging a handful of dough and squeezing off enough between the index finger and thumb to form the bottom half of a bun. This is placed on a greased baking pan and the process is immediately duplicated, pinching a slightly smaller doughball for the top. The repetitive motion and the resistance of the springy dough is taxing, and many a Mennonite *Oma's* muscular forearms give testimony to the rigours of this labour.

Epigraph

Patrick Friesen is a gifted Canadian author. He has written many works, from poetry to stage plays. Like Mitchell Toews, Patrick was born and raised in Steinbach, Manitoba, a distinctive place that forms a basis for the fictional town of "Hartplatz" found in many of the stories in this collection.

Pinching Zwieback

Swimming in the *Bazavluk* 1

Groota Peeta..7

Nothing to Lose 19

Fast and Steep 29

Willa Hund 37

Died Rich..43

Without Spot or Wrinkle..67

The Raspberry Code 79

Fall From Grace 89

The Peacemongers 101

A Vile Insinuation 121

The Sunshine Girl 129

The Grittiness of Mango Chiffon 141

Fetch 151

Breezy..161

Rommdriewe 171

A Heckuva Thing 183

The Worth of Sparrows 195

The Narrowing 209

In the Dim Light Beyond the Fence..225

Plautdietsch/Low German Glossary...241

The Zehen Family
(and other notables)

A number of recurrent characters in this manuscript are members of the fictional Zehen family, residents—past or present—of the imaginary Canadian prairie village of Hartplatz where much of the action is set.

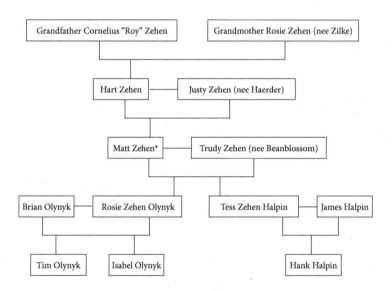

*Matt's younger sister, Edith Zehen, appears in "The Grittiness of Mango Chiffon." Matt's friend Lenny Gerbrandt and his older brother Erdman are recurrent. Diedrich Deutsch and his family and friends are in several stories set in Winkler, Manitoba.

All characters are fictional.

Swimming in the *Bazavluk*

It's cool here in the shade along the shore. That Janzen boy brought bottles of beer from his uncle's brewery way out in *Schoenwiese*. We all have some. I drink two, and some of another. It's a strong brew and it spins my head. I feel brave and happy. It makes me feel like I do after church, when we all sing until the building shakes.

I watch the other boys wrestling in the shallows. We are at a bend in the river. The *Bazavluk* meanders so. The soil is fertile here, the fields so green they hurt your eyes. I hear many people want to build more canals for irrigation. Some sly farmers want to fill in the oxbows because that is the richest soil of all and would increase their land holdings. 1873 has been one of our people's most bountiful years ever, here in South Russia, but even so, there's talk we might leave here altogether, so who knows?

I think about the boys and which of them I could fight. I imagine how I'd hold the boy down and make him say, uncle. It wouldn't be that Klassens' Jakob. He is such a big, strong guy. The best swimmer and always wants to race, and one time he let

1

me win on purpose. It was so easy to tell he swam slowly. That *domma Äsel*. I could beat him if I practiced. The flies tickle the hair on my legs, and I swat them away. I shouldn't think such *willa* thoughts, but it feels good sometimes to dream wild things that might never happen.

Father is going to travel with some other important men, church men and the *Brandaeltester* who's the boss of the fire insurance, to visit places in the world that want us Mennonites to move there. "Free land!" they say. A new Eden? Lots of families want to leave for Canada or someplace else. Some even say the soldiers will come for us soon—to break their promise and force us into the army. I can't understand the soldiers. Most of them aren't much older than me. They are given a place to live, food and clothing—such fine boots!—and for that they do whatever is ordered. Maybe they're afraid too—the *gulags* aren't fussy who they take. Father says our dear Saviour will help us in the world, but we must pay attention. "Our fallen nature and our *weltliche*, worldly lusts..." he says, can be our heavenly downfall if we're not careful. Sometimes I fear Father loves repentance more than he loves the Lord, but I believe he is right about being less worldly.

The Klassens don't want to leave *Borozenko* Colony, not as planned for next year or anytime after, for that matter. They are so rich, with dairy cows yet, and mulberry trees, and the best land—soil black and sweet smelling like rising dough. It never floods, their land, and they have so many workers that the place looks like a bee hive, especially at harvest. They have the best farm around, easy. They want to stay and see if things can be fixed. My father says it won't work. Nevers not, even with money for bribes. He says things are changing and we will lose out here in the colonies.

Then one of the boys calls to me: "Hey, Zehen! We're all

2

going to swim to that big floating tree trunk and ride it down to Neufeld's place. Are you coming with?"

"Sure, let's!" I bundle my clothes and hat beside a boulder and run down to the bank. The sun feels good on my chest and I wade in before the others. The swift water tugs at my legs. With an eddy in its trail, the big elm tree drifts towards us. It's an old, thick-trunked tree, shorn of all limbs. At the base, the broad, tangled root stands round as a plate and washed clean of clay. It protrudes from the surface like a half-wheel. The tree trunk swings in the current and reminds me of a sea monster from the Russian storybook we have at home.

The river is a friend to us here. A friend and yet, one that can be cruel. Icy cold and treacherous after a big rain. I wonder about the rivers in other places; like Canada where Father thinks we might want to go. He says it's colder there. I think of skating, of geese chasing me like they do on our cattle pond, my skates cutting white arcs into the ice as I escape the angry birds who try to run me off. I think of snow falling on my tongue, of chopping frozen firewood. I imagine the smell of cows in the barn in winter. In Canada, there will be no barns. Only trees, waiting to be cut. A longer winter over there, they say, but flat land where we can farm just like here.

I'm swimming fast now, over my head by far, and I'm way ahead of the others. I'll show them. I'll get there first and act like Jakob might—sitting astride the log like it's Hilltop, their big plough horse. I'll clown and yell and show everyone I can swim good too. But then I'm tired and I'm tired, and the log gets past me and I swallow some water. I try, but I can't touch. My nose is full and I have no air. The river pulls me to the bottom, where weeds grab at my legs. I am going down, but I must go up.

I open my eyes in the green haze. It's quiet and still. But

3

before the next thing, there comes a rough yank, and I feel a hand grab me. My head comes out of the water with a splash and Jakob is close by, looking in my eyes. He is stern, or maybe it's more cross, but he also looks afraid at the same time. The other boys come to see if we're alright and we all paddle slowly back to shore, carried by the current. I climb up among the rounded rocks, coughing and blowing my nose. They watch me from the river's edge, eyes shifting, until Klassens' Jakob points at me and says, "Zehen, be careful, once! Some things look simple, but they can easy hurt you if you don't know what you're doing." Then he grins and yells, "Don't try to drink the whole river!"

He says this in a big voice, but not in an unkind way. It's all true and I know it. I feel sick and my hands won't stop shaking. I find a place to sit and rest, drawing up my knees and resting my forehead on them, eyes closed. Water trickles down my back and slowly I catch my breath.

"Are you excited for your father's trip?" Jakob asks. He has come up quietly, leaving the rest of the boys splashing in the water. "Everyone is talking about it."

I look at him. He is silhouetted by the sun, and I close one eye, holding my hand up to block the glare. "It'll be strange to have Father gone for so long," I reply.

"Yes. I hadn't thought of that, but that's right. It puts a lot on your family." He sits beside me and picks a flat reed, peeling it lengthwise into green ribbons. His hands are tanned brown and the skin is puckered around the nails. "No more swimming in the *Bazavluk*. You'll be busy at your place. So many things for you and the others to keep up with. And preparing to go to Canada or wherever the delegates say we should go."

It's time to be grown up, I tell myself again. When Father goes away there's only Mother, me and Cornelius, and our three

4

little sisters. The neighbours will have to help. "My family will be counting on me," I say to Jakob. "Plus, the new world we're going to won't be one of ease. There is penance to be paid. Our earthly desires must be left here. No more '*Gierigkeit,*' as Father calls it, the greed and wanting that leaves us unfulfilled."

"He must be wise, your father. That's why he was chosen to go. Sounds like you have been listening to him."

A gull skims over the water. The sun is bright shining on the river and my eyes are tired from squinting. I'm sleepy and my head feels thick. Long blades of sawgrass rub against my legs, rough as a cat's tongue.

"Your father, he's not a minister, but he sometimes sounds like one."

Father couldn't be a minister because he had been shunned. He changed his ways and apologized. The brethren took him back in the church after he repented, but he could never be a clergy. I was sure Jakob knew this, but again, he was careful in what he said to me, even when we were alone. Part of me wants to sneer at him, "Here is the great Klassens' Jakob being kind to the twice-shunned Zehen boy, Johann." But instead, I say, "I think life will be so different, wherever we go. Everything will be thrown in the air. Not as it used to be. Not at all."

"The first will be last," Jakob says, glancing at me with a quick smile. As he speaks I notice the boys coming in from swimming. Jakob continues, "But even with all the change, we must have faith. It's simple, isn't it? Trust the Lord and be there for one another."

"Many waters cannot quench love; rivers cannot sweep it away," I recite. It is the Bible verse Father has written in charcoal on the roof beam of our hayloft.

We are quiet after that, watching the boys joke around and roughhouse on the shore.

"Jakob, thank you for helping me, out there in the river."

"Of course, Johann. Why not? But I know that was just *späle*. You were doing me make-believe, *joh*?" With that he scrambles up and gallops down the bank, his stride long and mud flying off his feet. "One last swim before we go!" he shouts to the others who turn, cheering, to wade out with him.

I look at them for a minute, hearing their voices echo among the shore elms. I dry myself with my shirt and get dressed. It's soon time for evening chores.

Groota Peeta

In 1964, my eighth summer, make-shift fruit stands lined the Number 12 Highway along its approach to Hartplatz, in Southern Manitoba. Local entrepreneurs in borrowed trucks had motored to the distant orchards of the Okanagan and back. The fruit of their labours was announced by the signs that had sprouted along the highway: "Fresh! B.C. Cherries!"

At their roadside stands, the sunflower-seed-cracking vendors eyed us suspiciously when we pulled up on our bikes, dimes at the ready. "No free tasting!" they would warn, wagging wary fingers at us, calling us what we were, *schnoddanäs Tjinge*. My nose may have been snotty but I still resented the name.

I remember seeing strangely dressed boys of about my age hanging around. They had soup bowl haircuts and wore boots that looked like they had seen some real work. Some cowshit too. Banished from the proximity of the produce they had helped pick, they roughhoused and pelted rocks at telephone poles as their fathers collected our payments.

A few weeks later when the school year began, and the

playgrounds and classrooms were jammed with children, scrubbed lye-soap clean and wearing new clothes, I saw the cherry truck boys again. Unlike me, they did not have a new plaid pencil case and fresh-from-the-box Dash runners. They looked and acted much as they had beside the highway. I saw them puffing on corn silk roll-your-owns in the windrow of trees along Barkman Avenue. They gathered there like hobbits, all bony knuckles and patched denim overalls.

A shy, freckle-hided elf, I hovered nearby in curiosity. I heard them speaking Low German, which I only barely understood— my German lingo being restricted mostly to common slang phrases, cuss words and "barnyard descriptions," as my mom put it. A long and bickersome family history, spanning generations, continents, exoduses and shunnings, had made English the designated language of our household.

"Who are those kids, anyway?" I asked my friend Scottie as we walked home from school.

"They're from Mexico, Matt," he said, kicking a discarded Rogers Golden Syrup can.

"But they don't sound Mexican. They talk like my *Opa*."

"Well, yeah! They're Mennonites."

"Shouldn't they be from Russia then? Or, like, Europe?"

"Not these ones." Scottie shrugged. "Our Sunday School sponsors one."

Our Zehen family was Mennonite too, but not much given to churchgoing. This was the first I had heard of Mennonites from Mexico and sponsorships.

We played baseball at school that warm fall and it soon became apparent that while these new kids were not much for rules, they could really hit and throw. Some uneasy alliances were made but for the most part, our games were tense contests of "Canadians" against "Mexicans." Neither label was wholly accurate, but we were kids slinging names at one another, and our political correctness had no beginning and our playground animosity knew no end.

Finally, after a scuffle broke out over a controversial fair-foul call, an official Battle Royale was suggested to settle our differences. The rumble would begin as soon as school let out. Our field of glory was to be the parking lot behind the nearby Evangelical Fellowship Church. Fighting on school property meant expulsion if you were caught, and we were keen to distance ourselves from that consequence.

As we filed in for our last classes—Art class followed by Devotions—the so-called "*Meksikaunische*" crew looked confident. They were outnumbered three to one but seemed unconcerned. One boy poked his finger against my new corduroy jacket sleeve and said, "You're gonna really get it from *Groota Peeta*!" Again, my Low German failed me, but even in English the phrase "Peter the Great" meant nothing to me, although "Big Pete" might have got my attention.

The four-o-clock bell rang, and we dashed to the cloakroom to don our brave apparel and make for the battleground.

We didn't know exactly how to start. Congregated in shuffling clumps on opposing sides of the gravel lot, it was almost as if we needed a teacher or a pastor to organize the activity. But it was up to us to finish what we started.

"We should get garbage can lids and have a stone fight!" one of our gang suggested.

We considered this option at length. We were still weighing the relative merits of artillery versus infantry when everyone stopped talking and stared, open-mouthed, at our foes.

A boy of about six feet in height had joined them. He stood

among them like a thin balsam growing up from a cluster of ground-hugging juniper. A lone emissary from their side strode with reckless bravado toward us, carrying a white handkerchief.

"No fair bringing a big brother!" one of our side called out.

"He ain't no brother. That's *Groota Peeta*. He got here yesterday with his *Taunte* Lena."

"He's too big! No fair!"

"He's twelve, but he's anyways gonna be in Grade Four—in our class. He starts tomorrow."

Our side's tactical advantage was gone—escaped and bounding away like a rabbit freed from its hutch. We put our heads together as we did in our football huddles on the green grass of Barkman Park. *Groota Peeta's* threatening presence had inspired us to unite. Eventually, Scottie spoke for us all as we decided what to do next: "Fighting is against our religion anyway!" Our hasty council agreed. We voted for peace. Had we swords we would surely have beat them into ploughshares, but having only garbage can lids, we dropped them in clattering surrender. There were catcalls and more than a few chicken cackles from our opposition, but no battle took place that day.

A few days later, I made *Groota Peeta* my first pick for our lunch-hour ball team. He ambled over, and I fitted him with my dad's ball glove, brought in anticipation of this exact circumstance. I addressed him haltingly in my pidgin *Plautdietsch,* "*West du* first base *späle?*"

He gave me a bemused look, clearly knowing what I wanted but not impressed with my delivery.

"Oh, I can speak English, there Zehen. I ain't no Mexican. And yeah—I'll play first base," he said, taking his place there and smacking a bony fist into the glove I had given him.

"Nice mitt," he said with an oblong smile, then fixed me

with a stink eye that I did not soon forget. But he could do more than glare. He could also gobble up grounders and hurl lightning bolts across the field. The game ended when he, with a bat that looked comically small in his hands, smashed the ball into Plumber Unger's garden, far beyond the schoolyard fence.

Peeta became Pete and we came to know each other. I found in Pete a boy whose physical dimensions not only made him stand out but who was far advanced beyond me in other significant ways. He drove a truck on his parent's farm, he smoked but "only 'OPs'—other people's—because they are so beastly expensive here!" He had mechanical, carpentry and other adult skills to a proficiency level that awed me and most of my friends, and turned many of our male teacher's faces red with envy and shame. After only a few months however, the differences between us, and many were pronounced, did not seem that important. Somehow, first through our common love of baseball and later in other ways, we had earned each other's trust. We became fast friends, finding many unsuspected commonalities. To our mutual surprise, we were each "just regular guys" with many shared interests despite the "us and them" we had been so concerned with before. As for our past conflict, Pete and I both knew I had been in the wrong. For his part, *Groota Peeta* had the good grace to mention it often, in the company of others, and with obvious, grinning enjoyment. The sign of a true, uninhibited friend.

* * *

Many seasons—decades—after meeting Pete, whose full name was Peter Peters although that super alliterative handle somehow never brought him any ridicule, I sat on the wet bleachers at my granddaughter's fastball game. I thought of Pete that day, as I often did at ballgames. He and I had gone our separate ways in adulthood, though we still were able to pick up quickly when we did happen to meet.

My granddaughter's team was the Visitor in a small town west of Hartplatz, near Winkler. I found a seat on the top row of the rickety stands. A floor mat from my pickup truck served as a makeshift seat cushion for the late May contest. I was happy to be there. Baseball had been gone from my life for quite a few summers now, and it was good to be back. I liked this old ballpark with its painted backstops, where in the coming summer months tall ironweed stems and winding thistle would grow close to the wooden planks, kindred in their effort to escape the mower's blades.

"Hey Jake, I think the rain's done for today," a man said as he climbed up to the row in front of me. He smiled at the fellow seated there and sat beside him. I had introduced myself to Jake already, and we had been chatting about the Blue Jays' chances that year.

The two seemed like regulars at these games. Both were about my age or a few years older.

"How are you, Arnold?" Jake said to the new arrival.

"Oh, it goes to hold out. You?"

"Same," Jake said, accepting a handful of sunflower seeds.

The two men cracked and spat, clearing their throats and murmuring as the teams went through their infield warm-ups on the damp diamond.

Our Hartplatz team came to bat first. After the leadoff batter struck out, I did not recognize the player up to bat next. Must be a new kid, I thought.

"Man, dis oughta be good," Arnold said quietly, then yelled. "Easy out!"

I looked away as he shot a sidling glance in my direction and then focused on the batter's box. The girl wore a discreet head-scarf beneath her batting helmet. The scarf came up from under her uniform tunic and covered her neck and the back of her head.

"She one of them border crossers?" I heard Arnold speculate. He touched his head, indicating her scarf. "She's got a *Düak* on," he said, using the *Plautdietsch* word for headscarf. The other man, Jake, shrugged and dropped his remaining seeds onto the ground. He snuck a glance at me, but I quickly looked away.

After working the count full, the batter hit a sharp drive over second base. Her bright eyes beamed at their bench as she reached first base safely.

"Great hit, Maria," our coach shouted.

"Pretty good at bat," Jake said, giving me a friendly smile.

The next batter bunted, advancing her. Then my grand-daughter lined out to the pitcher to end the inning. Right back at 'er, I thought. Jake smiled at me and I shrugged my shoulders. "Can't steer it," I said, recalling a baseball axiom I hadn't used since grade school.

Next, Maria, the girl who had just got a hit, took the mound and threw hard. The home crowd watched anxiously as she struck out the side, overpowering the batters. A natural.

"She's too tall," Arnold grumbled, standing. He put his hands in his pockets and turned to me. "Your pitcher—she's gotta be older den fourteen, right?" He prodded again when I did not answer. "She looks older than fourteen—but it's hard to tell with them…"

"Well, if that's the rule, I'm sure she's no more than fourteen. I'm sure our coach would follow the rules. Maria's new on the team and, I'm afraid I don't know her or her family." I kept my voice even and quiet, speaking slowly. Jake gave me a slight head nod when I finished.

"New?" snorted Arnold. "I bet. Where's she from, anyway?"

"Corner of Friesen Avenue and First Street, I think." This won me a small chuckle from Jake, whose face I noted had grown slightly red.

"Eh? Whatever," Arnold said, scoffing. He returned his attention to the game, clapping his hands.

Several innings passed, and the game remained scoreless. Both pitchers were throwing well. As the game progressed, it became apparent that the two men hunched in front of me were deep in conversation. It did not seem altogether friendly and they had forgotten about baseball.

Cold, I hurried back to fetch a jacket from the truck. When I returned, Arnold and Jake had left the bleachers and were standing on the edge of the parking lot. Their posture and raised voices told me something was wrong.

"Well, we grew up in a 'sanctuary city' too!" Jake said, his frustration clear in his voice. "When our ancestors—the *Väavodasch*—left Russia, Manitoba gave us land, a home! Our parents were refugees too, yours and mine... everyone in their village. We, were just like they are now!"

"Those were different times," Arnold sputtered. "Our people came in peace!"

"Acch. Same manure, different pile!" Jake replied with disdain. "You think these people are here to start a war? Give your head a shake. They're refugees—they aren't here for a vacation, eh?"

"*Nay, nay*! But, we got invited," Arnold replied, biting off the last word like a curse. "And anyways, well, nobody really GAVE us nothing! We worked the land, cleared it and picked rocks—it was just scrub brush before we came!"

"Listen, Buhr! It was Métis land before we came! Some of

14

it, anyhow. They had the deeds. 'Scrips' they were called. The government promised to compensate them, but they took years, and never paid *nuscht*! Dragged their feet. Did you know that? Eh?" Jake fought to maintain his composure, kicking at a patch of crumbling asphalt as he spoke. "The Métis scattered after a while. We pushed them off, if you ask me. As good as. Never did seem right to me."

Arnold—Arnold Buhr, I now knew—lit a cigarette and held it in a cupped hand while he thought, his head bowed. "Our families feared God and wanted nothing but to live together without war. Can these illegals say the same? Some are terrorists!" He faltered, realizing that he was shouting.

I was listening intently. Their clash was the sort of thing you found online, but seldom heard out loud. It was ironic too: these two were so like each other. And both of them so like me, I thought grimly. I had forgotten this was a place just north of the U.S. border, on the front lines of refugee traffic—African and Middle Eastern families fleeing hatred: ethnic, religious, and racial. Plus, most of the inbound people were also poor and empty-handed. Upset and boiling inside, I went back to the bleachers to keep myself from speaking up. Jake was doing fine without me.

When we were young, Jake and Arnold and I, when we were children on the playground life was simple and pure.

We were gallant and brave. We saw the things that needed to be done and we had the strength to do them. We had rectitude of spirit and shared, all of us, a kindred nobility that drove our actions and guided our beliefs. All of these wonderful traits were born into us, a part of our innocence and the clarity that all children possess. Our common human traits.

When, in those school days, the emigrants from Mexico

arrived, something happened to our innate belief that everyone is equal. We lost it, but not through our own negligence. We were taught a new belief—one of discrimination. There were adults who wanted us to believe that the "Mexicans" were different. Their reasons sprang from greed and fear: "*Those people* work for cheap, they're out to steal our jobs!"

I watched the kids on the field. They were lost in the game. Their perspective was one of carefree pleasure even as they competed with all their hearts and wanted their side to win. They were beatific, in a way. Blissful and radiant and lost in their simple *späle* with the only rules having to do with balls and strikes, fair and foul. Rules that seek to erase bias, not enforce it.

After twenty minutes, with the game still scoreless in the last inning, Jake returned to the bleachers wearing a wool Mackinaw. He took the same spot, just in front of me. I looked back to the parking lot but did not see the other man. As the teams switched places on the field, Jake looked over. "Sorry about Buhr. He's a loudmouth, but he doesn't usually get so outta line."

"It's a tough situation," I said, voting for peace once again.

"Maybe. For me, it's clear-cut. Our family settled here at first, way back in the eighteen hundreds, then migrated to Mexico much later. My family and a bunch of others ended up moving back here in the Sixties, flat broke. Well, not *here* exactly but over in Hartplatz, where you're from. The churches were generous, but not everyone in the town was welcoming when we arrived, so I know what that's like."

I nodded, swallowing. "You say the Sixties?"

"Yeah. Fall, 1964. I didn't speak a word of English when we got to Manitoba."

I stared at him and shifted in my seat. I studied his face and wondered if I should ask him if he was in that group that came over to our school. Could it be? The boys from the fruit trucks. Some had stayed in Hartplatz—I knew most of them but many had scattered as their parents found work elsewhere. I knew that my childhood friend Pete, *Groota Peeta*, had eventually made himself a good career in Winnipeg, but he was the only one of that group I had really kept up with. I wondered if I asked Jake about *Groota Peeta*, what he would say. Instead, I spoke about our common history:

"Yeah, my dad's family came in 1874, from South Russia. They settled in Gruenfeld—now that's called Kleinfeld—and I don't think they had much. They spoke German and thought maybe Canada was ruled by a generous Queen who would look out for them. They left a lot behind." As I spoke, I thought of the long-ago grade-school Battle Royale with "those *Meksikaunische,*" and I felt an uneasy guilt I thought I had disposed of. I felt the sudden weight of the words I had used to comfort myself, "rectitude of spirit... a kindred nobility."

Just then, Maria hit a long fly ball, and her bench howled in delight. With one out, the runner on third tagged up and then trotted in with the first run. The visiting team was ahead.

"Well, how about that! Looks like the out-of-towners are making it interesting," Jake said with a wink.

"They always do," I said. "They always do."

Nothing to Lose

Dust hung in the heavy midsummer air, settling almost imperceptibly and with clinging persistence on the rosehips and yarrow and fescue and crocus growing alongside the road and down into the ditches. Nearby dry fields awaited a summer storm; the first large drops would land as heavy as pats of butter

The man's arm hung from the window of the bread delivery van. He tapped his wedding band absentmindedly against the *Hartplatz Bakery* logo painted on the door. Viewed from above, the van carried enough speed down the flat country road to raise a vee-shaped plume of fine white dust, like the wake of a boat.

Inside the van, a residue of *Prairie Rose* flour dusted the man's hair and stood out on the peach fuzz on his ears and the sloping nape of his neck. He shifted down into second gear and eased the clutch back out, making the motor race and the rear wheels check on the sandy gravel, adjusting their pace to the new ratio and slowing for the intersection ahead. The geometric roads drew a pale yellowish cross in dark green alfalfa fields. *"ARRÊT"* the sign demanded, in the de Salaberry Rural Municipality, north

19

of the town of Hartplatz. The panel van rolled to a stop, and the driver—the owner of the bakery, Hart Zehen—revved the engine once and then turned off the ignition. He sat in the close heat of the vehicle, the radiator ticking rapidly and crickets and frogs keeping time from their hiding places in the grass.

A male red wing blackbird swooped down towards a bulrush with its three-toed feet splayed out to grasp the brown, cigar-shaped spadix. His wings flared open just in time to stall and spill enough speed for landing. Trilling, the bird cocked its head, and then took off as quickly as it had come, leaving the bulrush swaying.

Hart checked his wristwatch again. Still 20 minutes early for the wedding delivery to the Giroux Hall. He knew the manager there and he did not want to spend any extra time with him. The order for 80 dozen *Zwieback* called for him to bring the buns by 6:30.

He opened the door and it creaked, piercing the quiet. Swinging his legs out, he pushed off the seat edge to land with both feet, a dusty plop on the road. He looked back at the sky to the northwest, where, impressively, an impasto storm cloud was building. It was dark purple at the bottom and startling white higher up, contrasting with the cerulean prairie sky. The thunderhead hung with menace, gathering bulk as Hart stood far below—an Israelite facing the giant Philistine.

The radio came on loudly after Hart leaned in and gave the key a quarter turn. It carried a baseball game from Minneapolis, the signal skipping in off the cloud cover to the south.

"Killebrew, the young first baseman, leads off this inning," announced the play-by-play man, his flat Midwest accent pinching off the words and sounding foreign to the Manitoba baker. "Ball one! A curveball that Harmon left alone. Good eye; it bounced in the dirt in front of home plate."

Imagining, Hart sat on his haunches in the crossroads and flashed a sign for fastball. Deliberately, he adjusted his imaginary catcher's mask with his right hand and presented a low target to the pitcher: a single rogue sunflower plant growing in the stony edge of the northbound lane. The sunflower sat atop a thick green stalk, its speckled face staring unblinkingly toward the baker-turned-catcher.

"STEE-rike!" the announcer shouted. Hart gathered four or five smooth hardball sized stones and laid them near where he crouched. He tossed one towards the sunflower that stood tall and attentive in the angled evening sunlight.

Several batters later, Hart was sweating lightly, enjoying his pantomime ballgame.

"One out, runner on first, the count two-and-two on the Twins number seven hitter," said the sing-song radio baritone. "Pitcher looks for the sign... he nods and reaches up into his stretch... pauses, holds the runner momentarily... now he delivers—THE RUNNER GOES!"

Hart grabbed a stone, crow-hopped up and fired a low, hissing bullet to where second base would be—an oiled cedar telephone pole across the ditch.

"BOCK!" The rock hit the pole just right of center, denting the wood. The crickets and frogs fell silent as one, then slowly renewed their cheering chorus.

He grinned as the voice from the radio, full of static, blared, "He throws him OUT and the batter goes down swinging to end the inning. Strike him out, throw him out! Washington zero, Twins zero. We'll be right back after this message from *GRAIN BELT BEER!*"

Hart checked his watch again, the leather band, stained white with sweat, dried in a jagged line. He jumped into the seat

21

and started the low-slung van, spinning the tires and shooting stones out behind the back bumper.

Feeling strangely exultant from the exertion of the make-believe ball game and in anticipation of the $40 cash he would collect on this Saturday night, Hart slewed the *Chevy* around the last corner to his destination. His tires clattered the thick boards of the bridge deck, the sound echoing off the hall's white-washed stucco walls. He wheeled around tightly on the packed dirt lot, braked hard, then backed up to about ten feet from the "Deliveries" door. Hopping out, he spun ninety degrees on the ball of his foot and flicked the door shut. He snapped down on the lever handle to open the left rear door and then side-stepped to do the same for the right. Every motion was athletic, rhythmic, and economical—practiced thirty times that day alone.

Inside the van were two stacked trays filled with bags of fresh buns. Saturday was the traditional *Zwieback* baking day—for events and Sunday afternoon "*Vaspa*," the cold meal of buns, cheese, jam and coffee prepared the day before the Sabbath. Still warm, the scent of the buns filled the air: yeasty, with the faint sweetness of caramelized sugar and scalded milk. The stacks stood side-by-side and a pink delivery slip was taped to the top of one of the clear plastic packages. Hart patted his back pocket, feeling for the invoice pad, then picked up one of the stacks, stepped to the delivery door and knocked deftly with the hard toe of his shoe.

He paused to listen and, hearing the lock open inside, backed up slightly to make way for the door to swing open.

"Well, well, right on time," said a thin man with a clean white dress shirt and a red tie tucked into the buttoned front. He stood smiling with his hands on his hips in the doorway, a silver tooth glinting in the evening sun. His sleeves were rolled, and a blue anchor was tattooed on one of his corded forearms.

"Where's the regular driver—Nightingale?"

"Night off. His twins' birthday today," Hart replied, hugging the trays like the waist of a polka partner as he brushed by the taller man into the kitchen. His leather soles slapped on the painted concrete floor as he walked into the room carrying the awkward metal rack. He raised his eyebrows questioningly.

The manager, Tamsyn, hesitated and then pointed back into the room where several pots sat boiling on a large range top, wetting the wall with their steam. "Put those buns next to the stove, on the left." As Hart walked by for the second load of buns, Tamsyn asked, "You the hockey player? Zehen?"

"One of them," Hart replied, smiling, his front teeth cut at an angle from a high stick, small scars like crossbones on the ball of his chin. "My brothers played too."

"You don't play no more?"

"Not no more. A little baseball in the summer, but the bakery keeps me pretty busy," he said, stacking the second load of buns on top of the first. After wiping his forehead with the back of his wrist, he opened the invoice book and pointed at the top copy, "Forty bucks, *see-voo-play.*"

"Eh?" Tamsyn squinted, pausing in mid-motion as he pulled out a leather cash wallet on a chain. "You are obviously not French." He put the emphasis on the last syllable: obvious-LEE.

Hart smirked. He shifted his weight from one foot to the other and thumbed the edge of the invoice pad, making a rippling sound.

Tamsyn unzipped the heavy brown pouch. He picked four tens free, then rubbed each one between thumb and forefinger to make sure two bills had not stuck together. He gestured towards Hart with the money. "You had a try-out with Detroit, I hear."

Hart shrugged his rounded shoulders; his head down as he

marked the invoice—"Paid: Cash"—and signed with his initials. He thought fleetingly of the long-ago try-out camp in Saskatoon; the big star players gliding around the rink. "Good check!" the red-faced coach had yelled to him as he climbed back over the boards in a scrimmage.

"I don't play no baseball but I played hockey for Ste. Anne, eh." Tamsyn held out the forty dollars to Hart. "I was a centre-man. That's a real credit to you. Detroit. The Red Wings. That's really something," he said the last with a look of genuine approval on his face. "And you had nothing to lose, right? You go an' give it your best shot and let the chips fall. Right?" He nodded to himself after speaking.

You got nothing to lose, right? Hart remembered one of his brothers saying this to him when they made the deal for the bakery, dissolving the partnership.

"Lots to lose," he had replied, "same as you." Hart and two of his older brothers, Barney and Dennis, had originally bought the small bakery from their uncle. After a year of argument and indecision, as they worked endless hours to grow the business, Hart wanted to end the three-man partnership. "I don't make a good partner," he told his wife, Justy.

The terms were blunt. Either the two brothers bought him out or he bought them out; the price was $5,000 per share, either way. They got to choose—stay or go. Hart had wanted the partnership to work but it had not and he believed this was the only fair way out. At first, they had scorned him, Barney barking at him, "Screw you, Hart! Let's go get a beer at the pub. Man! Who crapped in your porridge?"

Hart stood his ground.

His father stayed out of the fray, sticking to his shoe repair shop—in the last years before an overdue retirement—and letting his boys work it out among themselves. He saw the friction. The three men were competitive and strong-willed. Stubborn, as he had raised them. Finally, the brothers wavered, their anger rising when they realized he was unyielding, resolute: "Yeah, you've got nothing to lose. If the bakery goes broke, you can always fall back on hockey—make a career and play in the States." He said nothing.

"Hey! YOU! What the hell's wrong with you?" Tamsyn stood close to him, waving the money, and snapping his fingers with his free hand.

Hart came out of his reverie. "Okay, okay," he replied, stepping back. He took the forty dollars, passed Tamsyn the invoice and nodded, mumbling thanks.

He walked towards the van and stopped to stand with the sun in his face, watching heat waves rising off the highway three miles away and glimpsing bright flashes of cars and tractor-trailers. The land was flat. A few miles north, east or south and it began to roll, taking contour from shallow rivers or gravel ridges.

While looking to the west and the immense prairie that spread from here to the Alberta foothills, Hart thought of his time on the coast with his brother-in-law Bill, commercial fishing north of Tofino. Wild Bill, sitting in the tiny, heaving cockpit of the boat, one rubber boot propped up against the cracked windshield, laughing as Hart choked on his first cigarette.

What if I had stayed on? Hart wondered. He recalled how Bill wanted him to stay—equal partners—and Hart could play for the local hockey team. But, as he told everyone at home, he was only sixteen; how could he? Besides, back then his father needed him to help in the shoe shop.

Walking slowly, he paused, letting the dust of the parking lot settle on his feet. He watched as it rose and reached up to grasp him; holding him there like a fly to tape. Hart thought of punching a batch of dough early that morning, the first blast of escaping yeast gas hitting him, so strong he could feel it like a fan blowing in his face. Like most mornings, a few drops of sweat dripped from the tip of his nose or the line of his jaw, mixing into the dough as he lifted and folded, grunting at the live weight. He thought, as always, how he was in the bread: his sweat, his salt, his DNA; his quiet hopes, and his sadness or his joy. He baked it all in.

Folding the bills, he tucked them away and walked to the van. He was eager to leave.

Tamsyn stood in the shade of the doorway, staring out at Hart. "Now I know why you didn't make the Wings," he called to the stocky baker, who was about to slam the cargo doors shut.

Hart looked back at him, unimpressed before he even heard the conclusion.

"Head case," Tamsyn said, tapping his temple with two fingers.

"Is that right?" He thought of his mother standing in her kitchen on the checkered tile floor. "If you can govern your temper, you can govern this town," she would say to him. "Same as hockey—don't retaliate," chiding, smiling with her hazel eyes.

Breaking like a skater, in short, quick strides, Hart went back towards Tamsyn, who was caught off-guard. "They taught you about head cases in Ste. Anne, did they? Gave you a degree and sent you to work cooking cabbage for weddings?"

Tamsyn held up his open palms like a highway flagman, hoping to slow the burly man's advance. "Hey, hey. Take it easy there. I didn't mean nothing, but you were just kind of daydreaming. That's all."

Hart stopped in front of him. "Okay, sure. You didn't mean anything. That's good, Tamsyn. Shake." He stuck out a thick-fingered hand. Tamsyn raised his arm and Hart thrust forward, engulfing Tamsyn's slim hand and squeezing it so that it caved in backward, creasing into a concave. The small bones clicked as they flexed inwardly, against their natural inclination. Tamsyn's knees buckled, and he dipped, pulling back his hand from the crushing grip, but Hart tugged, forcing Tamsyn off balance.

"Shit!" Tamsyn blurted as his grey dress-trouser knees hit the dirt just outside of the door sill, his teeth gritted.

"The reason I did not make the NHL," Hart began in a measured voice. "Was..." he paused, then suddenly let go of the kneeling man completely. Tamsyn, who was still straining to pull his hand out of Hart's, pitched backward.

"Not tall enough," Hart said in a low, quiet voice, looking down at Tamsyn and then holding out a hand to help him up. "Only one defenseman in the league was less than 5'7." He stepped back and turned towards the gibbous cloud above him, smelled the rain coming and said over his shoulder to Tamsyn, "The bakery business has no height requirement."

Fast and Steep

Hart's breath hangs in the air around his head. The sunshine makes the tiny splinters of floating ice into glinting flashes, gone in an instant and replaced by fresh volunteers, a radiant halo. His long woollen scarf, creased canvas parka and red toque are all hoary with frost. Heavy leather work mitts, wet and steaming, cover his hands.

After first laying out a winding trail in the snow and marking its course with twigs, he sets to stamping and packing the snow into a shallow concave chute about two feet wide. With the course laid and the top layer of snow warmed by the sun, he drops to all fours to shape it with palm and balled fist. The toboggan run begins on the steps of his small house, continues over the yard, across a rutted, ice-filled road and down into the nearby creek bed.

Following two afternoons of work, Hart is satisfied with his effort. A new garden hose uncoils reluctantly, its rubber memory stubbornly retaining a corkscrew pattern in the raw cold until hot water persuades it to relax. With a thumb over the sputtering end, he mists the run, glazing the surface with new ice. It vaporizes on contact, shrouding the slide in a white cloud. He drags the hose through the snow to soak the run's entire length, his face a frown of concentration.

"Hey, Lord of the Slides! How'm I 'sposed to do dishes and laundry?" Justy calls from the kitchen window to her young husband. "No hot water!"

He grins and waves a non-answer back to her. Hunching to light a smoke, Hart thinks hard about the physics of momentum, if there will be enough to slide his son and the wooden toboggan up the far incline and let them stop gently on the other side of Old Tom Creek.

That evening, Justy asks, "Won't it be dangerous to have Matthew slide across the road like that?"

"There's no traffic because they only plow the road on the far side of the creek. This side stays plugged. No one but old man Funk and his tractor use it, and I asked him not to drive over the run."

"Okay." Justy thinks about the parallel road on the far side, but trusts Hart. "Funk, eh? I thought he was blind? Thought you two didn't get along?" she says with a wink.

"As an umpire, yes, no question. Blind Jake. But he does okay driving that old cornbinder tractor of his. Sees better in the clear winter air, I figure."

"If you say so. I'll have some coffee if you're getting up, please."

* * *

Hart putters on the slide each afternoon after his early-rising workday in the bakery. Sculpting in the afternoon's waning light with a broken-handled spade, he scrapes the cupped run. "Don't want no chatter," he says over and over to himself, like a mantra.

He imagines Matthew's toboggan whisking down the run.

To build the course for speed and safety, Hart imagines every inch, testing and fussing. He sees it in his head: a swift initial acceleration down the concrete steps and across the sloped yard. Then a fast scat across the flat of the ice-packed road, bank left, and drop into the creek. **Watch now!** In the creek bottom at terminal velocity, a deeply slung right-hander peels the toboggan around forty-five degrees, laying it almost on its side, so steep is the bank of the curve. Ten feet later comes the sudden upshoot of the far incline. At the last, there is the level ice of the road on the far side. A coasting, clattering conclusion.

"Just like the Lockport roller coaster!" Hart says aloud, looking up at the sloped creek bank from his surveyor's crouch at the bottom.

With a squint, he sights through the borrowed transit, making sure the rise is not too sudden at the far end where the speed will bleed off and the toboggan will—ideally—just barely top the crest.

"Man-oh-man, yer really playing for serious!" Funk says to Hart from the road where he stands, hands in pockets.

"Don't wanna launch my little guy offa that far bank," Hart says without looking up.

"About that..." Funk shuffles down the embankment and holds out a worn silver hardhat from his past employer, the feed mill. There are several paper egg cartons compressed into its hollow crown. "That's for padding..." A red lightning bolt is freshly painted on each side. "And that's for speed."

* * *

Hart makes the last preparations. He polishes the chute with boiling water and a drag made from a jute flour sack. The corners are given a trial run by a test pilot—a thirty-pound bag of flaxseed

31

tied to the toboggan—to check the angles and the banking.

"Top-dressing 'er, eh, Hart?" Funk says on arrival, ever the willing sidewalk inspector. "When's da first run?"

"Sunday."

"Morning?"

"Think so."

"Mmm. But ya know, actually, dat works pretty good 'cause I been feelin' sick. Like I gotta cold. I have scared that I gotta miss church dis Sunday. So maybe I can come watch."

Hart cocks his head. "You can't take illness lightly."

"Nope. You never know. Nevers not."

* * *

On Sunday, Justy and Hart dress the boy in his parka, snow pants, mittens and boots. Hart's red scarf hangs down Matthew's back to the floor. The lightning bolts on the helmet seem to quiver with impatience; they point with electric vitality at the door as the boy waits to get outside, knees jouncing rhythmically.

"He looks like a lawn ornament," Justy comments, tapping her knuckles on the shiny helmet.

Hart has already broomed the snow off the run. The little boy jumps up and down, suspended between his parents' hands. Hart kneels down to tug on the chinstrap of the feed mill hardhat.

"I waxed the bottom of the toboggan," Hart says, running his bare hand over the blonde staves. "You hold on here, to the rope, and put your feet under here..."

"In there?"

"Yep, right under the front part, where it bends up," adds Justy. "Rear back a little when you first start going…"

"And lean into the curves," says Hart, starting to feel jumpy.

"Are you going too?" Matthew asks, looking back and forth between them as he sits holding the braided rope.

"Sure, but this first time is just for you," Hart says. "We want to watch you go!"

Hart and Justy look up and down the roads that parallel the creek. The smooth surface glistens white in the sun. No tire tracks. Tall, furrowed piles of graded snow block the roadway entrances at each end.

"I see our neighbour has taken a sporting interest." Justy nods at the freshly plowed windrow blockades just as Funk himself comes towards them, walking, legs stiff, from his house. She waves at him and he gives her a thumbs-up.

"Ready?" Hart asks a minute later.

The boy's lips press together and he hunkers down like an Olympian. "Go!" he yells through the red wool scarf, "Go!"

Hart and Justy, one on each side, give him a slight pull back and then shove him down the stairway precipice. Matthew looks so vulnerable, but it's already too late to reconsider. The toboggan skims across the yard and patters wood-on-ice across the road and around the first bend. Then the boy's helmeted head drops out of sight as he plunges down the embankment. A second later—like the crack of a whip——he shoots out of the chicane, the toboggan loose in a skid. Just as it seems sure to tumble off the course, gravity regains its hold. Finally, the toboggan rises up the bank and comes to a crunching halt on the far side.

Funk cheers from his post at the top of the creek. Knees bent and one arm waving, the old man jangles a cowbell, raising a din and hollering. Hart does not breathe until he sees the boy wriggling out sideways, kicking his booted feet free of the curled sled nose. Roly-poly in his snow gear, he scrambles up and runs back to the house, shouting and tugging the toboggan behind him, his short legs churning.

Justy and Hart watch transfixed, tears welling in smiling eyes.

"I love you, *Hart*," she wants to say, just like that. She wants to tell him that and how their little family is everything for her now, even the prairie winter and Funk's noisy damn tractor. "All of this. Now and forever," she'd tell him, but she knows that's no good, that he'd just stiffen up and crowd her out. Give him time, she thinks. **Hart is still just a boy, really. Mom says these years go by the quickest, but I've got to let him get used to it at his own pace. Look at Funk. His wife died inside of a year after they were married. Her and the baby both gone, and her just seventeen.**

She sucks air in through her teeth and it seems like they might crack from the cold. Looking at Hart, she can feel him through her winter clothing—no need for words. She senses his pleasure in her and in their son. It's there like a cat purring in her lap. Even if she found herself, a lifetime later, pushing a walker, hair in a grey bun, and with Hart long gone to his man's grave and beside her no more, at least she would have had this. Petal, leaf, and stem growing as one. **It's more than most and today is mine forever,** she thinks. **Come what may. Come what may.**

Justy hears Hart pull in a breath—halfway between a laugh and a sob—as Matty clambers up the porch steps. She sees her son as if in a home movie—like the ones the missionaries showed in the church basement; the people's rigid movements in fast-motion and energetic. Everyone is talking at once, all bright eyes and Funk's bell clamours from the road.

It is they who remember, not the remembered, who get to decide history, Justy thinks. **I hope our little Matthew remembers this day, our joy, his part in it, for as long as he lives.**

"This year, I wish it wouldn't melt," Hart says, voice thick. Arms and bliss encircle jacketed waists as the young parents hug.

Justy bends to kiss her little boy, his cheek as cold on her lips as an apple from the cellar.

From the top branches of the leafless poplar beyond the creek, two crows call to each other as if by name. Their voices ring clear in the frozen air. Justy is reminded of her *Oma*, bundled in a chair, her skin fragile and transparent as wax paper. "When the blackbird is singing, bad weather is bringing," she counselled, her accent thick and beautiful. "But *Oma*," Justy had wanted to say, "they sing every day."

A car passes crosswise on Barkman Avenue, church-bound with frosted windows. It trails a plume of white exhaust.

Hart sets the toboggan in place, gets Justy settled and then pulls their son up the slippery porch steps and helps him to sit on his mother's lap.

First, one crow flaps from the treetop and then its partner follows. Their black bodies are sharp against the pale sky and their wings make a swooping noise in the still air.

The car driver brakes to watch the tobogganers. Hands scratch to clear glass. Faster now with two aboard, mother and child slip over the glassy edge and into the steepness, the smoothness, hurtling down the toboggan run.

Willa Hund

The church ladies are seated in a circle in the living room. "Justy?" they call. I'm alone in the kitchen making a snack for everyone.

"Justy? Come here and join in!" that Debbie Dearborn says. She thinks herself so big. "Deb" like she wants to be called, is the church choir leader and her husband owns that Case tractor dealership yet too. She went to school with my sister when Neeta had her troubles and had to go to the hospital in Selkirk. "Not right in the head," is what some rude people said about Neeta's spells. We just called it the "*willa Hund*" because it was like some wild dog that possessed her from time to time.

I watch them through the archway. They laugh in sudden unison, then touch their hair, pick lint from their skirts. Sarah Neufeld, the Pastor's wife, blushes because her joke made everyone laugh so loud. She clears her throat. Once. Then again, putting a napkin to her lips.

"It'll just be a minute, ladies." My voice is rough, like a stone boat scraping over the field in Little Russia where I grew up. A

37

place on the wrong side of the tracks in a town without tracks, as I like to say.

With care, I pour hot water into the teapot and close the lid. It makes a porcelain jingle that sounds like it's saying "prosperity." My cup is nicely fixed-up with something special. My little secret. Vodka from the bottle Hart hides in the garage. I think he knows I know. He doesn't care—maybe even likes it when I take a little. I spread a package of expensive store-bought cookies onto a crystal platter, thinking how that ought to make them jealous—on two counts—and deliver the food to the coffee table.

"Oh, but *terrible* fancy," Deb Dearborn says, reaching out with two hands to take the tray. "You shouldn't fuss so!" she adds, extra loud and I think, there she goes again.

They twitter through pursed lips, heads nod, then bow.

All tits and teeth, I call them inside my head. I learned that saying from one of those British *Carry On* movies in Winnipeg. It makes me feel hot inside my head when I think those words, and imagine saying that to the church ladies and watching their faces. Say it like those strange Englishmen in the movie, with their accents that sound like they are sitting on something sharp. I wish I could be brave and funny like that and just not give a rip, like those men do in their movies.

Everybody's talking and talking. With their eyes on me, I feel the *willa Hund* inside of me pulling like it's a real dog, a mean dog on a chain. My head feels all full up and I want to go peel a hundred potatoes or scrape that paint stain on the basement floor or do something to quit thinking over and over about how they... how they're better than me. Or whatever. I know what they're really thinking about me, even if everything is all *joh-joh-joh*...

So, I sneak off downstairs and then I can breathe again. "*Jauma!*" The mop and pail are in the hall and I slide them in the way of the door and then slip into the bathroom. I snap the latch shut. Safe and alone in the quiet of the bathroom, no bigger than a closet.

There's a lighter and smokes hidden in the medicine chest. I light a menthol and blow smoke through my nose and watch myself carefully in the mirror. Chin up, one eyebrow arched like Barbara, that woman from Vancouver who gave a poetry reading in the school library. That was the first time I ever heard a full-grown woman use the F-word! And everyone else looked down with red faces when she said that and I just wanted to jump up and yell for the joy of it, or, I don't know for sure what!

So proud, the church ladies are. Important families and big-shot husbands. But look! My clothes are better, our house is bigger. I have an automatic garage door opener, for goodness sakes! You just push the white button.

Leather soles click on the tile floor outside. It's Ruth. "Justy! Where are you, *Mejahl?* Sarah spilled! Do you have some Comet cleanser? Justy?" Ruth's accent is really good. She sounds like an Englisher. Very proper and *Winnipegsch,* like my city cousins.

"Oh, Ruth! I'm here and I just have to tell you how nice you always sound! I mean your English. You don't have an accent like me! You are like my mom's Winkler friend, Mrs. Rudolf Deutsch. She is so terrible smart and treats me like we're, you know, equals, ("Call me Rosalyn.") even if she is seventy and won the medal and graduated high school and I'm not even thirty and just barely passed. And her and her sister Myrtle with their husbands long dead and already on pension and them raising their nephew, Diedrich. Anyway, she speaks like that, Mrs. Deutsch does. She reminds me of the lady at the perfume counter in the Hudson's Bay Store in Winnipeg, only without all that make-up, but talking just as good as her. And I wanted to tell you that..." is what I *wish* I could say to her but instead, all I say is, "Yes, Ruth. Just a minute, please. A Justy minute, you know."

"Okay."

I flush the toilet with a sigh, give my hair a flip and drop the cigarette into the swirl so it gets all the way gone.

Through the crack of the door, I hear Ruth's thin voice again, "Sarah didn't just spill. I mean, she did, but, she brought up too. Quite a lot. In the kitchen."

Oh, but! *Dietschlaund!* Everybody's pregnant. Everybody's always pregnant! I'm happy I'm not, but I wish I was? Whatever, whatever. I think another baby will come soon for us. But who knows? Leave it with the Lord, is what they say. Ho, but.

I hear Ruth fidget outside in the hall. "Sarah said she'd wipe it up. She just wants to know where your cleaning goods are kept. I'll help..."

"That's so sweet of you, Ruth. Thank you. The *Comet* is under the kitchen sink. Take the pail and mop along with, can you, please?"

Standing on the aquamarine blue toilet lid, I swing the window open. I look out and see it's not that far down to the concrete walk. I could easy make it. Sneak out quietly and go sit in one of the junk cars behind the body shop next door. I could put on lipstick like Anne Bancroft in the movies and practice to make my accent sound not so strong. But I don't have my jacket and it's too cold.

"Okay, sure. But, are you all right, Justy? You don't sound so good."

"I feel a little yuck, so..."

She says, "*Nah joh,*" and leaves. I feel fine, of course. *Willa*, but fine.

I light another smoke and close the window to just a crack. No need to climb out! I'll just stay in here until they leave. Hoo-boy. Was it the special secret I added to my tea? Did that bring on the *willa Hund*? Or maybe it was all of them being here, together, at once, in the new house; all of them using big words and bragging about their husbands and children. Going on about what all they are doing at church—their missionary support *initiatives*. And everyone had to say "initiative" at least twice. And talking about volunteering. And fellowship. And Arts Council. I am yet so stupid! How embarrassing—I thought it was Art, like Arthur, a man's name: "Art's council." I'm so glad I didn't say anything.

I hear them get up from the living room and walk past the kitchen. They're coming down the stairs now, all talking at once. Like cedar waxwings, in a flock, turning in the sky, then landing as one. Beautiful in a way, but still capable of turning on you. Hurting you to make things better for themselves. "I'll just stay here in my safe little place," I whisper to myself. I open the window and wave the hand towel to get the tobacco smell out.

Ruth calls out to me if I'm okay and I answer, talking in my girly voice—my *Mejahl* voice—nice and high and meek like hers, "No, no, I amn't that sick. I'll phone you later."

The women talk quietly. I hear the wooden hangers clatter as they get their coats, purses snap open and shut, keys jingle and they call goodbye like we're all best friends. And as I'm listening something happens inside of me and before they can leave I run out of the bathroom waving my hands around and I'm saying how nice they all are and how glad I am they came. I am "gushing" at least that's what Ruth says to me later.

"And Deb, that dress looks sooo nice. It's new, *joh*? And brings out your blue eyes!" Ruth looks amazed and comes next to me, smiling like crazy.

And I'm talking and laughing and hugging them and

thinking how easy this is, really. And how it's just like sliding down the big toboggan hill; you just get started, and away you go! The door closes behind the last one and I can hear them drive off, but I can't tell for sure whether or not I can still hear them or if they are really gone. It's like the slowly growing silence of the choir, at the end of a hymn.

Only Ruth is left, beaming, her face red and looking at me and looking at me. I help her on with her coat and then from out of some *willa* place way down inside, I look at her and yell,

"What the fuck! That was a fuck of fun!"

And she opens her eyes wider than ever and then starts laughing so hard she starts coughing and spit comes out of her mouth and tears are on her cheeks. She sits down with her coat half on and half off and I plop down beside her and after we stop laughing, in a really quiet voice, she says back to me, "Yeah, that was a fuck of fun!"

After she leaves, still giggling a little now and I go to the garage. I feel *morschijch goot* and happy I did such a bold thing, even if it was only in front of my friend, who is nice and quiet and will keep it secret, especially because she said the F-word too. "I have to be more like that. I have to be bold." I say, looking behind the paint cans where Hart keeps the vodka.

I remember just then about Cornie Dyck, a *Russländer* boy who moved to town when I was little. He was so small and thin and shy. He always hid in the tall rhubarb when we played baseball at school and the boys called him Rhubarb Dyck. I think if I don't watch out, that I will become like him and all the "tits and teeth" ladies and the Hartplatz men who once called the little Dyck boy names and are still just as mean as ever will gobble me up and spit me out. If I let them. I don't want to be a little Russian boy in the rhubarb.

Died Rich

"I am a true sea-dog with balls the size of cantaloupes!" Diedrich shouted, slashing at a snowy tree branch with a cutlass made from a broken broom handle.

"Diedrich! Diedrich Deutsch!" Doctor Rempel shouted from an open window. His breath turned to frozen vapour as soon as the words left the warm sedan. "Do you want a ride to school?"

Diedrich dropped his weapon but not his fourteen-year-old swagger. He walked towards the familiar waiting car that sat idling on the rutted ice of the street. A plume rose from the tail-pipe, fouling the blue of the Manitoba sky in the little town of Winkler and when the engine backfired, a perfect white smoke ring shot out, twirling with delight.

"Hurry up, swashbuckler!" Doctor Rempel said with a friendly smile. He hawked and spat, then tossed out a cigar remnant and rolled up the window with a pumping arm.

Diedrich got in and slammed the door. His window fogged immediately.

"Now, did you say, 'cantaloupes' or 'antelopes'?" the doctor

43

asked, steel wool eyebrows wagging. His nose was a purplish red and the pores on his cheeks stood out like moon craters, complete with a coating of grey dust—the same fine material that accumulated on the interior surfaces of the round-fendered four-door.

Diedrich offered a winking reply, "Which is bigger?"

"Ho-ho! You sounded like your dad just then. You did. You're looking like him too. Seen him lately?"

How likely is that? Diedrich thought. He thought these bold words, but just shook his head no, adding a quiet scoff.

"How about your aunts then? They doing alright? Still living in that farmhouse on the edge of town, right?"

"By Plett's potato fields," Diedrich said.

"How long you been with them now? What's it, two years?"

"You know," Diedrich said slyly. "Aunty Ros says you are my father figure. I heard her say that to Aunty Myrtle. Anyway, to answer your question: Since Grade Seven."

"*Joh-joh.* How come you're so smart? You sound like a social worker, not a pirate. Eh?"

Diedrich made a "huh" sound in his throat and looked out his window in reply.

"And now you're in Grade Nine, eh? In high school. A future matriculant in the class of '65. *Cum Laude*, no doubt. Your family has a fine history of brains and determination—and not a little of either! I delivered your daddy, you know? I swear he tried to kick me after I slapped him on the bottom." He grinned at the thought, then grunted with effort to steer the lumbering car onto the school street. He halted, tires sliding, in front of the school steps. A small boggle of teens stood on the curtilage—off school property—the snow packed down with footprints, sunflower seed shells, and cigarette butts. They turned to watch Diedrich disembark, the door squawking as he pushed at it.

"Swing it hard!" Rempel hollered. "Give my greetings to Myrtle and Rosalyn, buccaneer!"

The door clanked as Diedrich flung it shut with two hands. The boys watched him.

"Hey, buccaneer," Ronny Graefer sneered, "how come the doctor has to give you a ride?"

"Yeah, what makes you so special? You sick?" said another.

The biggest of the boys stepped forward and grabbed Diedrich's sleeve. The old woolly garment, a refugee from the church basement, threatened to part at the shoulder seam. "Hey," he said. "Us guys are talking to you."

His name was Morton and he was the son of the Phys. Ed teacher, Mr. Smullett, a new resident who was an "Englisher" from Winnipeg. It was only the Smulletts' second year in Winkler and the family was a gossip favourite, discussed by residents with mild, unspecified suspicion. Morton had earned the unfriendly *Plautdietsch* sobriquet, "*Moazh.*" It meant "ass."

Moazh was over a head taller than Diedrich, but Diedrich was most concerned for the wellbeing of his jacket, the only one he owned. Without stopping to think, he lifted his boot and stomped down on *Moazh*'s foot. Protected only by a clean white Converse basketball sneaker, the result was as Diedrich hoped. *Moazh* jumped back cursing and Diedrich made a streaking getaway, churning through fresh snow and up the steps, shouting, "*Moazh!*" into his floury wake.

In Miss Feeblecorn's classroom, his new homeroom this semester, he found his name written on a piece of masking tape affixed to a desktop. "Deidrick Deutsch." He stared at the penned name tag as he hung his jacket on the chairback.

"Young man," the teacher said, raising her voice and pointing at him with a ruler from her post on the raised floor near the blackboard. "You should put your jacket in your locker. I think you know that…"

He nodded and said, "Yes, ma'am, from now on. I forgot."

She mouthed, "O-K" as the announcements crackled from the loudspeaker.

*　*　*

He steered clear of *Moazh* for the rest of the day. After school, he snuck out through the janitor's room at the back of the building. On his way out, he paused to scoop a handful of green granules from the paper drum marked, "Sweeping Compound." He held the mixture under his nose, sniffing the refreshing chemical tang, and then put the crumbly concoction in his pocket. Cutting diagonally across the playground, Diedrich set a course for the *Thrift-T Car Wash*. It was a self-serve coin-operated business that he cleaned several times a week, his after-school job.

He found his tools in the pumphouse: a square-edged spade, a wheelbarrow, and a heavy length of steel reinforcing bar bent into a "J" at one end and a welded "T" at the other. One of the pumps hummed a short electric tone and then jangled to life. The copper water pipe that led out through the block wall to the car wash stall quivered like a hard-struck tuning fork.

In the unoccupied car wash stall, Diedrich began his regular routine. He blocked the entrance with a sawhorse and left the waterlogged overhead door open for light and ventilation. He coaxed the re-bar tip into the grillwork of the steel floor grate. Lifting and backpedaling, he skidded the cumbersome cover off, revealing a grave-sized pit in the concrete floor. At the bottom of the cement-walled tomb lay a six-inch thick layer of grey-green sludge. A septic reek grasped him in a foul embrace. He dug a handful of the minty sweeping compound from his pocket and took a deep *Pine-Sol* scented breath.

"Ahh... ambrosia," he sighed, squinting one eye and then discarding the compound into the hole.

With the wheelbarrow placed next to the edge and armed with his spade, Diedrich hopped down and began scraping out the half-frozen slurry of car wash residue. The loud rasp of the shovel hid the sound of a vehicle approaching. Just in time, he looked around to see the sawhorse lying on its side. A pick-up truck rolled towards him, its crooked teeth spelling out "*MERCURY*." He ducked just in time to miss being clipped by the front axle. The truck pulled up to the wheelbarrow and then continued more slowly, the wheelbarrow chattering and screeching as it slid sideways against its will. The vehicle stopped above him and the doors opened. Feet appeared, including a familiar pair of pristine *Converse* high-top runners.

"Hey, hey, little Deutsch! Who's the ass now, eh? Eh? Now you're the *morch*—Ronny, is that how you say it?"

"Yep, *moarrzzzhhhh,*" was faceless Ronny's phonetic reply, emphasizing the buzzing-shushing last syllable sound.

"Ha-ha! Hear that, moarzzhh? We're goin' for a *Pepsi* now. You wanna watch my truck for me while you're down there? Tell ya what—I'll shut the garage door so you and my truck stay nice and warm in here, eh."

Diedrich watched as the feet drew near to the wheelbarrow, dumping the dead-rat-motor-oil stinking muck on the sloping floor. A few seconds later he heard a quarter clink into the coin box on the wall and then the rush of water in the wash wand. Soapy water ran into the pit. He scraped a canal in the sludge so it could drain away. The wand fell with a clatter and then propelled itself backwards like a fleeing cuttlefish until it jammed in the corner of the bay. *Moazh* and Ronny left, their laughter echoing above the hiss of the spray.

As soon as they were gone, Diedrich began crawling out, turning his head sideways to fit under the truck. Watery slop smeared his jeans and the chest and sleeves of his black jacket. No sweat, he thought; it'll all wash out. But once he emerged, he noticed the rip on the seam where the sleeve attached to the shoulder.

* * *

Walking home in the failed light, he thought of all the things he could have done, retaliation planned with dark precision: piss in the gas tank, empty the tires or drench the pick-up's interior with the wash wand. As he cut across Plett's plowed field, pebbly white snow on dark furrows, he shook away his scheming and began preparing the lie he must tell his aunts to lessen their anger and dismay. He'd accept the black spot of their blame he decided, but not the punishment.

* * *

"Dear Miss Feeblecorn," Diedrich wrote in his neat, small cursive. "I have hung my jacket in my locker. Thank you for reminding me. I also noticed that you are spelling my name wrong. There is an easy way to remember: died rich. That's what I'm going to do, live a long life and die rich. You can remember it easy this way—I'm going to be the student who died rich, indeed. Spelled died but pronounced deed. Diedrich."

He stuck the tape from his desk to the bottom of the page as evidence. Folding the note carefully into thirds, the way Aunty Myrtle taught him, he put it on the teacher's desk before school started, tucked with one corner slipped under the edge of her blotter.

After the class sang, "God Save the Queen" and recited "The Lord's Prayer", Miss Feeblecorn taught them about decimals, her tall, slanted numbers gathering like a crowd of bystanders on black pavement. The chalk dust lit on her green sweater and she picked bits off her sleeve as she assigned a problem to them.

Walking slowly down the aisle, arms crossed, she approached Diedrich's desk. He looked up when the soft tap of her square-heeled shoes paused beside him. She bent down from the waist and whispered, "See me at lunch, please, Diedrich." He nodded, smelling the faint fragrance of *Jergens Lotion*, reminding him of his mother. A distant memory.

"I just wanted to confirm that I received your note," she began when he went to her desk at the break, after eating his sandwich.

"Okay."

"That's a very creative way to help others to remember the spelling of your name. I appreciate your telling me—I use tricks like that to remember names all the time."

Diedrich blushed. He put his hands in his jacket pocket. He glanced at the shoulder seam, now neatly re-stitched courtesy of Aunty Rosalyn. She had washed it too, hanging it to dry in the glowing, orange-toothed grin of the kitchen's portable heater. He caught a whiff of detergent and the outdoors smell of clean wool.

"Of course, we don't want to think about dying, necessarily, but it's okay to have big dreams. We are such stuff as dreams are made on, are we not?"

"Pass it!" a high-pitched shout from the playground soccer game interrupted his consideration of her comment. He took a half-step back with one foot.

"Oh, I'm holding you up. Sure! You get out there and get into the game with the others."

As Diedrich turned to leave, Mr. Smullett came in, a whistle dangling on a lanyard around his neck. "Anita," he said, then glanced at Diedrich and corrected himself, "Miss Feeblecorn.

Here are the sign-up sheets for the boys' basketball team. Please announce it to your class and invite anyone who wants to try-out to put their name here."

"Shall do, Coach. Here you go, Diedrich, you could be the first to sign-up. That way," Miss Feeblecorn added, her eyes shining, "everyone will see the correct spelling of your name!"

Diedrich shrugged but stopped and looked at the foolscap sheet. It was divided into three columns: Name, Grade, Position.

"Does it cost anything?" he asked, looking up at Mr. Smullett.

"Only your time and sweat," he said, grinning at Miss Feeblecorn.

"When do you play?"

"We practice at noon-hour in the gym—that way the bus students have a chance to make the squad. We play in the evenings, four home games and four away games and then the championship tournament is on a Saturday."

Diedrich pouted his lip, thinking of his job at the car wash. He could play.

"'Kay, give it here, once," he said, reaching for the sheet. He took it to his desk and wrote his name and grade into the spaces provided on the top line. He paused. His gaze passing back and forth between the two teachers, he asked, "What should I put for 'Position'?"

Smullett held out a flat palm to the top of Diedrich's head, "I'd say, 'Guard'. Can you dribble, shoot and pass? Can you run fast?"

"I can run fast. I can shoot, I think." Diedrich smiled at Miss Feeblecorn, and she replied with a determined face paired with a stabbing, upward hand gesture. "Shooting?" he wondered. He smelled the *Jergens Lotion* again and handed the paper to Smullett, thinking, what does he mean, "dribble" and "guard?"

"Okay," Smullett said, shuffling backwards, "I'll mark you down as a guard. See you tomorrow at twelve. Wear your gym clothes."

* * *

"When it's this cold, it always occurs to me that some of the creatures from Hell, the ones who were the borderline cases, the ones who just barely missed going to Heaven, get a short furlough. A vacation from Hades. I imagine the gatekeeper of Hell to be wearing a sharp business suit with a tailored shirt and tie—maybe a string tie—and that he would not be sweating, not even armpits or bum crack. He would just be there at the gates, bathed in flame and molten sulfur, near the hounds. That fiend would be crisp and clean as a brand new twenty-dollar bill, frosty as a Fudgsicle fresh outta the freezer," Doctor Rempel said, his Roosevelt moustache jouncing.

Since basketball tryouts started, there had been a cold snap, and he had taken to driving Diedrich to the car wash on working afternoons. He also bought a pair of lined, leather work gloves for the boy. These were kept in the old *Lincoln* so that the doctor could also use them when he scraped the frost off his car windows.

Rempel continued, "'Where the Hell do you think you're going?' the gatekeeper would ask—his little joke—and the borderline hellions would hand him a note. On Satan's private stationery, stamped in blood, a short message, a hall pass if you will, from the Devil. 'Please allow these lost souls a brief respite from the heat. They may walk from the Winkler Collegiate Institute to the car wash, accompanying young Diedrich Deutsch to his job. Once they cool off to their satisfaction, they are to promptly return. No playing billiards, no consorting and no sexual congress, no consumption of strong drink. No dancing, either," Rempel added with a silky smile.

The two drove in silence for a block and when the car stopped at an intersection, the doctor waited patiently for a number of boys and girls to squat down behind the *Lincoln* and grab the bumper. He pulled away slowly, gradually accelerating until the kids could be heard squealing and laughing as they slid along the ice-covered street behind the car.

"But what if they *did* some of the things they weren't supposed to?" Diedrich asked. "What if they played pool or drank a cold root beer from the Dairy Whip, or what if they didn't go back to Hell? Then what?"

Doctor Rempel toggled the turn-indicator as they turned onto Pembina Avenue, towards the car wash. The bumper-shiners let go because Pembina, freshly gravelled, was too gritty to *rutsch*. "Well, exactly!" Rempel said, reaching into his tweed coat and finding a cigar of reasonable length. He lit it while Diedrich waited for him to continue, and the Zephyr idled at an intersection. They paused, watching as a teacher led her line of waddling children across the street in their bright snowsuits, two-by-two.

"If the lost souls are already in Hell, borderline or not, they can receive no further, greater sentence, right? Here on earth, if you receive the death penalty, that is the maximum. In the same way, if you are in Hell, what worse place is there? If there is a Super Picante Hell filled with angry skunks, it's not mentioned in the Bible, and you'd think they might have pointed that out!" His conversation tailed off as the car wheeled onto the car wash yard.

"So, okay," Diedrich replied. "They can't be punished any more, they are already ten out of ten, so they play hooky. Then what?" He looked around for the leather gloves.

"Oh, Lordy, I wish I could figure that one out," Doctor Rempel said, puffing on his cigar. "On one hand, I suppose there's nothing matters at that point. They are Hell-bound souls that have escaped, conditionally. If they come to this realization—if they see that they have beaten the system—what then? I hesitate to say this to such a tender boy as you, youth's impressions lasting lifelong and me your older male mentor and all, but that knowledge of having beat the Devil might almost be better than Heaven!"

"*Oh, bah nay...*" Diedrich said softly.

"Listen. To get to Heaven, you play by the rules. You sacrifice some earthly pleasures, many examples of which you yourself will soon face in relative abundance in the coming years, even here in Winkler." He tapped ash from the cigar. "These imaginary borderline folk from the evermore obviously did not fully embrace self-denial and hence, wound up in the basement suite. Now, what if these prisoners of eternal damnation, out on their cold-weather day pass, recognize the infinity-sized loop-hole? Imagine the joy, imagine the freedom of knowing that, for all eternity—*nothing more matters.* My dear Diedrich, I suggest that wondrous revelation is not only better than Heaven, but worthy of a whole new religion in support of it. What say you? Are you my first convert?"

"Thanks for the ride; I have to get to work," Diedrich said, sliding out the door into the frigid prairie gloaming. He paused, imagining the condemned, newly released from Hell. Then he added, "Yeah. The worst punishment they could have got is to be sent back to H-E-double-hockey-sticks and that was gonna happen, eventually, anyhow." He flipped hair out of his eyes, then pulled his toque on. "They couldn't be threatened!"

"Yes! But would they feel brave because they were safe, or because they were totally, eternally unsafe? So, what's the diff?"

Diedrich trudged to the pump room, confused by the strange conversation. He stopped and walked back to the open window

53

on the driver's side, from which a blue cloud of *El Producto* emanated.

"Yes, my acolyte?" Doctor Rempel said.

"What you are saying is that you want me to be brave? Period, end of story?"

"You got it. Period, end of story."

"Alright. I think I'm pretty good at that." Diedrich said.

"Be better than 'pretty good'. Be the best there is at being brave. You are in this little *Darp* on the smooth, flat bottom of an ancient sea with your aunts, me, and some others here who know about you and the bad things you've endured. So, you're safe. On the other hand, the things that have vexed you will continue to do so, and new adversaries and evils will threaten you on your path. So, you are unsafe."

He stoked the cigar with hollowed cheeks, bringing its tip back to crackling life, then similarly revved the flathead when it sputtered and seemed about to stall. "It's cold and my window's frozen open, so hurry up," he said, nipping at a silver flask he slipped out of his coat. "You have exactly thirty minutes before my tail lights you will see."

* * *

Early on school day mornings, the thump-thump-thump of a basketball could be heard in the deserted hallways framing the cinderblock sanctuary that was the Valentine Winkler Collegiate Institute gymnasium. Periodically, the echo of the ball dribbling would cease, followed after a few seconds by the metallic clash of the steel supports that held the basketball backboards. Diedrich Deutsch created this syncopated melody as he ran from end to end, barefoot, practicing his dribbling—first lefty, then righty— and taking an awkward shot at each end of the court. Panting and red-cheeked, he stopped just before the bell rang to alert teachers and janitors that the front doors would now be unlocked. Diedrich gained early entry through the janitorial staff entrance, courtesy of Mr. Schellenberg.

"No work boots on the gym floor!" Schellenberg had scolded on Diedrich's first morning, kneeling as if in prayer to apply a wetted thumb to one of the black heel marks left behind by Diedrich's work boots, his *Steewele.*

"*Vedaumpte groote oabeit Steewle!*" he had said, rising up and glaring down at Diedrich's dirty footwear. He followed this pronouncement, curse word and all, with a blast of air through his thin nose. Then he beckoned for the ball and with unexpected skill, banked it into the basket directly above him, spinning it like a top off the backboard.

"English, not Low German!" he quipped, winking and retreating quickly to continue his morning chores.

After a few weeks, Mr. Schellenberg paid him no attention, except to peek in on occasion to ensure his *oabeit Steewle* interdiction was being upheld. Alone under the buzz of the blueish lights, Diedrich sat on the bleachers and rubbed at the soles of his feet, pink and blistered in places from their taxing laps on the polished hardwood. Just then, Coach Smullett came into the gym on the way to his small office.

"Hey-hey!" he shouted, "look who's here early workin' on his game!"

He pointed at Diedrich's bare feet. "It looks like Schellenberg gave you the heck for wearing street shoes on the floor, eh?"

Diedrich nodded. He was on the team's "spare" list and although still allowed to attend practices, he had not yet made the team, officially. Being discovered in the morning by the coach was a happy accident that he had patiently contrived. He wasn't a particularly guileful boy, but knew that extra effort could not worsen his chances. Doctor Rempel had commented, "Can't hurt," and Aunty Ros had said the exact same thing when he asked her.

"Why don't you have your runners on? Forget 'em?"

"No. I don't have any. Ernie Froese lets me wear his old ones, but I can't keep them 'cause he has to save them for his brother Jake. They don't really fit me anyway."

"Hmm. What size you take?"

"My boots are tens, but they are a little big, yet. A lot, actually."

Smullett spun on a creaking rubber heel and walked swiftly to his office. He swung the door open and reappeared a minute later carrying a pair of worn *Converse* All-Star high top runners. One lace was red and one blue.

"These old clod-hoppers—they're eights—have been in the lost and found since last year. You are welcome to them. Also, we have a game on Friday night in Plum Coulee. Can you go?"

Overcome with excitement, Diedrich held the shoes as if a priceless, fragile prize. He flopped down on the gym floor and immediately began trying them on, first holding the dark gum sole of one flat against his bare foot. Tying the laces, Diedrich took some rapid stutter steps, each squeal like music to him. He licked his fingers and cleaned the rubber soles the way he had seen older players do at practice.

"Grippy!" he said to Smullett. "Thanks, Coach! *Väl mol dankscheen*! Thank you!" With that, he peeled away across the floor at top speed, rounding into a U-turn and flying back to Smullett, finishing with a bounding lay-up—sans basketball—his fingers riffling the dangling cotton string of the net.

* * *

The sweaty starters sat on the bench while the second string stood in an encircling crescent. Crouching low in front of them, Coach Smullett swallowed his excitement and carefully went over his notes. "We are behind by only four points and their big guy…"

"Number forty-four, that big, giant *Schanzenfelder*?" Ernie Froese asked.

"Yes, yeah, forty-four, he's got four fouls. One more and he's out!"

Diedrich listened, arms folded, weight on one foot above canted hips. He stared intently into Smullett's eyes as, arms waving, the coach described how they would pressure the guy with the ball in the second half. ("*Dutch Blitz*!" was Ernie's uninvited translation.)

As the scoreboard clock sounded and their huddle broke up, Diedrich spoke. "Not to change the subject Coach, but when do I get in? I can take the ball away from those guys, easy."

Smullett ignored the comment and sent the team out onto the floor.

When Diedrich turned to sit down, he found no room on the player's bench. He could stand or choose instead to sit on the first row of bleachers in the midst of the Plum Coulee fans. Several of the nearby spectators recognized his predicament and began mocking him, laughing and jeering.

"Hey number eight, why don't you sit down? Ride the pine!"

"Yeah, you make a better door than a window, not? *Sat die dol, Jung*!"

"Eight don't rate!"

Anxious to get out of the spotlight, Diedrich spun around and backed in, wedging himself on the crowded bench right beside the coach. Smullett slid sideways, hanging one chino-clad cheek over the end.

With the game tied and only a few minutes left, *Moazh* fell

57

heavily. He limped off the floor and when Smullett turned to look down the row of eager replacement candidates, Diedrich shot up, yelling, "I know what to do!" and sprinted to the timer's table to check-in. Smullett sputtered, but the referee blew the whistle and the game resumed.

Red and blue laces flashed and Diedrich was everywhere at once, frantically chasing the ball, his slim form darting in between and around the taller players. Within seconds he stole a pass and despite missing the open shot and the subsequent one he gained off a scrappy rebound, he was there when his teammate Ronny Graefer scored. The same thing happened twice more. Diedrich did not contribute directly to the score, but WCI pulled ahead and the buzzer blared to signal a timeout by the home team.

"Eight is great!" said a pretty girl with bright blue eye shadow, calling from the stands. Diedrich hid behind the coach. Ernie Froese, who scored twice thanks to Diedrich's rabid dog antics, slapped him on the back. "Way to go, there, Deutsch!"

* * *

Doctor Rempel's breath wheezed in and out. He concentrated on the *Converse* All-Stars that sat on the *Lincoln*'s bench seat between him and Diedrich, peering through smudgy glasses perched on his rutabaga nose.

"And that's how you found them, in your locker?"

Diedrich nodded, his chin lifting off his chest.

"Yeah. I could smell something was wrong, though. The melons are totally rotten."

"Right, I'm getting that," the doctor replied, sniffing. He used the red tip of a wooden match to pull back at the tongue of one of the runners. They were packed with a viscous, runny filling of rancid fruit. The shoelaces were slit down the middle and the canvas uppers were in ribbons.

"Kind of funny, don't you think, that cantaloupes were the weapon of choice? Eh? Remember?"

Diedrich snuffled in reply. Rempel quickly said, "Coulda been worse, coulda been rancid antelope!"

Diedrich snickered despite his best efforts, then forced himself to look serious. "What should I do?"

Rempel mused. He retrieved and offered a clean folded hanky to the boy, who took it and blew his nose hard.

"Hey! That's for polishing my glasses!" Doctor Rempel said, feigning anger. "Okay, look. What do you want? Justice? Revenge? A get out of jail free card? What?"

"I just want my runners," Diedrich said.

"Really? Whoever did this deserves some knuckle justice. Me? I'd want to kick his *Moazh*."

Diedrich blew out a puff of air.

"I'll take you home. Leave the shoes with me. Get a good night's sleep and I'll see you in the morning. Sound good?"

After a long, clearing breath, Diedrich hummed, "Um-hmm," and wiped his nose on a jacket sleeve.

"Here. Keep it," Rempel said, tossing back the hanky and wrinkling his sea lion nose.

* * *

The next afternoon at the car wash, Cornelius James Rempel, M.D., sat in his rusting '42 *Lincoln* Zephyr and smoked. He watched the boy work, a study in efficiency and diligence. After scraping up a shovelful of sludge, he rocked its weight back and used the pendulum momentum to heft the load up to the apogee. Up and over the lip of the barrow it went, him twisting the blade at the last to spill its sodden cargo.

Still so young, he thought. Whip smart. Mature too—a stoic. Unlike his weasel of a father on that count.

"How far that little candle throws his beams!" Rempel said aloud. His speech disturbed a sparrow that pecked at his cigar ash outside on the yard. He wondered too at the boy's ability to allow a kind of yieldedness to govern his life. Like the much-respected *Gelassenheit* his old *Brüderthaler* pastor used to rave about, ("Submit! Leave your cares with the Lord!") except, as for Diedrich, there was no need of an omnipotent God. "This boy Diedrich relinquishes himself to the care of the world and all its grace and all its vicissitudes—come what may, come what may," he whispered to himself. There was, he mused, much to be learned from this boy who never sought to teach.

He had asked Diedrich earlier what he wanted—justice or revenge? "What about you, Rempel?" the doctor said now to himself, eyes regarding his reflection in the mirror. "What do *you* want?"

The sparrow, satisfied that there was no nutrition in the black scatterings on the snow, beat a whirring retreat. Rempel watched it go. **What *do* I want? To have no regrets—free as a bird**, he thought. **To relinquish. To achieve serenity.**

Leaning back in his seat, he remembered Rosalyn, back in high school. A year behind him, she had the best marks in her grade and beat him in the school spelling bee. He faltered under her confident stare back then and added a fatal extra "n" to "panache," giving her the win. He thought of how her and Myrtle had stepped up when Diedrich was abandoned. With no pay, only an eternal reward, they had taken on a head-strong teenage boy with an absentee father whose appearance was all the boy would ever inherit.

Diedrich hurried towards the car, whacking the leather work gloves against his dirty pants and the sides of his boots, as if challenging them to a duel. "All done, record time!" he called out.

Swirling back into the old Zephyr together with a shock of cold air, he rested a hand on the box holding the rotted evidence, his defiled All-Stars.

"Okay, Doctor, what did you decide?" he asked, applying his hanky to his reddened nose.

"I decided... I decided that you and your aunts—not me—should be the ones to decide. Not me, sir. But I, of course, have some ideas."

Diedrich waited for the doctor to continue as Rempel pulled the car up onto the macadam esker that was Pembina Avenue. "Myrtle and Rosalyn will be home now, yes?" he asked.

At home in the small, wood frame storey-and-a-half house, Rempel sat across the kitchen table facing Diedrich and his two spinster aunts. Following small talk and tea, he told the whole story to the sisters. He answered their initial questions, then laid out his plan.

"First, I believe we need to confirm, with absolute certainty, who did this. It seems quite obvious to me that the vandal is the coach's son, Morton," he looked at Diedrich, who affirmed with a nod. "His father should be given the evidence and..."

"Sorry to interrupt, but Morton said something to me," Diedrich said. "Guess I should have told you before, but at school today he bugged me about the shoes."

"Who else knew about them, about your runners?" Rosalyn asked.

"No one. Only Doctor Rempel, and now—you and Aunty Myrtle. Today Morton, he said to me, 'How do your shoes smell?' or something like that."

She looked at Rempel, eyebrows raised. "Go on, please Cornie."

"Fine. That's out of the way, then! Morton's guilty, he's our man.

61

Doctor Rempel worried with fat fingers the pocket holding his cigars. "I went and talked to Coach Smullett earlier today. I wanted to know how he would approach this, how well he knows his son."

All eyes in the kitchen were on him as he continued—bedside manner activated, his voice rumbled like an advancing tank. "I believe Smullett is a decent man. I met him this morning before school. I went to his car and showed him the shoes. As soon as I showed Smullett the ruined runners, his face turned bright red and he said, 'Morton!'"

"He knew right away?" Rosalyn asked.

Rempel nodded slowly, a hand cupping his beard, fingers combing the grey whiskers. "He did. I'm not sure how, but Smullett was convinced. Is convinced. He said that Morton would buy new shoes and apologize in front of the team."

Diedrich seemed neutral, unaffected by this news but looked like he suspected there might be more.

"I said... well, I said we'd think about that."

"Why" Myrtle said. Rosalyn sat up tall in her chair.

"Oh, I don't know. Something didn't sit quite right. I wanted to see what you two had to say." He looked at Rosalyn.

"You were right to hold off, Cornie. Here's what I think. I am afraid that boy is what some might call a bad egg. He's not going to give up this little power struggle quite so readily. In fact, Morton could blame Diedrich for showing him up and making him appear weak. Or he could blame his dad—the coach. He'll blame anyone else but himself. I suspect—fear, really—that the only way to get him to leave Diedrich be, now and forever, is to push him right to the edge." Rosalyn paused and then made a cutting motion with her hand. "Diedrich should challenge him to a fight."

62

"Oh, my!" Myrtle said, shifting in her seat. "You may be right, Rosalyn, but it's the coach's job to manage the team and it's also his job as a father to discipline his son. Right? Plus, the shoes were free in the first place. A gift from the Coach Smullett. A very thoughtful one, too."

"All true," Rosalyn acknowledged. "Plus, there's turning the other cheek, something that I've thought about a lot..."

The room was quiet for a moment.

"I'd say...You're both right," Rempel stammered, caught in Rosalyn's gaze. Eyes that could stare an eagle blind. "But, in this case, I think I agree that this Morton misery will visit us again if we don't cut it out entirely. Now's the time to excise it," Rempel replied, thinking of Rosalyn's decisive gesture.

The tiny kitchen was quiet again. This time the muffled clatter of the sump pump from the crawlspace below broke the nervous silence. It jumped to life with a throbbing beat.

"You two *really* think that if Diedrich challenges Morton to a fight, the other, apparently rather larger boy will back out?" Myrtle said, her voice raised slightly to overcome the noisy pump.

"If I know my bullies, yes, that's what I think will happen. Between his guilt and his weak character, yes. *Oba, joh*! One hundred per cent. And, just to be on the safe side, Cornie can be on hand. He is a doctor, remember—to make sure it's just a little dust-up. A cut lip never killed anyone."

"How will that, *excise* the problem for good, as the Doctor put it?" Myrtle asked, one eyebrow hitched.

"Morton will be shamed, by his own doing. He will find himself trapped. You see, it's all the same whether he declines to fight... if he fights and loses... or—especially—if he fights and wins over Diedrich who is smaller and younger—Morton is shamed. In all cases, Diedrich is the more honourable, the bravest."

Doctor Rempel thought of his earlier advice to the boy.

"If, however," Rosalyn continued, "his father, or the school, or any of us step in, then Morton will escape the trap."

"How so?" Myrtle questioned, still not fully convinced, although she was now leaning in her sister's direction.

"Morton will become the victim, and our Diedrich will be nothing but a *tattle-tale*. Plus," she said, taking in a breath and tapping her finger on the tablecloth like a gavel, "it will leave the door open, or even *invite* future animosity from Morton. Reprisals against Diedrich. No one likes a tattler."

Myrtle drummed her fingertips on the table top, almost as if a Morse code reply. Doctor Rempel studied their faces and added a summation.

"As is my practice in the case of a fishhook mishap. You do not cut the flesh. You take the hook, push it all the way through and snip off the barb. Then ease it out."

Myrtle's brow crinkled in concentration. The others watched her for a reaction.

"Diedrich," she said, turning to face her ward. "I never thought your Aunt Rosalyn or I would push you into a fight. That is not our way! But we agree that in this situation, a bold approach is best. What do you think, *Jung*?"

"What took you guys so long?" he sighed.

Rosalyn touched Diedrich on the shoulder. "It's your decision. Still, we'll pray on it."

* * *

The old Zephyr gurgled asthmatically, shuddering in place on the street in front of WCI. A small flock of sparrows took turns flitting to a scattering of seeds beneath the open driver's window and a cluster of elms across the street.

A shoebox under his arm, Diedrich was one of the first to

skip out of the entrance doors after the final school bell rang. He trotted towards the gurgling car with a light gait and popped the passenger door open with a smooth one-handed motion.

"So? Tell me! How'd it go with Morton? What happened?" Doctor Rempel asked in a rush of words as soon as the Diedrich got in.

"Oh, no big deal. He said sorry. At lunchtime, Morton bought me new shoes with Christmas money from his *Opa* in Morden and he's gonna come to the car wash and help me for a week."

"Huh? I hope you mean Morton, not his *Opa*," the doctor said, unable to resist the chance to tease and using it to hide his surprise. Before Diedrich replied he turned away and kicked at the accelerator, suddenly annoyed with the halting idle. "I thought you were going to challenge him to a fight?"

"Who, his *Opa*?"

"Ha. You got me back." Doctor Rempel slipped him a dour, side-eyed look, buttered with a smile.

"I don't mean to change the subject, Doctor, but Morton an' me are going to go to Winnipeg with his cousin Theodore on Saturday. To the U of M. They have glass backboards in the Bison fieldhouse. We're gonna shoot around and then watch the team practice."

"So—what?" Rempel said, incredulous. "That means you and Morton are friends now?" The big V12 car engine grumbled, and Rempel adjusted the choke lever on the dash.

"I guess. You said be brave. You said, 'be the best at being brave. Period. End of story.'" Diedrich said this plainly, all the while with his eyes on Doctor Rempel, a frank expression on his young face. "It wasn't as scary as you grown-ups figured."

"Okay. Okay. As simple as that." Rempel said, imagining

how this resolute young boy, the ruined shoes brandished like loaded muskets, would have approached the bully, pushing down his fear, looking up at his stronger, older foe. Not knowing what to expect but somehow confident that he'd emerge with the best of all outcomes. "...for I am gentle and humble in heart," the doctor thought, the passage clear in his mind.

"Anyway," Diedrich said, leaning forward to tune the radio dial. "You get the *Stones* on this old bucket?" He grinned playfully and then shoved the shoebox at his chauffeur. "Take a look, these runners are really neat! One lace red, one blue!"

After dutifully inspecting the boy's treasure, with their diamond tread soles and crinkly paper wrappers, he put the car in gear and began up the street. The engine fell into synchronization, dropping down several octaves and then spitting out a white smoke ring that spun rearward, rising against the Prussian blue of the winter sky.

Without Spot or Wrinkle

A dintless blue sky looks down on an energetic young father. The man, Hart Zehen, trails along behind his young son Matthew who rides his tricycle along the sidewalk of Main Street in their small prairie town. It's a red-knuckled place ringed by farm fields.

Matthew is permitted a certain territory by his mother, Justy. He may cross Barkman Avenue and then carry on west for two more blocks along Main. Then about-face and return. That boundary gives him a passing view of several businesses and their activity and commerce. His daily route includes the *Vogel's Economy Store*, a print shop, a gas station and best of all, the imposing edifice of the new credit union.

The building is a showcase with large windows trimmed in expensive aluminum. The only ones like it in town. The structure is low-slung and modern, and father and son admire it equally. The *Hartplatz Credit Union* crouches on the margin of the street and features hewn stone of different colours, and newly poured and finished concrete steps. The sidewalk fronting the structure has been dressed with a broom in a wavy pattern and when

Matthew pushes his trike to top speed, the hard rubber tires make a pulsing sound across the striations.

Together, Matthew and Hart study the detail in the sidewalk rectangles. Each one is bordered with a unique geometric pattern. Grandma Zehen has done research at the town's brand new and still nearly empty library. She tells them the pattern is called a "meander." "It's a design that was popular in ancient Greece, and it means 'winding path,' like the Red River or the Roseau, or the road to Stuartburn." She tells Matthew this as she tucks him in for a drowsy afternoon nap.

"But why is it on the sidewalk by the credit union?"

"That I don't exactly know! In German, to meander is to *rommbommle*. That's about a twenty-buck word, wouldn't you say?" she says with an exaggerated wink. "So, maybe…" she traces a line in the air with her finger. "Maybe it means that to go forwards, sometimes you have to go a little backwards? Retrace your steps?"

* * *

Early one morning, as he does every day, Matthew turns on the television set in the living room of the boxy little house where he lives. The antenna on the roof stands alone, one of only a few to offend the prairie horizon here in the town. Television is new and not entirely trusted by the conservative townspeople made up of mostly Mennonites, but also Lutherans and German Baptists. A strictly led population accustomed to stern sermons that admonished all and served warnings and penance in equal measure.

A motionless black and white test pattern fills the TV screen, silent but for an electric hum. Outside in the crab-apple tree, mourning doves announce the coming of day with their fluted song.

Next door, Matthew's father Hart is already well beyond the *eins* and the *zwei* of his work day. His shirt is wet with sweat from toil near the oven. The Zehen bake shop is less than a hundred yards from where the television fascinates the young boy.

An hour later, Barkman Avenue comes more fully to life with the bright chirping of a children's program on the TV and his father's return from the bakery.

"I'm late!" Hart shouts, rushing into the house. In full stride, he peels off his sloppy wet t-shirt, balls it up and—like a wrap-around goal in hockey—tucks it into the corner of the laundry hamper. He gives Matthew's hair a tousle as he sails by.

"Hey Matt, I gotta see a man about a horse!" He flashes a happy smile and closes the bathroom door with a click.

Minutes later he's clean-shaven and ready for business in a crisp, collared white shirt and white baker's pants. A black belt encircles his trim waist. He pats his back pocket for his wallet and snatches the bakery ledger from the hall table.

"Off to the Credit Union, I see," Justy says, her red head coming up from a mound of baker's aprons heaped on the kitchen table. She pauses in her never-ending cycle of washing, drying, sorting and folding. Mugging for him, she wraps an apron around her neck, a faux Hepburn scarf of coarse cotton.

"Today's the big day. I'll be back with the money, honey!" For that, he gets a quick peck on his *Aqua Velva* cheek.

"For luck, Hart," she says, and then adds a snap on his backside with one of the aprons. "And that's for later," she says with a wink. The screen door barks and he's skipping down the steps and cutting across the lawn to his meeting.

The world lays out before them, these three and soon-to-be four, beneath the watching sky. Their small bakeshop is boom-ing. A loan from the local brethren will allow for modernization and expansion; a freshly printed chequebook that makes money appear as if by magic—or possibly, as some claim—in response to prayer.

* * *

The quiet boardroom is another prairie box, rectilinear and oppressively neat from its long wooden table to its wall of cabinets and down to the square-tiled floor. It smells of furniture polish and *Sherwin-Williams* paint. More than that, the place smells like money. A framed dollar bill looks down from the wall like a coat-of-arms, Elizabeth Regina overseeing all.

A young man in a muted grey pinstripe suit begins the conversation. He cocks his thumb and points a Luger finger. "At which church are you a member, Mr. Zehen?"

The room crackles with silence. The baker fusses with the loan application page in front of him as he composes an answer. Fidgeting to stall, he tries to align the page at a right angle to the table edge. How can he say, "I do not attend, I'm not a member?" He can't. Slowly, he takes the application and folds it once and looks out the window.

"It's traditional to have a pastor's recommendation on the application," says a second pinstriper from across the smooth expanse of cherrywood. Then he quickly adds, with a slither, "Not a formal requirement, mind you."

A farm truck, manure spackled, seems to look at Hart through the plate glass with a sorry smile of rusting-chrome and then backs away from the curb. It's dinged up and the muffler has been missing for a while. Hart listens to the kettledrum exit. **Things to do, places to be,** he thinks, wishing he could join in the retreat.

The third man clears his throat. Hart's ledger is open on the table before him. He pauses and pats a loose fist on the tabletop lightly before he speaks. This is not a hand that has seen much sun, or gripped a shovel handle recently, or cinched tight a leather belt around a horse's girth. The man's skin is thin, so pale it appears lavender.

"It's not just a matter of collateral, Hart. Character, community standing, faith," he pauses, hitches his shoulders and then continues after glancing at the two grey-suited men flanking him on that side of the table. "And of course, industry ratios, that type of thing—that's what we look for," he says. "This is, after all, not *our* money."

He offers the last bit with a hand pressed against his chest like a lace hanky. Elizabeth Regina looks down, a savage smile on her green lips. "It's our members' money and we are charged with the responsibility of investing it wisely. I know you understand. As a businessman and as a... a brother." He closes the ledger with a soft thud. As he does so, the neat rows of numbers seem to protest—the zeros calling out in open-mouthed desperation.

* * *

The meeting ends. Hart pauses in the sunshine outside of the building. The sidewalk's chalky white concrete dazzles his eyes. He sets out, ledger in hand, leaving the meanders and their indirect windings behind him.

Plan B, he thinks, almost saying the words out loud. **Just going to have to see what old Heid at the Royal will say. He seems like a straight shooter, for a banker from out East. They call it the Royal Bank, but maybe he'll take a look at my numbers, common though they may be. Maybe he'll see it my way.**

As he crosses over the crown of the newly paved street, Zehen's footfalls echo from the macadam to the masonry façade of the bank storefront. Manager Heid looks out and waves hello through the greenish glass. He is stout with smile lines at the corners of his eyes. A grass-stained baseball rests in a small gold cup on his desk and there's a red ink blot on the pocket of his shirt. His suit jacket is off and his cuffs are rolled back over thick forearms in anticipation of the coming warmth of the day.

* * *

"So, the *Royal Bank* gave you the loan, eh?" Peter Vogel says, looking down through his spectacles. "I bank there too, you know."

"No, I didn't know that. I mean, Heid told me, but I thought… well, it just seemed more likely…" Hart replies awkwardly, then stops talking.

The two men blow on their coffee, sip, and Zehen murmurs approval. Vogel, the taller and older of the two and in whose kitchen they sit, motions at the table like a *Sharif* at an oasis. Brown buns and a jar of raspberry jelly await. Vogel arches an eyebrow.

They sup conversationally, chewing buns and slurping hot coffee. Hart feels comfortable here, as he always has. A place of friendship and the home of his mentors. The house is connected to the business, a dry goods store. Allies of Hart and his family, the Vogels are educated people who travel each year. Broadway ticket stubs and a glossy program from the *Metropolitan Opera* are their receipts; diplomas of a sort.

"You wait, Hart. Your bakery will do fine and then they'll all line up for your business. You'll get a better deal then too. Remember that and be kind, but still firm, when they show up."

"Wäa aunhelt, dee jewennt," Hart says, his Low German pronunciation suspect.

"That's a good one. 'You'll win if you persist.'" Vogel nods and smiles at his wife who rinses at the sink in the small, brilliant kitchen—gleaming porcelain and plated steel. "Your dad, he wanted to start a new church. Way back. Didn't go over so good around here. The men, they called him and his friends the '*Pepsi Cola Gemeinde.*' Not much respect for their would-be congregation, one that only met in restaurants, eh? Plus, your dad's first wife—as you well know—was Polish. Catholic, yet too. And his *Vater*, your *Opa,* he got kicked out of church, see? Oh, but that was some dirty business. Filthy dirty. *Schwiensch.* They said his team's bridles were too showy. Now the grandsons of the guys who shunned him, they drive *Cadillacs.* A Caddy, you know, that's a *real* show pony!"

Peter Vogel taps his wedding band on his cup as he thinks. "You know, if only we could all live in our village the way we used to—a shared pasture, shared water, shared labour. Heid, you know, he's a Scot from Windsor, Ontario. He has a firm hand on the idea of being fair—helping his neighbour, no matter who or *what* he is. Not a church man, that Heid, but he acts more like one than some others, in my opinion."

Ann clicks her tongue and nods, looking out the window.

"They forget the old ways, those guys in their fine suits, bought new. In fact, we all forget, with everything so fancy these days. It's distracting!" He takes a long breath and peers at the refrigerator. "Annie, do we have no butter?"

She pauses in mid-potato, peeler steady, and hums. She seems to have not heard her husband's request and steps towards Hart. "You know, Hart, how you are seen in this community, don't you?"

"Yes, Ann, I think so."

"I believe that for some, especially those who consider themselves the leaders, that you hold a certain status here. Because of your family history, partly."

Hart listened and blew on his coffee.

"They watch you and how you don't accept the rules that put them in their positions. For you, the old wounds—shunning and the hurtful consequences that remain for generations—are part of your unhappiness with the 'ruling class.' You see them as believing, against their own teachings, that they are greater than certain others. Greater by far than those who were here in this place before us; greater than other religions, both old and new."

Peter Vogel nodded in agreement, murmuring quietly.

"You, on the other hand, they see as being incomplete. The absence of what they'd call a serious church life puts a spot on your identity. It is unspoken, unwritten, but as firm as if Moses himself had handed it to them on a tablet."

Satisfied with what she has said, she dries her hands on her apron, and pulls down on the silver handle to unlatch the fridge door. Hart feels a puff of cool air on his arm.

He is comforted by her words. That and the aroma of fresh baking and perked coffee, the angled sun through the open window and the easy back-and-forth—partly English, partly Low German—makes the room a pleasant sanctuary. He believes what Ann Vogel has said and knows the Vogels are helping him to see things clearly.

"Here," she says, pushing the buns closer to Hart and Peter. "IF this and IF that... Too many things to ponder for you fellows. Too many ifs. Like when I was a girl, and it was time to get up and go into the barn, us kids would complain, "If only we didn't have to milk the cows..." Then *Opa*, he would always say, '*Wenn "wenn" nicht wäre, wäre Kuhscheiße Botta!*'"

"You know that expression, Hart?" Mr. Vogel said. "I told Heid that one last week, when I went in there to sign things up for another year. "If, if, if... If not for *if*, cow shit would be butter!"

Hart chuckled and watched Vogel who stirred his coffee slowly, without the tinkle of metal against china.

"We talked for a while, me and Heid. He said he might not be able to take risks as much anymore and that he liked my business because it was secure. I told him right back that without him taking some risks, there wouldn't be no secure businesses and he'd be out of a job! 'Back to Windsor for you!' I said, 'But if you have my safe business secure in your bank, then that means you can afford to help others who aren't so safe. Because, what's just a small loan to you, is a terrible big something to a young couple, just starting out.' Mr. Heid, well, he understood. He saw how, if the risks are—you know—shared, everything keeps moving forward. But only IF the risks are shared."

"If, if, if," Mrs. Vogel sighed and stepped towards the table.

Mr. Vogel leaned back in his chair and smiled at her. His wife Ann was wide-shouldered with a kind face. She beamed back, eyes bright, and set the blue dish of butter on the table in front of Hart with the faint ringing sound of glass-on-wood.

"*Nah, Peeta*, I want to tell Hart about his great grandfather, *joh?*"

"*Joh, joh*— go ahead!"

"Okay, so back in Russia, that Cornie Zehen got himself in some trouble with the church. And not just once, but twice! Each time, he suffered the ban. He was kicked out by the ministerial group and was shunned by the community..."

"As if *they* were without spot and wrinkle," Peter Vogel added.

"Like those Ephesians liked to say," Ann replied. She sipped her coffee and carried on. "So anyway, your great *Opa* was repentant, in each case. And, in the way things went back then, he was given the chance to come back into the church after a certain time away."

"He was invited back, but some will say that it was partly—maybe mostly—not because he was entirely forgiven, or because he had even learned his lesson, but maybe more because his absence as a young man of strength, influence and economic importance in the *Darp*, well, let's just say he had earned some special consideration, you see."

"Sounds like maybe his leniency was there for more than one reason?" Hart said.

"That's it." Peter replied. "The ban on him was hurting the whole community, so in the spirit of the common good, he was given a reprieve." He cleared his throat and shifted in his chair.

"Plus, in the normal way of things back then, if you were kicked out and then let back in, you still could never be a minister. For that there was no reprieve..."

"Except, it seems to me that Great Grandpa *was* part of the clergy, right?" Hart said.

Ann and Peter exchanged glances. "Sure. *Joh*," Ann said. "The ministerial gang, they declared when your Great *Opa's* skills were needed most, that he could have his bans, uhh, *retroactively revoked*. Expunged."

The three sat for a moment in the quiet of the kitchen. A soft gust of wind made the cottonwoods outside sough and rustle and a fresh leafy scent blew in through the open window.

"Funny how that worked, *joh*? Peter said, his thick eyebrows raised high. "And then, he was yet too named one of the official church delegates to go to North America. That's a big responsibility! Coming here to look things over and see how the deal was for everyone to leave Russia and move to Manitoba."

"Yes," Ann agreed in a voice calm and sure. "And he did well for his people, all things considered. He sure did. Anyway, Hart... like Peter says, don't be surprised if those credit union guys don't

76

reconsider some time in the future. Just bake lots of bread until then and be ready for them when they come."

The Raspberry Code

My friend Leonard Gerbrandt, Lenny, was wiry and tall for his age and he had big dimples and a giant Adam's apple. His mom worked for my parents at our little bakery and she was an elegant beauty reminiscent, to me at least, of the movie star, Hedy Lamarr. Nora Gerbrandt was dark haired and slender with high, rouged cheekbones and large brown eyes. I was just a little kid, but I felt weak when she was near; the scent of her perfume confusing me through a kind of permeating intoxication, although I would never reveal it. Especially to Lenny, who was as tough and unyielding as a Manitoba March storm.

Their dad was an ex-cop. Mr. Gerbrandt had been a good baseball player and was a rugged guy. I often pictured him as a Hartplatz version of American actor Robert Mitchum. Mitchum married Lamarr and they begat sons and daughters, including Lenny, who, in later years, taught me how to roll a corn silk cigarette and do a catwalk on my bike. The Gerbrandts were made of stern stuff. Lenny's older brother, Erd, was thick-limbed and towered over all of us. He was friendly but I knew him to also possess a temper, if pushed. I'd seen Lenny take things too far and rely on Erd's good nature. That was a mistake I never made. Lenny's two sisters were younger than us and so, not so much a part of our small troupe, though I knew them to be clever and funny, able to tease Lenny and sometimes get the better of him. This was most true of Rebecca, the one next in age to Lenny.

Their dad was the town cop but then joined the army. When he came back, he was not the same anymore. He had run out of whatever it was that made him Robert Mitchum, the big raw-boned cop who got Hedy Lamarr. Instead, Mannfred Gerbrandt sat alone in the Hartplatz men-only beer parlour and got quietly loaded every day.

Luckily, Nora was as smart and as tireless as she was pretty. She worked eight hours at the bakery making doughnuts and jambusters and raisin tarts, and she made the kids' lunches for school, paid the bills, did the laundry, mended clothes, made dinner for them all and much more. She kept the family together, mastering her fate in so doing.

Lenny and Erd had chips on their shoulders. They knew their parents were special and that their dad had been changed unkindly. They knew their mom was pushed beyond what was right and that things could have—should have—been different.

Every year or so they would move, carrying wagonloads of belongings down the street to the next rental house. Mr. Gerbrandt made a pension, but he mostly drank it up and Mrs. Gerbrandt could not keep up payments. So, they rented houses and sometimes fell behind. Lenny wore Erd's hand-me-downs and my mom would sometimes send home a roast or a pot of soup with Nora, under cover of exceptional circumstances like, "I was defrosting the freezer and the food all thawed!"

I figured if I had a crush on Nora Gerbrandt, Lenny felt

similarly about my mom. Like JFK and Khrushchev, however, we had mutual assurance and we spoke not of this.

Early that fall, there was a day when Lenny was going to miss school for an important dentist appointment. He was a sucker for candy and his sweet tooth—many of them in fact—were rotten. In confidence, he told me he was going to the dentist to have several teeth removed, some cavities filled, and some other serious work done. Lenny said he would miss one day for the dental work and one day for convalescence. He was embarrassed and swore me to secrecy.

Second only to the Hedy Lamarr beauty of Nora Gerbrandt was the beguiling feminine charm of the Gidget-like Ms. Froese, our teacher. Of course, "Ms." did not exist then, only Misses and she was one. Around five feet tall, bobbed blonde hair, saddle shoes, cashmere sweaters and rocket bras. I am sure I had no distinct thought then of that conically constrained part of her anatomy, only that it was soft and pleasing when she leaned over to help you with a problem and happened to make fuzzy impact with your head or shoulder.

Miss Froese was sweet-natured and young, and I remember the utter sadness I felt when, later that same school year, on November 22, she ran crying from the room after telling us that school would be cancelled for the day because of what had happened in a place called Dallas, Texas.

The next day we returned to school and added, "America the Beautiful" right after our normal singing of "God Save the Queen." A big box of *Kleenex* sat on her desk and was empty before Science that afternoon. Baseball and the Kennedys were things about the United States that our well-traveled neighbour, Mr. Vogel, had made certain that I appreciated, so I felt a special kinship with Miss Froese that desperate day in November.

Lenny's dental reckoning was months before the events of Dealey Plaza, but I already had a crush on Miss Froese by then. I was happy to clean chalk brushes after school, run to ask the janitor to open sticky classroom windows on hot afternoons, or agree to appear in the class play. If she had a need, I agreed. So, it was not surprising that when she asked where Lenny was on the second day of his absence, I raised my hand, eager to share with Miss Froese the solemn news. Though under oath to keep this quiet, how could it harm to tell HER? She was, like me, only concerned with Lenny's well-being.

"Yes, Matthew?" she asked, seeing my upraised hand. "Do you know why Leonard is not here again today?"

"Yes, ma'am. He is at the dentist. His teeth are all black from too much candy and he's getting them fixed. He is terrible brave and he probably won't even cry," I reported in detail.

That day was Friday. On Saturday afternoon, as I collected interesting rocks from the laneway that cut between my Grandma Zehen's large raspberry patch and the back of the bakery next door, Lenny pedalled up to me. He let his bicycle fall clattering as he jumped off.

"Zehen!" he shouted, through a clenched jaw still tender from the dentist.

"Hi, Lenny," I said, standing. "How are your teeth?"

"Why don't you ask Eleanor?" he said, scoffing, "or Ruby, or the Hiebert twins or…"

"Wait," I yelled, putting my hand up to stop his rushing words.

He paused and then slowly reached over and pushed my shoulder, staring hard at me all the while.

"You," he said, leaning back as he took a breath, his eyes never leaving mine, "you told on me."

"Did not!" I said immediately. I would never tell on someone, particularly not Lenny.

"It's just like telling."

"Is not."

"Is too!"

I stopped. He was right. I looked away to the back of the bakery, where a tall baker bent over a burnt bun pan, scraping loudly with a wire brush to clean the surface. Gummy black residue fell into the tall grass and dandelions, and some on his shoes.

I had no intention to embarrass Lenny, but that is just what I had done. When I thought about it more carefully, rotten teeth were not a thing to be proud of, nor something you announced to the whole class. And not to Miss Froese. *Especially not* Miss Froese.

Lenny reached over deliberately and pushed again; his gaze still intent on me: a barn cat with a cornered mouse. I resisted a bit, a hard look on my face, hiding fear. He saw this and smiled, then rolled up his sleeves like cowboys did in old-time movies. Prepared in this manner, he posed awkwardly in front of me, leaning forward, almost tipping over. He pointed to his chin.

"Hit me," Leonard Gerbrandt said, in a mocking tone.

I stood with my hands hanging loosely at my sides. I shook my head and looked at his sister Rebecca who had rode her bike over to us and was our shared witness and presumably, our mutual second. Rebecca shrugged in my direction, meaning, "Don't ask me!"

"C'mon," Lenny urged. "Give me your best lick. I ain't scared."

"Who said you were scared?"

"*You're* scared," he replied, nodding slowly. Rebecca nodded in cadence, sensing his teasing tone and activating her tough Gerbrandt side

"C'mon, c'mon, scaredy-cat. Scared to hurt your hand?"

At this, Rebecca giggled and I stood more rigidly, turning a quarter turn sideways and spreading my feet.

Lenny touched his chin with a thin finger, bobbing his head slightly and chanting softly, "Scare-dy, scare-dy, scare-dy," in rhythm to the bobbing. Rebecca picked up the chant.

I bent my knees and made fists. Rebecca stopped singing and Lenny quieted, stepping back before catching himself and—with a forced casualness—he leaned forward again, tendering a jutted jaw.

I supposed he would hit back and supposed he would hit hard, but the chanting and Rebecca's complicity had been too much. Lenny should hit me first. He should hit first because I was wrong—I hurt him and he should hurt me back. But I wanted to take a swing because I was mad from the scaredy-cat chant and my anger overcame the ignoble shame of striking first.

I folded my thumb on top of, not beneath, my fingers, the way my dad had shown me. Then I cocked my arm and hit him square on the cleft of his pointed chin just as he glanced at Rebecca.

"Ugnnn!" he grunted, his head snapping sideways and his knees giving way. He staggered back, confused, and fell in a puff of raspberry patch dirt just as my grandma came churning head-long out of the house, all ahead full.

"No, no, no, nooo! No fighting, boys. *Matthew James Zehen*! You stop right now." She bore down on us through the raspberry bushes, her apron snagging as she ran down the narrow row. There was flour on her hands and her glasses were pushed up on her red forehead.

She arrived as Lenny scrambled up clumsily, reaching for his bike handlebar in case her arrival meant flight.

"Leonard Gerbrandt! Why are you fighting with Matty? You

boys are such good friends. You are pals—not *brutes!*" she said loudly.

"Rebecca! Go home now, please. Come another time, yeah?" she commanded, her tone less stern towards Rebecca. She pointed in the direction of the Gerbrandt bungalow a block south.

Lenny continued to pick up his bike, thinking he was to go also. She grabbed my arm hard, surprising me—but not really— with her grip made strong by the stubborn resistance of a million *Zwieback* buns pinched. Yanking me, she took hold of Lenny's rhubarb-stalk arm, but gently, and pulled him toward her.

"Put down that bike, Lenny," she said. Then she asked, "Who hit first?" her head turning owlishly from Lenny to me and back. "Who?"

I looked down, as did Lenny. "Me, Grandma," I confessed quietly after a too long pause, my eyes still down. Lenny immediately looked up at her and said evenly, "I told him to," pointing to his red chin.

"How many times? How many punches?" she said urgently, looking at Lenny, imploring the truth.

"Just once, Mrs. Zehen," he offered, looking at me a little stink-eyed because he was starting to suspect that, because of Grandma's apron-flying arrival, I was going to get a pardon.

Lenny resented Grandma's intrusion. In his mind, he was handling things just fine because his code of honour called for him to start the fight by inviting me to take "my best shot" and then—despite this obvious disadvantage—absorb the blow and subsequently *put a beating on me,* as he would say. The cowboy code. Robert Mitchum, there among the raspberries.

As much of a beating as those pipe-cleaner arms could give, that is. Tough and wiry though he was, his seventy-five pounds was thinly coated on an angular five-foot collection of sticks. He was destined to add more than a foot and 100 pounds by the time he could trade his bike in for a car, but in 1963, he was as thin as picnic Kool-Aid.

"Matthew," she said, "is this so?"

"Yes, ma'am."

"Don't ma'am me, *Jung*! Is that true? One punch?"

"*Joh*, Grandma," I said, nodding gravely.

"*Nah-joh*," she said, pivoting sharply to spin her body behind me, planting her palms on my shoulders and clamping down with clothespin fingers to hold me still.

"You," she demanded. "Lenny, you hit him back and then the fight is over." She glanced up to see if Rebecca was safely on her way home. She was, walking caterpillar-slow and with her head turned to watch.

Lenny took a half step back, glancing first at me, then up at the square-jawed, flour-dusted praying mantis that held me immobile in her grip. His head oscillated in a slow-motion no. She continued decisively. "Matty hit you. You hit him. Fight over, shake hands and come in for a piece of Saskatoon pie." Grandma too had a code.

Before he could say no, or move, she reached across and pulled him a little closer. Then she nudged me forward with her knees and pointed to my freckled chin. "Right here, Lenny. One good one."

Lenny stroked his jaw (still hurting, I hoped with childish pride) in a pose that unconsciously copied his father's deliberate way of pondering an issue. He looked closely at me with Grandma's sturdy Prussian finger targeting my chin.

"I won't tell," Grandma added; a sparkle in her eye that Lenny caught but could not process. Then finally, she concluded irresistibly, "Pie *and* ice cream."

As Lenny pulled back to deliver his best hockey haymaker, Grandma released her hold on my shoulders and I could hear her breath as she sucked it keenly through her teeth.

I let my head turn and my legs buckle the way Dad had shown me and so the punch did little damage. Either that or Lenny had pulled it a little. Maybe some of both. I fell, landing hard on the square toe of Grandma's shoe and that hurt more than my chin. Getting up, I saw that Lenny had a quizzical half-smile on his face as he looked first at me, then at Grandma.

She marched off briskly ahead of us, laughing and scolding all at once, telling Lenny to bring his bike away from the street and for us to wash our hands in the lawn sprinkler before we came in. And leave our runners on the porch. And would he and Rebecca like to stay for night?

I said, "Sorry I told," to Lenny. He nodded once emphatically and replied that he was sorry he got so mad. We had Saskatoon pie, our dishes and our lips stained purple.

After we ate Lenny felt my bicep and said, "You hit hard, Zehen."

"You too, Gerbrandt," I said back to him. "Hey, Grandma..."

"Yes?"

"Is it okay for Lenny to have another piece of pie and you remember about the ice cream, right? And I would have some ice cream too, of course."

"Of course," she said. She opened the freezer and then held the brick of ice cream against my neck, "Here's yours," she said in her high laughing voice. "And Lenny can for sure have another big piece and ice cream too."

Fall from Grace

A well-thrown crab apple, ripe and soft of skin, makes a distinctive sound when it hits a metal STOP sign: a pulpy *splat* followed by the ringing vibration of tin. The many crab trees along Barkman Avenue were ready for this duty, branches slung low with dark fruit by August. When I think of my childhood in Hartplatz, that's what I see. My friends and I would fill our pockets, alternately eating and throwing them at targets like signs or telephone poles. Blackbirds watched from the tall reeds, their bodies spattered like ink spots in the swaying green ditch across from my parents' house.

The playtime restrictions for young girls and boys in our small town were not high security. I was, in theory, supposed to stay on this side of Reimer Avenue, two blocks west. This gave me access to the fire hall, Main Street, the *5¢ to $1 Store*, and other distractions including Loeb's lumberyard. If I say we often played in the Loeb yard—amid any number of dangers and without adult supervision—you will get a sense of the loose restriction placed on us. All the same, I did have *some* restrictions. I was not

89

supposed to climb the conical sawdust and gravel piles in the compound. My mom had read of a boy who had been swallowed up while playing on top of a pile of sawdust and the tall, fragrant pyramids in the sleepy yard were like rattlesnake nests to her.

Mom knew I sometimes strayed inside the chain link fence that marked the Loeb grounds. But she—and she alone—also knew that her interdict against climbing the giant sawdust and gravel piles was fine with me; heights often made me woozy.

One afternoon in the heat of August, my friend Scottie told me that his older brother had been throwing crabs at cars. I shook my head, perplexed.

"Moving cars?"

"Yeah."

"Why?"

He made a face, deeming my question unworthy of a verbal reply. I left it there, and we continued our excavations in the sandbox.

A few days later, Scottie came to Grandma's where I was playing in the yard. His older brother Dave stuck his head around the corner of the house, scattering pecking robins from the lawn.

"Matty Zehen!"

"Hello, Davey."

"Is your *Oma* here?" Davey and many others in our town called their grandmothers and all grandmothers, "*Oma*." My dad was not a Low German speaker so we mostly called her Grandma. Davey wanted to know if she was around because he knew he was not one of her favourites. Grandma always said Davey was "trouble." She held this opinion for several of the kids I played with, but in Davey's case, I tended to agree.

"She's inside, but I think she's busy."

I had experienced Dave's leadership in the past—his time

at the helm of our spring flood raft and our subsequent capsized result should have been enough to teach me a lesson, but I was slow to accept some truths about some friends. I should have known better that day too when he, after exchanging cordialities, suggested an expedition to the roof of the curling rink.

"*What?*" I said. "Why?"

"To throw crab apples," he said, as if the answer should have been obvious. "Cars drive by and you throw a crab at them and when it hits them, they stop and get out."

"Yeah, right… and then they chase you and beat you up."

"No, they don't, 'cause if we are quiet, they won't figure out where we are. After a while, they just go away. It is *terrible* funny."

There was no doubt that we would be caught. I imagined with dread the sound of my dad's leather belt slipping from the loops of his pants, his face looking stern and sad at the same time.

I began a stammering refusal. But Davey, reading my thoughts, retaliated with the all-powerful chicken cackle. My resolve first weakened and then capsized, familiar green creek water gushing over its decks.

"When?"

"Now," he said, pushing out his bulging pockets and letting a few crab apples fall out onto the yard.

The curling rink stood facing Creek Road two blocks from our house. It was a squat arch-ribbed structure. On the building's front façade, a faded plywood sign read *Hartplatz Curling Club* in the hand-brushed font of the local sign-painter, Hans Heinrich Friesen. The words were framed by red, white and blue curling houses—circular bullseyes that looked like the markings on a Spitfire's wings.

A large barn door on the whitewashed plywood back wall gleamed in the sun. Davey took us to the weedy field along one side of the rink. This empty property served as a storage lot, filled with assorted pieces of farm equipment, old trucks and other derelict machinery.

Among them was an ancient *Case* combine. Rusted dark orange, it stood beside the rink, almost touching the building's sloped roof. As Davey showed us, by climbing up the hopper ladder on the combine, you could jump across to the roof and land beside the two-by-four cleats that acted as a ladder to the roof peak. This cleat ladder began about six feet above the ground, placed in this way to discourage unauthorized use.

Adults and tall kids could get on the roof quite easily, but smaller kids like us had to use the combine's hopper ladder. Davey, having practiced and perfected the move required to clamber onto the cleat ladder, was an expert.

Heat waves rose above the roof in the afternoon sun, and when Davey landed on the black roof, he yelped from the hot shingles. He wasted no time, hopping sideways onto the ladder rungs, bleached white from the sun. Davey scrambled up to perch on the peak.

"Scott next!" yelled Davey. "I'll help him up and Matty will go last," he instructed. A good plan: Scottie was six years Davey's junior and one less birthday than me.

"How do we get down?" I yelled.

"Easy," Dave said, pointing to a pile of sand near the front. "You just slide down and jump into the sand. No problem," he added with palms upturned.

Scottie climbed the combine, giddy with excitement. He jumped onto the roof with no hesitation. He was so light he seemed to stick to the gritty surface and then scooted onto the ladder. Davey was waiting to stretch out a helping hand.

Emboldened by the brothers' easy ascent, I climbed without

fear and jumped across. Making an expert landing with one hand already on a ladder rung, I continued up. I took care not to bark my knees on the abrasive shingles, bare-legged in my cut-off jean shorts as I was.

A few apples tippled by me, falling from Davey's pockets. I watched them as they dropped into the grass below. I noticed several unfriendly-looking pieces of dinosaur-toothed hay-mowing equipment directly beneath us. One bouncing crab lay slashed in two, showing its white core and black seeds. A sudden feeling of floating washed over me when I looked back up.

Scottie was almost to the top when Davey began walking along the ridge, one foot on either side. He marched in slow and halting metre toward the distant front of the curling rink.

"C'mon, Matty," Scottie said. He waited in a crouch on the roof ridge, breathless above me. Then he began waddling along the crest, gingerly placing fingertips on the hot shingles for support, not quite trusting his ability to stand upright.

I got to the top and was surprised by the height we had reached, looking down on the nearby fire hall's flat roof, on piles of gravel in Loeb's lumberyard, and down even further into the dandelions and reeds growing in the creek far below us. Glancing again at the grinning haymow, I had an undeniable wave of nausea. My temperature dropped—it was as if I had run sweating and hot into a cold meat locker. I watched as Scottie, now brazen, scampered along the roof peak, his arms outstretched. Davey waited beyond him, leaning against the false front of the façade and cheering for me to come across.

The length of a curling rink is 146 feet, and with the ladder near the building's rear it was a long walk. I stared down again at the sharp scythe, maybe 20 feet below me. Unsettled, I looked across to where Dave and Scottie stood waving their arms, calling for me. I felt a second wave of nausea and vertigo; it staggered me as I began to release my grip on the top ladder rung and walk to the front. My runner slipped with a loud scrape on the asphalt shingle. Adrenaline surged down my backbone, tingling and sharp. The half-slip and my pained expression stopped the other boys' chatter in an instant. I caught my balance and gripped the roof peak. In that shaking moment, I was suddenly unsure of where I was, and why.

Adding to my confusion was the sound of my dad's voice, clear and nearby: "Matt!"

I swiveled my head to see him far below on the street beside the bakery delivery truck. His door stood open and the tick-tock voice of the blinker signal seemed to mock me: *slip—slip—slip!*

"Matthew!" he shouted, half fear, half anger. Perplexed.

"Dad!"

"What are you doing? Why are you up there?"

"Dad," I started to answer and then reeled. A swimming feeling passed through me as my foot slid down again, losing precious inches to gravity. "I'm STUCK!" I shrilled.

I adjusted my grip and reached back with a toe, feeling for a ladder cleat. At the same time, I heard the dull popping of crabs skipping down the roof, landing with nestling sounds in the grass. Davey was frantically emptying his pockets of evidence. He stood part-way down the far side of the peak, hidden from my dad. He glanced at Scottie and me and then slid down the roof and jumped onto the sandpile to make good his escape, bolting down Creek Road towards home.

"You and Scottie stay PUT!" Dad hollered, his voice like a bullhorn. Scottie and I did as instructed. I used my ball hat like an oven mitt to protect my hands from the shingles.

Dad ran to the building and cut through the tall grass. He

came around to the ladder side, climbed as far as he could and then easily stepped, with a small hop, onto the roof ladder.

Dad climbed up to me, "You OK?"

"Yes," I mumbled.

He looked across to Scottie and saw that he too was safe, his back braced against the false front. Dad's white tee-shirt was soaked through with sweat from the bakery heat, his sleeve was rolled up on one side and a package of *Buckingham* cigarettes was tucked in the fold.

He encircled my waist to hold me with one hand. Whispering curses as he touched the shingles, he said, "Put your arms around my neck. Feet around me, like a backward piggy-back."

I did what Dad said and he climbed down the ladder with me clinging to him like a baby possum. When he stopped, I lowered my bottom down onto a cleat. He was breathing hard into my face. He leaned back so our eyes were level and then said, "Sit still, okay knucklehead?" I nodded in mute agreement and he clicked his tongue and rubbed my bare head. He looked over to Scottie, pointed at him and said in a resonant, Sunday morning bass, "STAY THERE! I'll come get you."

* * *

That evening, with all safe, I sat at the kitchen table pushing my food around on the plate while Dad was outside on the cement porch steps, smoking cigarettes and drinking beer from a case of *Carling Black Label.* I could see him through the screen door as he took two bottles out and returned an empty into the box. He used the edge of the cap of one full bottle to pry the cap off the second with a hissing snap.

"Send Matty out," he said to my mom, who stood beside him taking puffs from his smoke.

Hearing him through the door, I went out to stand beside

him in the still air. It was almost dark, and columns of mosquitoes buzzed over the tallest trees in the Beanblossom's yard across
the street.

He was a little drunk and when I sat down, he smiled at me,
front teeth cut at a slant where a hockey stick had sheared them
off.

"What did we find out today?" His eyes were soft and kind,
his forehead wrinkled as he awaited my answer.

"What do you mean, Daddy?" I stood beside where he sat.
From my vantage, I could look down on his head and see where
his curly hair was thinning.

"What did you learn when you were up on the roof and you
got stuck?"

"I guess I learned not to go there."

"Nope." He took a long sip. The bottle gurgled and I could
smell the yeast in it mingled with the odour of dry sweat from his
shirt. "You can't learn what you already know, buddy."

I studied the grass growing up between the sidewalk blocks.
"Yeah, but I didn't know I was *that* scared of being up high,"

"Yeah, but," came my Grandma's voice from behind me
as I faced Dad. She had walked up to us on the lawn from her
house next door and stood with two glasses of lemonade. "We
should call you 'Yeah-but, the boy who always has an answer.'"
She laughed her soprano laugh and handed me a glass. "You've
already got a drink," she nodded her big chin at Dad, who hoisted
his *Black Label* at her in reply. She used the other lemonade glass
to make a cooling swipe across her forehead. A mosquito stuck to
her wet glass and she picked it off and flicked it away. "What did
you learn, Matty? Tell Daddy."

"Should you have gone there, with Scottie?" Dad hinted,
smoke puffing out with each word. He ashed his cigarette into

the red cardboard beer case beside him and tapped his foot a few times, looking straight ahead towards the frog cacophony in the creek. Grandma stroked my neck, where the brush cut receded down to peach fuzz, then sipped her lemonade, motioning for me to try mine.

I tasted it, glad for the interval, and puckered my cheeks. "Sour."

My dad looked down at me and said, "Keep working on an answer for me, Matty. Right now it's bedtime, buster."

I took a big gulp of the freezing drink—enough to make my forehead hurt for a second—then handed the glass to Grandma and gave Dad a kiss on his prickly cheek.

"Climb into bed, but no higher," he said with false sternness, winking at Grandma.

Then I was in my darkened room with the window wide open, the sun set but the western horizon still lighted. Mosquitoes ticked with unrelenting determination at the metal screen, drawn by the blood taint on my breath. The wood floor was warm on my bare feet as I stood near the window. I was hidden from view in the shadow. The sun set before me, sinking behind the *Economy Store* silhouette and every dust mote and dragonfly stood out in the golden backlit glow. I could see Dad pulling up weeds with one hand, an empty beer dangling from the other as he and his mother chatted. His cigar-thick pinky finger was jammed down into the stubby brown bottleneck. He and Grandma walked aimlessly around the yard, slapping mosquitoes and speaking in subdued tones.

As they came closer to my window, Grandma's piercing laugh punctuated Dad's baritone. Sheet lightning flicked and ominous distant rumbles made a background overture as he described the curling rink incident to her, his voice rising in his enjoyment of the story. They both stood still as he described the last:

"And then I climbed up and the other kid was stuck too. He was against the front and I had to walk along the peak to go and get him." He stopped his narration to smile, looking down and rubbing his neck.

Grandma chuckled, her gaze on him, full of light and adoration.

"Then Denver Funk drove by, right when I was in the middle of the roof, and yelled at me, 'Don't break your ankle, Zehen!'"

Grandma shrieked, her eyes shut and she crumpled down onto one of the nearby seats on my swing set. She was racked with laughter for half a minute while Dad stood, kicking at the ground, grinning and self-conscious.

Mom leaned against the bedroom doorway behind me. She wore a mint green sleeveless top and white peddle pusher pants. Her hair was pulled back into berets on the side of her head, and she smelled like suntan lotion. Later, just before she went to bed, she would smell like *Noxzema* cream.

"Do you remember the story of when Daddy was eight and he broke his ankle?" Mom said.

"Kind of," I said.

"That Denver," I heard Dad mutter.

"Haw!" came Grandma's high choir voice.

I looked back at Mom.

She smiled her most special smile. She smiled it bright and she said, "Your father broke his ankle jumping off the roof of the skating rink into a snowbank with Uncle Shoesnick."

"Oh yeah?"

"And you know where that skating rink used to be?"

"Where it is now?"

"No, almost. It was right where you were today when you got stuck on the curling rink roof."

"Oh." I was just seven, but I could see it was both a funny and a serious thing.

"Uncle Shoesnick got in trouble, 'cause he was 14 and your father was just eight. And Grandpa Zehen was very mad, and he said that because Daddy couldn't play hockey anymore that winter, neither could Uncle Shoe. And Uncle Shoe got *real* upset."

"So, he had to work in Grandpa Zehen's shoe shop all winter and that's why they called him Shoesnick, right Mom? Like lots of people call Grandpa, *Schusta*."

"Right. And Uncle Shoesnick stayed mad at Grandpa for a long time. And a bit mad at Daddy too, but not too much."

I nodded and looked out at Grandma and how she looked at Dad as he talked to her about the bakery business.

My mom's touch settled light on my shoulder and it guided me to the bed. She knelt beside me, her strong hand on my back. I said prayers ("and God bless Mom and Dad, and Grandma and Grandpa, and Scottie too...") and then she tucked me in with a thin sheet in the hot, quiet room. The thunder was closer now, but still not close enough to smell the rain. A fly buzzed against the screen.

"Mom," I said, raising my voice a little to make sure she heard me.

"Yes, Matty?" she replied, as a dog down the street barked at the thunder.

"I think I know what I learned. I learned that I should not have taken Scottie there, 'cause he's littler than me."

She turned back and smiled a proud smile. Then she fussed with my covers and asked, "Where was Davey, Matt? I thought he and Scottie came together?"

I glanced away in silence, up to the corner where bits of paint had come off the ceiling and you could make a face out of it, if you concentrated.

"Mom?" I said again as she waved goodnight and started to leave.

"Yes, honey?"

"Will I have to work in the bakery like Uncle Shoesnick had to work in Grandpa's shoe shop? Can I still play baseball when I'm eight?"

"We'll see," said my dad.

He was standing outside with Grandma, the two of them looking in the window. Their silhouettes, side by side, looked blurry through the screen, and I could see Beanblossom's crab tree behind them. In the gloaming light, tinted by the dull metal screen that was once black, but had since been faded by the sun, their faces were sepia tone like an old photograph, a hazy shade of summer.

The Peacemongers

After a scrub ball game, we sat in the shade of the park's plywood toboggan slide, and somehow the conversation wandered from baseball to the philosophical. Our Mennonite elders taught us peace and how to live in a congregation and a community, if not a colony, and our greatest collective efforts as a people were directed at prevention and resolution. Other, less noble efforts concerned denial and a callus refusal to face the conflict that found us. Sometimes this denial worked its way deep down into the compressed community like ice in a rock fissure, until the pressure was too great and the rock broke along the hidden fault line.

"I'd fight you, but it's against my religion" was a statement that not only would *not* be laughed at but one that might command some respect. Turn the other cheek and love thine enemy were taught in Jesus' name and, in many cases, practiced. At our young age, however, such Sunday School principles were discarded when the blood ran hot. While we knew and accepted these higher ideals, the rules of the jungle applied in the playground.

Our stern conversation on that day was this: "If there was a war tomorrow... and you were old enough, would you go?" Many in our group quietly admitted that they would not go. Most were inclined to bravado—at least there in the shade of the slide—and said they would go to war.

I thought of my dad and my grandparents and how they all became quiet when we sat in front of our TV, and the announcer discussed the growing crisis in Cuba. The international emergency was distilled into a simple formula by the CBC newscast. The U.S. had found evidence of nuclear weapons in Cuba; Russia was steaming ships to the island loaded with more weapons and soldiers, and President Kennedy was all but openly accusing them of preparing to wage war on the U.S.A. Cuba was close to the tip of Florida, close to the famous Cape Canaveral launch pad and millions of Americans.

All of this seemed plausible to my parents. Dad said Cuba was only as far away from the Florida coast as it was from Hartplatz to Pembina, North Dakota. This reference made it real to me. Pembina was where one of the TV stations was re-broadcast from, reaching us at the dim northern edge of its range.

It was also a place where Roger Maris of the Yankees had played high school and minor league baseball. Maris was from North Dakota, born just a few beet fields south of us. A man from Pembina who looked a lot like Maris but with a suit and thick eyeglasses, read the news each night on the Fargo station. My parents often listened to him in addition to the CBC telecast, despite the snowy screen, to hear about what Kennedy and Khrushchev were doing.

There were other signs that everything in the wide world beyond was not quite right. One of the Loeb brothers had just built a house near the new elementary school, and it had a special room in the basement; a fallout shelter. Atomic bombs were apparently giant explosives that could be aimed at various targets, like the cities in Japan that were destroyed at the end of WWII. They were now delivered by rocket, not dropped from a plane. Upon landing in a brilliant flash ("Put your heads down on your desks and don't look up!"), the bomb released toxic, radioactive "fallout" that lasted for weeks or longer.

I will never forget the smell of my wood desk as I lay my head down on it when we did an "Atomic Bomb Drill." The odour of varnish and ink. I recall too the sound of all of us breathing quietly, the classroom unnaturally silent except for the occasional hiss of steam in the radiators, the sound ominous and sinister, rising up from the boiler in the basement.

The bomb shelters, containing food, guns and other implements of survival behind their dense concrete walls, were—to us kids—the ultimate fort. Still, we were disquieted by the presence of one of these doomsday shelters in our tiny, peaceful Hartplatz—even if it was only the indulgence of an ostentatious rich man. The U.S. aimed their weapons at places in Russia, and the Russians aimed theirs at U.S. targets, including air bases and missile launching sites. Nearby Grand Forks had a massive air base, and their planes' contrails could regularly be seen far, far above Hartplatz in the deepest blue of the sky; specks of silver spewing a faint watercolour plume of white.

I remember the day my grandpa and Mr. Vogel stood on the sunny sidewalk outside of the post office and looked up at the faint parallel lines etched high in the sky. They held their palms up to shade their eyes against the glare of the sun and sucked their teeth, estimating how high the planes might be and if they were "fighters" or "bombers."

I had collected a hatbox full of brightly coloured plastic disks from cereal, tea and chocolate milk containers. The company had promoted its goods by including a slim, clear plastic bag with two free disks in each package. The disks had a company logo moulded into the back, and the front carried a colour image of an airplane. Hundreds of aircraft were in the collection, such as Von Richthofen's red tri-wing, muscular P-51 Mustangs, and obscure Fokkers—German warplanes that carried the name of a Dutch aeronautical engineer on pictures provided by a Swiss chocolate company. These Fokkers were—like Mennonites—possessors of a convoluted Northern European ancestry.

There were also DC-1s like the one that would—a few years later—carry my proud parents to the Grey Cup football game in Vancouver. The picture of them boarding the plane in Winnipeg sat in a place of honour on our bookshelf for years—Mom and Dad topped with newly-bought hats they never wore at home; my dad in a felt fedora and Mom in a movie star pill-box. Their young black and white faces were flushed with excitement as they climbed the rolling steel staircase standing up against the side of the riveted aluminum jet.

I pulled out a handful of *Nestlé* airplane disks from my pocket and showed them to Grandpa and Mr. Vogel as they peered at the U.S. planes far above. "They are either B-29s or F-10s," I offered, handing them each an illustrated disk. "When they get to Russian airspace," I continued with authority, "the Russians will scramble MiGs like this." I handed them each a disk showing a MiG fighter plane with its sleek, swept-back wings. In the picture, the dull silver fighter stood out against fluffy white clouds, with the red hammer and sickle insignia the focal point of the image. The pilot, his football-like white helmet visible beneath the stream-lined, clear canopy, looked ominously resolute, if not ruthless. Except for the Billy Bishop Sopwith Camel, I had more MiGs than any other single disk. There was one in almost every package. "Beware the Red Menace!" they seemed to say.

Grandpa Zehen stared at me incredulously for a few seconds as Mr. Vogel chuckled, still looking up at the distant jet trails. "We're gonna scramble you!" Grandpa said, snatching the disk I held and pulling me into a gentle hammerlock in one motion.

* * *

When it was my turn to answer the "Would you go to war?" question, I thought of the people huddled in their fallout shelters as the soldiers bravely climbed into tanks and airplanes and jeeps to fight the war. I imagined the people in Miami (and Moscow), skin hanging from their burnt bodies like torn fabric as they wandered in a daze among flattened buildings in a Hiroshima landscape. I thought of Sargent Rock wading ashore in a hail of bullets on the cover of comic books at *Rexall* Drugs. I thought of my Uncle Barney, who had joined the Winnipeg Rifles and had made it as far as Halifax before Hitler was defeated. I recalled the great grey battleships tossing fearlessly on the *War at Sea* film— stark, grainy images projected on a white sheet in the Kornelsen school basement at a *National Film Board* evening sponsored by the local Arts Council.

"I think I would do whatever my dad said to do. I think my grandma would say to help by going to the C.O. camps and working extra hard. I think my dad would fight—he'd be a General, at least." I stated, without guilt or doubt. I thought of another thing and spoke up some more.

"My great uncle Ed went to war in the Pacific. He was in a camp there, for Prisoners of War. Grandma says it was a bad place. Uncle Ed told us a story once about how, like, hundreds of years back, our early Mennonite ancestors were getting picked on by these Roman soldiers. Each year they came to the ancestors and demanded money. After a while, they got fed up with the Roman guys and fought them. The ancestors didn't want to fight—they thought fighting and war was wrong, but they knew if they didn't stand up for themselves, they would just get pushed around forever, and maybe they would not make it. Anyways, my dad says that's why Uncle Ed joined up. He didn't want us Canadians to get pushed around either. That's why he didn't go to a C.O. camp."

"We fought a war against the Romans?" said Corky. I grabbed his hat and threw it behind him. He reached back to get it and said, "Also, what's a C.O. camp again?"

"I think it's what you can do if your minister will go to Winnipeg and say that you are baptized. The government sends men a letter saying they have to join the army. If they don't go, they have to go to jail. But if they are members of a Mennonite Church, my grandma says that the government promised they didn't have to be in the army."

"Just Mennonites?" asked Max Quakenbush, a Lutheran boy who lived on Barkman Avenue on the other side of Main Street. No one answered.

"Dunno," I shrugged. "My grandma says that in the Second World War, lots of Canadians fought and some Mennonites, like my great uncle went, and some, lots from Hartplatz, went to C.O. camps instead of the army."

"Yeah, but what's C.O. mean, exactly?" Corky asked, still struggling.

"Don't know. Some kind of *objector*—like, 'you're against it,'" I replied. "My grandpa went to a camp. He said he worked in the kitchen, and they had a big bread oven. Grandpa learned about baking in the camp."

"My grandpa did that way back in Russia!" said a boy named

Abe. "The camp was by a lake in a forest and all the guys worked as lumberjacks. He has a picture. It's marked '*Forsteidienst.*' He cut off his ring finger when he was there! It's shorter than his pinky!"

"Ho, but!" said Scottie, who sat cross-legged, his ball glove on the ground beside him and his hands holding an elm leaf, which he stretched between his thumbs, blowing against the leaf to make a squawking sound. "I'd like to be a lumberjack and chop down trees instead of shooting guys in the war. The war is neat too, especially the tanks and stuff, but lumberjack is really good. I would sign up for camp." he concluded, sighing, happy to have made his decision.

"I don't know if it was the same thing or not," Corky said, "but my uncles went to a forest camp in Canada. My dad wanted to go too, but his minister told the army guys that my dad had to stay to run the farm with my grandparents and my aunties. Someone had to keep growing wheat and whatnot. My uncle John learned how to sawmill out there at the camp. After the war, he got a job in Loeb's mill and worked cutting trees in Sandilands too."

I thought of Corky's uncle John who worked at Loeb's lumberyard. He wore a red vest and a plaid shirt and stood behind the counter at the lumber desk. He was a big man with very white teeth, and he would stand there smiling and writing down what you wanted to buy. My dad would always order lumber from him, and it always started out the same way. Dad would say, "I need some two-by-fours," and John would say, "how many and how long do you need 'em?" and Dad would reply "twenty pieces and forever!" Same joke every time. Then John would yell for one of the yard boys to come and load the order into our truck, his pencil poised over the order form, looking at my dad over his glasses.

"Twelve-footers," or whatever length he needed, was Dad's answer, served with a slanted smile.

Dad also talked about how John had been in a C.O. camp during the war. He told stories about it and how he made lifelong friends there. "Some were in the camp for other reasons, but most were there to follow the Word. That meant something to us and it was like our own private battle... to stay true to what we had been taught and to what we would teach our children." I heard him talk about this to my dad and other men at the lumberyard. He stood straight up and looked into the eyes of the person he spoke to. His voice was firm and he was not trying to convince anyone—he was just telling it. I was too young to understand everything, but felt like he was telling me the truth, exactly as he knew it and believed it.

When I was older, my cousin told me about what had happened with his dad, my Uncle Barney, an older brother to my dad. Barney had wanted to join the army and "do his bit." Grandpa Zehen disagreed and they argued about it. Grandpa wanted Barney to go to the judge in Winnipeg who was charged with overseeing petitions for a draft release on Conscientious Objector grounds. Barney went, but came home without a release. He would go to war not to a C.O. camp. Grandpa believed that Barney had been less than convincing in his testimony to the judge and had "thrown the fight" intentionally. A rift formed between father and son that took a long time to close.

"If I'm old enough to fight and perhaps even die, then I am old enough to decide for myself if I will join the army or be a C.O.," was the way my uncle and others saw it. Many more in our town took the path John from the lumberyard had and as an adult, I could see both as truths that demanded complete self-honesty and courage, either way.

As a child discussing it after our ballgame under a big prairie sky—and even now as an adult—I sometimes felt as though John and many others like him in our town believed, maybe secretly, that God was just the biggest, toughest, most bad-ass Mennonite of them all. As if God would do all the fighting for us, and He would take no prisoners. I'm not sure that made our desire to live a life of pacifism any better. Possibly worse. It made God seem like a kind of bully—always smiting armies and kings in the Old Testament that he didn't like and constantly fighting with the Devil. Like Archie and Don, older boys from Hartplatz who fought almost every day after school at the corner of Hannover and Kroeker, accomplishing nothing but scuffed chins and knuckles.

Mostly though, our town was a peaceful place. Friendly and easy going in lots of ways. Most people went out of their way to avoid trouble. I also tried to, but because my hair was bright orange and my ears stuck out like the side mirrors on a car and because I was small and hot tempered—conflict often found me. Grandma counselled to avoid it as long as you could; but that if you were going to fight, then you did your best and the other guy had to be ready. "He starts it, you finish it," she would say, her body in constant motion in the tiny kitchen of the house where she raised a hockey team worth of children—mostly boys, but also girls who had to hold their own with a swarm of brothers.

"That's what I told Uncle Barney when he joined up for the army," she said, her eyes far away as she shelled peas with a rhythmic cadence. "We didn't know about Uncle Ed then—he was listed as "Missing in Action" and we prayed every day. We knew this war was serious business, not just marching and uniforms, and if you go, I told Barney, it has to be to do what they send you to do. Come home alive and we can work out everything between

God and you once it's done." She was quiet for a moment and the only sound was the faint chime of peas landing in the bowl on her lap.

"Once you go over there to fight," she said, pausing in her chore, "...then there is no more peace. If you go, then you go to fight. You fight to come home."

* * *

We sat in the enveloping light as the afternoon waned; some boys climbed the greying wooden back side of the wooden toboggan slide that had been built in the park. It was a sixteen-foot-tall slide, sloped to forty-five degrees. In winter, the neighbourhood garden hoses brought water to the top and it sluiced down to create a thrilling slide that carried us on sleds and scraps of cardboard down the iced plywood ramp. The ice sluice created a long, bumpy path on the snow that ended in a fanned delta at the end of the run. After hurtling down, we pulled our sleds behind us and ran back up the two-by-four cleat stairway to the top of the ramp.

As we languished in the shade of the slide that summer day—a great, grazing brontosaurus of spruce, pine and fir—two cars pulled up loudly across the park at the ball diamond. Seven or eight teenage boys, most of whom we knew, piled out of the cars. We knew something was up because these teens did not often come to the park, instead preferring to cruise in their old cars or going for a swim at the gravel pits or hanging out at a drive-in restaurant. There was Johnny Fehr, a big tough hockey player; Corny Haerder, a cousin of mine from my mom's family; Dennis Fehr, Big Johnny's younger brother—a natural goal scorer in hockey; Fats Fehr, a cousin to Johnny and Dennis; and Tracy Lord, one of the toughest guys in town.

Two more were in Johnny's car, in the back seat. One was

Erd, the big square-shouldered older brother of my good friend Lenny, who was almost as big as Johnny and who played a solid defence on the town hockey team. Where Lenny was edgy and easy to anger, Erdman was more of a gentle giant. At least towards Lenny and I. Seated beside Erd was Richard Lord, tough Tracy's older brother who went by the name "Reb."

The Lords were originally from the neighbouring hamlet of Ste. Remaud, but they both had jobs in Hartplatz and so they hung around town with the high school boys. The Lord boys were "rough customers," as my grandma put it. They came from a family where the father was mostly gone, he had moved to Brandon for work as a welder and seldom came back—although the family depended on him for money and lived in his house in Ste. Remaud.

Reb was a wonderful diver and he spent hours at the town swimming pool diving off the springboard—precise jackknifes, spinning somersaults and towering swan dives. He wore leather jackets and pointy black *Beatle* boots that slipped on with elastic patches on the sides. These boots were dreaded as he was rumoured to be able to kick, or "shoot the boots," to a height of nine feet. Indeed, once he had kicked out a light bulb outside of *Fred's Lunch* and that was a good eight feet above the sidewalk, give or take a toe or two.

His younger brother Tracy was the one we feared most of all. He terrorized us kids and even though many of my friends' more wide-bodied older brothers might take him in a fight, they did not dare to take on *his* older brother, "Reb." So, Tracy was left unchallenged, and he took particular delight in torturing us little guys, who feared him openly and without shame. I dreaded going to my grandpa's distant shoe shop on an errand for Grandma because it would take me past one of the restaurants where Tracy hung out, drinking innumerable *Pepsi-Colas* and smoking *Export "A"* cigarettes.

On one such trip, he saw me and pulled me roughly into a vinyl upholstered booth, where Scottie already sat, likewise waylaid. Tracy pushed me in next to Scottie, then lit a wooden match with his thumbnail and held the orange flame under the heel of his hand. "Just getting' ready for Hell, boys, jus' gettin' ready," he said evenly while he grinned at us. Then he cuffed us each sharply and said we'd be taking a ride soon, "so stick around you little shits!" Scottie and I seemed like his favourite victims.

Of course, we left as he went to visit a booth full of girls and turned his back to us. He later caught us at the *A&W* and pulled us into the front seat of his 1949 *Ford* Fordor Sedan, our exit blocked by big Johnny Fehr who sat eating a burger against the far door. Tracy held the car keys up in front of my face and said, "Hey Zehen. Did you know this car is a magic car? This car is a LIE DETECTOR, and you are gonna be tested right now."

Johnny snickered, elbowing me a little but without Tracy's psychopath attitude. Tracy continued: "Okay, Zehen. Here's the first question: Do you like girls? Eh, Zehen? Do you like girls?"

I stared at him dumbly and then looked at Scottie who shrugged his shoulders and turned his palms up, his lip quivering. "C'mon Zehen—time's up," Tracy cooed, prodding me hard with the car key. I sucked in my breath and stiffened, involuntarily leaning against Johnny Fehr (Johnny *Fear* to us) and making him spill a bit of his root beer. He shoved me back hard, back into the key point which tore my shirt.

"Answer, little turd!" Johnny growled.

"No!" I said.

"No, what, ya snot-nosed *Schnoddanäs*?"

A redundant phrase but I chose not to quibble. "No, I don't like girls."

"Ohhhh. We'll see," Tracy said, gesturing with the car key. "Car," he intoned mechanically, "Does Zehen here like girls? True or False?" Then he pointed at the gas tank gauge, the red needle lay inert pointing at the E. As he put the key in the ignition and clicked it once, the needle animated and rose steadily past ½ and then slowly stopped, pointing directly at the F.

"F!" Tracy yelled, making the family in the car next to us stare. Johnny Fear waved a hand at them in annoyance, shouting sarcastically, "Take a picture!" to which they responded by looking away, except the small children in the back who stood on the seat staring unabashedly.

"F stands for what, Johnny? F stands for..."

"FALSE!" Big Johnny barked, despite a mouth full of food. "F stands for False, m' Lord."

"False, eh, Zehen? The lie detector Ford says that your answer is false. So, I asked if you like girls, you said you did not, and the car says your answer is false. So that means you DO like girls."

Johnny chimed in roughly, "Good thing, don't want no homos in here."

Tracy laughed just a bit *too* hard, bringing looks from the family next door, which Johnny waved away angrily, gesturing with pronged fingers for them to point their eyes forward.

"Okay, Zehen. Here's the next question. The lie detector *Ford* is all warmed up now. Tell us, Zehen—do you like ME, Zehen. Eh? Do you boys like me, Tracy Lord?"

To say yes, we liked him, was a lie—too easy for him to insert the key and generate the F response. Then what? If we said we *didn't* like him, what would happen?

"No. We don't like Tracy Lord." Scottie interjected with

unexpected calm, to my horror.

"Pardon me! What is THAT, shit-for-brains?" Tracy erupted, as Johnny Fear laughed, wheezing and spitting onion and saliva on the steel dashboard in front of him. Johnny clapped Scottie on the back and coughing, eyes tearing, said, "Good one, kid, good one!"

Spotting a pair of girls arm in arm, coming out of the bowling alley, Tracy suddenly lit a cigarette, gestured at Johnny to look and jumped out of the car.

* * *

I remembered all of this as we drifted slowly across the field to the ball diamond. We steered toward the edge of the group, away from Johnny Fear and Tracy and the two young men in the car. I went over to my cousin Corny Haerder, who was tagging along, far out of his weight class here. "What are you guys doing?" I asked him. He looked down at me and explained. Erdman had been in *Fred's Lunch Bar* delivering cheese for his uncle when he had come to the attention of Tracy, Reb, Johnny Fehr and Corny.

Tracy said, "Who's the queer?" in a loud voice. Erdman, apparently oblivious, had continued counting out change to the restaurant owner. Reb jumped up and strode noisily up to Erd and inquired loudly, "Hey! Didn't you hear what Tracy said?" to which Erdman immediately replied, smiling broadly back at the booths, many of which held high school girls, "Tracy? Which one is *she*?"

Corny whispered all this to me, with my friends listening intently. At the conclusion of the story, we unanimously exclaimed, "whoa!" or "oh but!" and Corny winked. He said to us, "Now Johnny and Reb are gonna make Erdman fight Tracy. Tracy wanted to fight him right away, but Erdman was chicken. So, the other guys grabbed him and made him come here."

Just then, Johnny Fear yelled, "Shut up!" We did and then he said, in a ring announcer voice, "Erdman called Tracy a girl. Tracy wants to fight, but Erdman says no. Either Erd fights Tracy, or me n' Reb are gonna pound the shit out of Erd."

"End of story!" Reb shouted from the car, where he sat next to Erdman. Then he began pushing him out, kicking Erd while Johnny reached in to pull at him, finally skidding him out on his back right out of the car and onto the sandy lane.

Grimacing, Erdman rolled onto his side and like a bear woken from hibernation, he was not pleased. He kicked out at Johnny's legs, who jumped back and yelled, "Now we're cookin'!"

Tracy stood snapping swift, showy kicks near the pitcher's mound, waiting.

Erdman, my friend Lenny's big brother, was big indeed. He had outgrown his boy's body and he possessed a chunky square-ness that made him hard to get around, even on skates. He rose, slamming the car door so hard it sounded like a gunshot, and Corny, who had been talking to me, whirled around like he had been yanked by a chain. So too, did Tracy. He stood near the mound in some kind of a martial arts pose, which looked suddenly ridiculous as Erdman, pulling off a white cheese factory delivery jacket, walked slowly towards him.

"Alright," Erdman said, "fist fights are against my religion, but you crazy guys are making me. So, let's fight."

"Now there's gonna be a war!" Scottie whispered.

We all knew Erdman could handle himself. I was a bit surprised to hear his religious position—the Gerbrandts weren't the most pious family I knew—but in Hartplatz, this point of view was an inalienable right. When one of Erd's clumsy but powerful body checks sent a rushing opponent into the boards, he sometimes had to defend himself with his fists. But hockey fights were different and the legendary Lord brother's boots were much scarier than sweater-tugging and off-balance hay-makers. But now something had happened and like the weather after the first frost of September, things felt different.

Tracy made some threatening kicks, leaping into the air as Erdman walked steadily forward. Erdman came up to the mound where Tracy stood and then started instinctively stepping back and to his left, quartering his body and raising his hands in front of his chest, fingers loose, palms down.

"C'mon, Lil Reb!" cheered Johnny Fear, earning a loud, "Yee-haw!" from Richard the Reb, who reclined on the car hood his hands clasped behind his head, fingers interlaced.

Tracy suddenly raced forward and jumped, straddling his legs in the air. Erdman stopped, watching as one foot came toward his chest. Then suddenly Tracy jerked it down to gain leverage and send the other foot flying at Erdman's head. Erdman flinched, glimpsed the boot coming at him and reached up to throw a forearm over the outstretched leg. Catching hold quickly with both hands, he twisted Tracy over in the air and forced him down, like bulldogging a calf at a rodeo. Tracy landed hard and could not prepare so his left cheek hit the pitcher's mound dirt first. He came up moaning, gravel and grass pressed into his red face.

Erdman shouted, "Ha!" as surprised as anyone, and Reb quickly sat up straight on the car hood, his fists clenched.

Erdman, backed off a step as Tracy scrambled up, wiping his face with a swipe of his hand, checking for blood. Seeing none, he hitched his shoulders and raised his hands in front of him, hissing swear words. He danced forward like a fencer, then led at the big man with a straight right hand. Carelessly, he left himself open and Erdman leaned back to slip the punch and slapped his flat palm against Tracy's open right cheek. The wallop sent Tracy to the ground again, this time falling on his shoulder; ducking his head to prevent another scrape on his bruised cheek. He failed though and a cut opened, and a trickle of blood ran down through the hair on his temple and onto his jaw, dripping off the tip of his chin.

Erdman, seeing the blood, dropped his hands in dismay. The smaller man rushed forward, this time jabbing well with his left and then sweep-kicking at Erdman's shin. The jab knocked Erdman's head back and he instinctively threw his arms around Tracy in a clinch to keep from falling when the kick knocked him off balance. They fell heavily together, with Tracy taking the landing on his left side, and again, his cheekbone. He pushed free and regained his feet, blinking and rubbing at his eye, which was already bloodshot and showing puffiness. Erdman got up, slowly slapping dust from his hands.

Reb stood in front of the car now; his feet spread wide apart, arms crossed on his chest.

Panting slightly, Tracy mimicked Erdman's boxer stance and waited for an advance. Seeing this, Erdman lowered his heavy arms and said loudly, "I thought you wanted to fight. C'mon." He beckoned with a crooked finger.

Enraged, Tracy leaped forward and Erdman used his superior reach to copy Tracy's earlier jabs, hitting him soundly twice. Tracy's left cheekbone was fiery red, and blue and purple, and that eye was completely bloodshot. Facing Erdman's bulk, Tracy was being exposed as an unpolished scrapper, who was more reputation than skill.

He regrouped and swung wildly, missing with his left hand and pulling himself forward. As he fell past Erdman, the larger man simply put his elbow into Tracy's path, catching his top lip and nose. The collision crunched audibly and beside me, Scottie and Corky said, "Ohhhhh." at the same time. The blow stopped Tracy short and he simply fell to all fours in front of Erdman.

"This fight is over," said Johnny flatly, stepping forward to slap Erdman on the back and hand him his white delivery jacket. "C'mon big fella, I'll take you back to your truck. Let's go." He waved Reb away from the car and hopped in. Erdman walked slowly around the front of the car, a predatory grin on his compressed lips as he walked by Reb, who watched him silently.

Erdman stopped and looked over at Reb, who had backed up a step to let him by. Sensing Reb's wariness, Erd hesitated, and then flashed a fake jab. Reb stumbled as he ducked, throwing his hands up and falling in a cloud of dust on the third baseline.

I frowned with mock sternness at Scottie who beamed back at me. "Do you like Tracy?" I asked him, my finger feigning the motion of the gas gauge needle. "No, I don't like her at all," he grinned.

* * *

A few weeks later I was over at the Gerbrandt's building a model airplane kit—a B-29 Superfortress bomber—with Lenny. Erd came over and sat with us. "So, that was some fight you had with Tracy," I said.

"Yeah. Wish that hadn't happened."

"But, still. You did good."

"Acch. Whatever. Tracy and me, we were both talked into that whole thing. I didn't have nothing against him and if I accidentally insulted him, well, I didn't know. Tracy *is* a girl's name sometimes and I didn't mean to tease him. Lots of guys make fun of *my* name—call me Turd man—..."

I gritted my teeth to keep from laughing. "Yeah. I wondered about that, why you and Tracy fought. It was plain you didn't want to. It seemed like Reb and Johnny Fear set the whole thing up. Like they wanted to see a fight, not be in one, and just got you guys to do it."

"That's true. And I knew it too. But after they threw me out of the car, I thought, okay, either I fight Tracy, or I fight both Johnny and Reb, or maybe all three of them! I saw pretty quick which way I should go."

"Yeah, it was kinda like a cock-fight or something..."

"Who you calling a cock?" Erd said, putting me in a friendly bear hug, both of us laughing.

"The good thing is," Erd said after we settled down, "I think maybe Tracy and all those guys don't want to do that again. I was afraid I was still gonna have to fight all those guys—Johnny Fear and Reb too—but it looks like they don't want to. I think maybe they'll steer clear. For a while, anyhow."

"Maybe they'll steer clear of Matt and Scottie too," Lenny said, crossing his thin arms. They already know not to mess with me," he added in typical cowboy Lenny style.

"Hope so," Erd said, "That way, at least it was all kind of for something good, even if, like Matt's grandma says, 'there's no such thing as a good fight,' but sometimes it sure seems like you don't have a choice, exactly.

A Vile Insinuation

My head spun and my lips and cheeks felt numb—too much July sun followed by too much beer. I sat on a picnic table in the beer garden. Our team was in Vita for a baseball tournament. It was over and we had lost in the final to a team from the States.

"Manna from heaven!" a voice behind me said as a full tray of beer arrived on the tabletop. It was Marty, the do-it-all short-stop from the winning team. He had been buying for our table all evening, using the fast-shrinking wad of fives, tens and singles that had been his winner's share. He reminded me of Mark Belanger from the Baltimore Orioles—big and tall, a smooth infielder.

"Marty the party," I said, sliding one of the foamy cups back towards him. "I have to drive, you know. It's quite a hike." We were near the US border.

"Nothing to it," he said. "Ain't no bulls on the highway down here. Not in these parts, not now."

"Sure, but I gotta get my friend's old car back to him before it gets too late. In one piece. It is true though, that the highways should be pretty well empty. Plus, once we get home, my cousin is the town cop on patrol. As long as the RCs are not cruisin' around, I should be OK."

"RC's? You mean Roman Catholics?" he asked, his face screwed up. "You Mennonites take adult baptism seriously!"

Our shortstop, Ernie Froese, did an exaggerated spit take, misting the table. It smelled yeasty.

"Hey! Quit wasting beer there, Milton Berle! It don't grow on trees," Marty said, pulling out his thick wallet.

"RCs are police—Royal Canadian Mounted Police. R-C-M-P or RCs for short," Ernie explained. "Where we're from, we have both town cops and RCs. The RCs are jerks; the town cops are guys we know. The town cops stop us and confiscate our beer. The RCs stop us and steal our beer."

Marty stopped fiddling with his wallet. "Why does one 'confiscate' and the other 'steal'?" he asked.

"Because the town cops share the beer with us later and the RCs don't," I answered. Ernie chimed in with a loud, "Right on!"

Marty chuckled and went through his wallet. "Well, dudn't matter anyhow—the bank is about empty." He flipped assorted keepsakes and pictures out as he searched for another dollar bill.

"It dudn't, dud it?" said Ernie, an eyebrow arched theatrically. "I got a buck but I think we're gonna need that for gas. Doctor Rempel's Zephyr guzzles gas, right, Diedrich?"

"Don't ask me those complicated mechanical questions, Ernesto, I am just a lowly driver, not an oil-change caddy and part-time service technician trainee at Janzen's ," I replied.

"Okay. I accept your limitations. And also, *kleiw die*!" Ernie replied drunkenly, staring at me over a poised cup of *Labatt's 50 Ale*.

Marty finished lighting one of my *DuMauriers* and tossed the *Bic* back at me. I was smoking his Marlies, so it was an even trade. "What the hell is *KLIVE DEE?*" he asked.

Ernie laughed. "Okay, you Yankee Martin Luther, here's what: "*kleiw die*" is *Plautdietsch*—Low German. It is my way of suggesting politely to Diedrich here, our stoic backcatcher and fearless late-night limousine chauffeur, that he go scratch himself. It further insinuates to claw oneself in an inappropriate place and manner. *Vesteist? Verstehen?* Understand?"

Marty, with a straight face, answered, "*kliewe die, Hund!*"

We all laughed. Marty—his last name was Schroeder, not Luther—then admitted that his mom was a Mennonite, a Fast, originally from Manitoba where so many Mennonite families had settled. He admitted that he spoke a few words of God's own language, words like "*Hund*," the *Plautdietsch* word for dog. We nodded appreciatively, toasting him into the brethren, "with sacramental suds," Ernie offered, gravely. As always, his mock-ery—what my Aunty Rosalyn called "*spott*"—was over-the-top, but entertaining and not out of step for our group of guys during baseball. I had played basketball and baseball with these fellows since I made Coach Smullett's basketball team way back when.

"What do you call it when you have too much sacramental wine?" I asked, riffing off of Ernie's comment. They shrugged. "Being in an altar-ed state," I dead-panned.

Ernie did another loud spit take and Marty began cleaning up the assorted cards from his wallet.

Another teammate of ours, Ernie's brother Dennis, joined our table. "You guys going soon?" he asked.

"Yeah, I am *hundmeed*—dog-tired," I said, directing the translation at Marty, just in case.

"What's that thing?" Dennis asked, pointing at an offi-cial-looking paper form on the tabletop, folded in half. It had dropped from Marty's wallet. "Selective Service System STATUS

CARD," he read aloud. The big first baseman stood beside me, harshly backlit by a string of naked 100-watt bulbs.

"That is President Nixon's draft lottery," Marty said, squinting up at Dennis from where he sat.

"How old are you, Marty?" I asked him.

"I turn nineteen next month, August 16," he said.

"Me too—August 22. So, what does that all mean?" asked Ernie, leaning forward to study the card.

Marty pointed at a printed number near the center of the card. "44 is my all-important lottery number. Hank Aaron's number, huh? His lucky number after he quit wearin' 42 in honour of Jackie Robinson. Anyhow, that means my birthdate has drawn 'Random Sequence Number' 44. So everyone born on that day who's eligible to be drafted is going to go—to be inducted—once Selective Services get to the forty-fourth birthday on the list. You are eligible once you turn nineteen." He sipped his beer, holding the card in one hand and staring at it.

"Right now, they are projectin' that they will call up until about RSN 130, this year" he concluded.

"So," I slid a beer out of the pack, "all those born on August sixteenth go into the army when the forty-fourth group is called up?" I asked.

"Yeah, it's a low draft number. It means I'm going to Vietnam, buddy, unless the war ends, ya know," Marty finished the thought, and his beer. "I'll be called up almost right away after my birthday. You betcha."

We were quiet for a minute. "Life During Wartime" by *Talking Heads* drifted across the beer garden from a boom box near the bar.

"You said your mom was a Menno from Manitoba, right?" Ernie asked.

Marty sat up, glaring at Ernie. He did not answer.

"No doubt you've thought of this, but why don't you claim C.O. status?" Ernie continued. "If your mom is a member of the church, maybe you can use that."

Marty flicked his cigarette butt across the table. It whizzed past Ernie. Exhaling smoke, Marty stood and sized up Dennis who was about the same height as him. "Conscientious Objectors ain't popular where I'm from. Besides, my mom already looked into it, and because I don't go to a Mennonite church—I ain't baptized—it wouldn't work. It's not like it was in Canada during World War Two, Mom says. Besides, that's not what I want." He folded the draft card carefully and put it in his wallet, slotted in among many pictures, notes, and ticket stubs.

"Your Mom's a Canuck. Yer in Canada right now—just stay here," said Dennis, in his deep Brer Bear voice.

Marty looked at him soberly and shook his head. "No way, man. I'm an American, plain and simple. Besides, I gotta tell you something about my birthday. You guys are the deep thinkers," he said, looking at Ernie, "so you need to know that I was born at exactly 11:52 pm on the sixteenth. I don't know about fate or karma and I sure as heck don't know about the will of God. For me, it's just a random draw—a lottery. See, the funny thing is that August 17 drew draft number 360…"

Marty reached down and picked up his glove and spikes, and stuffed the pack of *Marlboroughs* into his jacket pocket. He strolled out of the brightly lit beer garden, nodding at players from his team as he receded into the dark forest. I watched him ambling loosely across the sandy ground toward the parking lot, his tall form intermingling with the white spruce and black pine.

*　*　*

We drove Doctor Rempel's Zephyr slowly along the highway,

heading west past Stuartburn and Dominion City. Every few miles another deer would appear, eyes reflecting in the headlights, head surrounded by a cloud of mosquitoes; tail and ears twitching.

It was quiet, the radio being no good this far away from Winnipeg. The only sounds were the hum of the tires and the muffled burr of the engine.

"If not for the grace of God..." Dennis rumbled from the darkness of the backseat.

Ernie sniffed, "Mmmmm. Deep."

"*Kliewe die, Hund!*" I said, drawing tired chuckles from the brothers.

"If not for the grace of the Delegates who came from Russia to choose where us Mennos were gonna wind up, *actually,*" Ernie said, from the middle seat. "If some guy's Great-Great *Opa* had chosen to live in North Dakota, instead of Manitoba, we would have been in that Vietnam lottery with Marty too."

"From Russia with love," Dennis said.

"A lot of the new Canadian Mennonites left for the U.S. after they got to Manitoba," said Ernie. "My *Opa* said that the people from our church who left for the States did it because the land here was so rocky," he continued. "They left big established farms over there in *Molotschna*—in Southern Russia—and couldn't stand the idea of mucking around in the stumps and stones here. Plus, the flooding. So, when the U.S. offered citizenship, a bunch of them headed stateside and now they have huge farms. Sugar beets, probably some of the places right on the highway on the way to Grand Forks and Fargo."

"I hate to burst your bubble, but I heard that was bull," I said, just before spewing a bulging cheek's worth of sunflower seed shells out of my open window. "The border doesn't change the soil. I heard those people were kicked out because of some bickering, but mainly because they only came to Canada in the twenties, when so many had come earlier. The early ones left everything they had in Russia."

We were quiet for a while. "There was resentment," I added, looking at the two brothers who sat beside me, their faces dimly lit by the dashboard lights.

"Things happen for a reason, they say," Dennis said. "The first shall be last."

The tires droned. Deer peeped out from the ditch, their eyes like white phosphorous flares.

"I don't know about that," I said. "Just like Marty there, getting born just before midnight and that making what could be a life-and-death difference for him. Pure luck of the draw, I say. I don't buy your master plan and God sitting up in Heaven marking his bingo card with a felt tip marker." I filled up my cheek with fresh sunflower seeds. "Maybe some day I'll think that way, but right now, no way."

We drove in silence again. Ernie worked to repair a torn leather lace on his ball glove, concentrating and breathing noisily through his mouth. He looked up as we came towards a pair of deer, who stood chewing cow-like on the shoulder of the highway. They stared at the car as we approached and then the smaller of the two gathered its legs and suddenly leapt straight up in the air, like an African gazelle.

"Whoa! I've never seen that before! That's something they do, eh? It's called *stotting*. We just studied that in Biology. They do that to stay alive," Ernie said. "It's like—Hey, I'm small and agile, hard to catch! Don't bother with me—take the bigger, slower one."

"Don't mean to interrupt," I said, "but how do you know that shit?"

"I pay attention in class, for one..." His reply was interrupted by the radio as it picked up distant thunder and coughed static into the car's dusty interior.

"Hmm," Dennis mumbled, "That jumping deer trick... don't think that'd work for me."

"Nor Marty," I said, staring ahead into the yellow dinge of the headlights on the straight, empty road before us, the speakers squelching and buzzing as we drove.

The Sunshine Girl

Lenny travelled north on the highway. The intersecting mile roads offered a clear measure of his progress, with foxtail and bulrushes standing tall in the roadside ditches like summertime sentries. His truck tires sang on the soaked asphalt and the speedometer needle dandled somewhere just below fifty miles per hour.

After a while he grew bored with the sameness of his prairie surroundings and scanned the pick-up's spartan interior for diversion. His gaze caught on the large screwdriver resting in a holder mounted to the underside of the metal dashboard. It had a two-tone yellow handle and was the extra-long version: a full 20 inches of heat-treated chromium-molybdenum alloy. It had a "cabinet tip," meaning that the width of the flathead was no greater than that of the shaft—it was not flared.

The screwdriver was the biggest one they sold at *Barkman Hardware*. Its handle was the same colour and opacity as the syrup from a can of peaches. The tool's length was equal to Lenny's forearm from elbow to fingertip. The shank was as thick as a man's baby finger and had the Zen-like balance of a Japanese carving knife, providing a firm heft that he knew and trusted. Holding the screwdriver was like shaking the hand of a friend.

No amount of abuse, prying or cursing seemed to deter it or wear the thing out and the only harm that could befall it was loss. **That's where the custom holder comes in,** Lenny mused. Two galvanized steel U-clamps were screwed to the dog-chested curve of the dash—a single-purpose holster made to order. He always knew where the tool was and if it was not there, he didn't leave until it was found and re-sheathed. It was drilling the holes and fastening the screwdriver holder in place that made the old truck his, and Lenny knew that too.

Today was a rainy summer day, tea-warm drizzle from the grey belly of a staying-put cloud that sagged from the sky. The straight two-lane highway shone with a dull sheen as he and the *Chevy* came up behind another pick-up. Lenny could see right away that it was tracking crookedly. Instead of two neat, parallel tire tracks cut into the black velvet of the wet pavement, there were four tracks; two close-together pairs separated by a wider division of glistening roadway.

"His right fender is gonna arrive in advance of his left," Lenny monotoned to the interior, doing his best John Prine. Likely due to some chassis disfigurement, the truck was advancing at a five-degree angle. *Dog-tracking* in the parlance of farm vehicles, trotting hounds, and airplanes landing in heavy crosswinds. "Kind of a *Schmäahmoazh*," Lenny whispered to himself, using one of Matt's favourite German phrases. "Greasy-arsed."

He followed along behind the truck. The cab contained a big, round-shouldered man who was driving and a narrow, upright-sitting woman on his right. She had shoved herself into the extreme far side of the seat, her arm compressed against the door and her small hat touching the glass. Although the man glanced frequently and sometimes for extended periods at his cab mate, she did not return his gaze. The man, in fact, sprawled and gestured randomly and sent his considerable weight sluicing from side to side like thirty gallons of gas in a fifty-five-gallon drum.

"It's like he's doing the polka with himself," Lenny said quietly.

The pick-up he trailed was pale yellow—not even yellow but more like melon or September poplar leaf or maybe the shade of a pickerel belly but without the sparkle. **Rusted pretty bad, too,** he thought. The driver's side hung like a droopy eye, a hand or so lower than the right.

He was near enough to see the V-shaped dents in the top lip of the tailgate but not quite enough to discern the exact colour of the woman's hair. Honey blonde, maybe. Or, "strawberry blonde," as his cousin Phyllis from Winkler called her own shade, and she was right. He could tell this pale rider was young, wearing a new-looking "go to Winnipeg" jacket, not a barn jacket and that she—unlike the truck she rode in—sat up straight and tall. **Bet her dad is a preacher,** Lenny thought, amusing himself with the idea.

As they neared the TransCanada highway intersection, Lenny was reminded of his friend Sarah. She lived north of here, on a farm up near Hazel Creek. Her mother was best friends with his mom and Lenny had known the family as long as he could remember. Sarah's parents were "Uncle and Aunty" and Sarah was a cousin, but even more than that. She wasn't, after all, really a relative and that made it different. They had always been close, Sarah and he. Lenny didn't see her much anymore and he was reminded of that as he neared the corner, following the truck with its passenger who could have been Sarah, viewed through the truck cab window from behind.

The two vehicles both took the cloverleaf onto the Trans-Canada, curling off to the west. Lenny examined the driver ahead more carefully. He wore a *John Deere* ball cap—the trademark green and yellow made the familiar brand obvious even for a town kid like Lenny. The driver moved his head more than his body. He turned and twisted and nodded and canted and craned so much that Lenny felt his own neck becoming tired. The fellow was a six-footer, maybe a touch more. He could tell that because the driver's head reached about the same height as Lenny's in relation to the rear window in their respective trucks.

They rattled along over the rippling frost heaves on the highway, shifting up through the gears. Lenny could see the driver fussing with the shift lever. "Can't get her into third…" Lenny murmured.

The *International Harvester* truck, just like Lenny's *Chevy*, had a "three-on-the-tree" shifter on the steering column and they could be sticky. That stiff, mashing tendency of the transmission linkages was the reason for the big, amber-handled screwdriver and why it had such a prime location in Lenny's truck. The screwdriver was the tool used to free up jammed gear shifter rods when they—as they eventually always did—bound themselves together like the mating snakes of Narcisse.

Lenny gripped and regripped the circle of the steering wheel. The truck slowed in front of him, and the man heaved at the shifter arm with furious vigour but earned no avail—the old "Cornbinder" continued to slow down. Confident that he knew what the trouble was, Lenny followed them as they coasted onto the shoulder of the road.

Lenny sucked in and held his breath. He held it during the creak of his door opening, the gravel crunch under his boots, and the light tap of his knuckles on the driver-side window. He exhaled and breathed the wild fragrance of rapeseed, now coming into season. The patter of light rain sounded on the truck hood as the driver's window slid down. A bent toothpick toggled up and down in the man's lips and he sized Lenny up before speaking, regarding him with a slight backward lean of his torso.

"What can I do you for? Looks like you got more to say than a dog stuck down a well…"

"*Goon… dach*," Lenny replied in hitching *Plautdietsch*—perplexed by the heavily accented, unfamiliar expression the driver had tossed at him. "I just thought I'd check what was wrong. I been following you for some miles here and I'm guessin' you got a jammed-up gear shift."

The man stared blankly, searching for words. Lenny shifted his stance. He wondered if the driver spoke any other English or if his opening line was his whole vocabulary. The young woman passenger piped up from across the truck cab. Her accent was mild and she spoke mostly with the syntax of English sentences not Low German. Her voice was soft and soprano.

"Yes. The gear shifter on this truck sometimes gets stuck. Jake—this guy here is named Jake—gets stuck then too, it's like they're twins, joined together. Do you know what to do?" she asked. Jake sat unmoving but for the twitching toothpick. The young woman smiled just then and a small, sunlit crack appeared in the cloud cover above. Just a crack.

"He gets stuck, eh?" Lenny replied. "That's fine I guess, as long as I don't have to kiss him to revive him."

She of the wasp-waist stifled a laugh and quickly responded, "No, no. Sometimes it works to say his name three times, but that's only for emergencies."

"Har. Okay, sure. You just hang on, please, I might have another solution." He jogged back to his truck and pulled the screwdriver from its dashboard mount. It felt, he thought irrationally, eager to be set to work.

"Just shut her down, please, the truck engine," he said when back beside the open window. Still immobilized, Jake did not move but the young lady reached across with a slim, grey jacketed arm and counter-clock-wised the key with her gloved hand. The engine quieted with a final quivering jitter.

He slipped round to the front and unlatched the hood. With a grunt, he heaved it open, noting how it lifted without the telltale squeal of negligence. Lenny beheld a spotless, well-maintained engine compartment. He was both surprised and not. "Why should I have assumed that the driver's personal hygiene should match his truck maintenance habits?" was his guilty thought.

"Neat as a banker's desk," Lenny yelled, bending forward to peep through the gap between the raised hood and the windshield. Likewise, Jake and the woman were tilted forward to observe, like two surgical students leaning over a cadaver.

The tangled rods of the gear shifter told another story though. Like those of his truck, these were long, thin fibula of hardened steel—mysterious and arcane in their convoluted mechanical fluency. They connected from the steering column post and down to the transmission and articulated the shifter's position in first, second or third gear. The rods were like a translator, conveying the driver's wishes to the transmission below. The two heaviest, longest rods were locked against each other. With a practiced probe of the screwdriver's lone, flat tooth, Lenny slipped it into the criss-cross clench and pried.

"*Puh-whang!*" sang out the gear rods as they released in an ecstasy of metallic relief. Separating like uncoupled lovers, they vibrated for a brief moment and then sought their own private space near one another.

"You can grease the knuckle up a bit, right here," Lenny hollered, gesturing. Jake's narrowed eyes followed the pointing screwdriver tip. With hands drumming on the steering wheel, Jake nodded, coming out of his trance now that the truck had. The petite passenger paid attention too, leaning forward, her slender neck extended. She looked amused.

Lenny eased the hood shut and returned to the side of the truck, thinking, **"This guy's a little old to be taking advice from a young buck like me—I'm just a kid out running errands! I wonder what's up with him?"**

Jake started the engine and it idled smoothly. His foot pinning the clutch down, the big-bellied man shifted through the gears a few times and they did not quarrel.

With some rubs against his shirt, Lenny made sure the screwdriver shaft was clean and then nodded at Jake. He found his gaze turning towards the woman—**and who is she anyway? 'Jake's' daughter?**—when suddenly Jake blurted out, his shoulders hiking up as he did so, "I'd like you to meet my wife... my *Frü*, or that's what she's anyways gonna be, once we get there by Winnipeg."

Hiding his surprise, Lenny stuck his hand through the window and, in his most neighbourly voice, said, "Congratulations! My name is Leonard Gerbrandt and I'm glad to meet you and your fiancée. My friends call me Lenny." Jake shook heartily but when Lenny reached in further to congratulate his bride-to-be, Jake grabbed his arm and packed it out the window.

"Here, you can have that back now. We're da Schmietums. I'm Schmietum... Jake and this here is gonna be Mrs. Schmietum—Mrs. Jake P. Schmietum, to be specific," he said with a serious look.

As Lenny started to walk back to his truck, Jake whistled and said, "Hey, Denny! If you wanna trail behind us 'til we get to the Justice for the Peace, in case we get all hooked up under the hood again, that'd be a good plan… Or you can just borrow me dat *Schrüwendreia*, once."

Now it was Lenny's turn to freeze, so stunned was he by Schmietum Jake's overly familiar suggestion. And he was also wondering if the use of "Denny," which could be taken as slang for someone thin in German—he knew because he was sometimes called that—was a mistake or an intentional jab. *Take my screwdriver? Seriously?* **To hell with that noise,** he thought, hearing his father's voice in his head. **What if MY gears jam?**

Mentally off balance, he quickly regrouped. Loaning out his beloved screwdriver was, after all, in so many ways an opportunity to do what his mom and good old Mrs. Zehen, his friend Matt's Grandma, were always telling him to do. It was the Golden Rule, it was the law of the open road, and a modern-day expression of good Samaritanism all balled up into one grace-filled, yellow-handled act.

But saving him, just as he was about to sputter out an unhappy *yes* to Schmietum Jake and risk his screwdriver's fate—forever, he feared—Mrs. Schmietum Jake-to-be spoke up.

"Oh, *nayyy*, Jake! We couldn't *impose* on this young man's generosity by taking his obviously new and expensive screwdriver. What if we, on accident, were to forget to return it?" She wagged her head in exaggerated, school-marm dismay. "*Oh, bah nay!*"

As she spoke, she moved away from the grasp of the far door and angled her torso slightly towards Schmietum Jake and Lenny, her lips moist and… parted. **Or maybe she was not intentionally positioned that way. Maybe she was just readjusting herself on the worn bench seat? It could be,** Lenny admitted to himself, that his belief that she was using her body to send him a message was really just his conceit running wild.

"Sure. Fine. Keep your screwdriver," Jake allowed, and fumbled with the gear shift lever. "Jost follow us to the *Staut*, Denny," he called out, pointing towards the city of Winnipeg, his eyes never leaving those of his betrothed.

Lenny gave him a thumbs-up gesture and made a friendly wave to future Mrs. Schmietum Jake. Beguiled once more, he noticed that her lips were pink, her cheeks a smooth rosé and her blue eyes were large, complemented by feathery lashes, so dark and so curved. This he did not imagine. He felt unmistakably attracted to her and along with that came a shiver of shame. He thought of Matt's Grandma, Mrs. Zehen, and Sarah up north at Hazel Creek and his sister Rebecca. What would they think of all this? He heard Grandma Zehen's accusatory voice in his head: "What if the woman in the passenger seat looked more like Schmietum Jake and less like a movie star? Hmm?"

Good question, Lenny thought. Would I still be so wound up about her then? Would I have even stopped to help? Maybe, but if so, then only to show off my knowledge and to put my expensive screwdriver to use.

"You men and your *Schrüwendreia!*" he imagined Grandma Zehen saying, in a tut-tut voice.

Just then, "Starla Grieves," Jake's *Frü*-to-be called out, interrupting his thoughts and quieting the mental voices. She had introduced herself to him! Lenny heard her say it and so, obviously, did Schmietum Jake who pumped his window shut, grunting with effort.

Taking a few steps back towards his truck, Lenny heard Jake's voice. He saw Jake's head nodding emphatically as he spat words out. The driver door was ajar with Jake gripping the inside handle.

"...none of his beeswax, anyhow!" Lenny overheard Jake say to Starla Grieves in a hissing whisper. Jake pushed the door open and heaved himself out, eyes flashing, pantlegs tucked into new cowboy boots. The door clanged shut behind him.

"Thanks for all da help, eh?" Jake said, coming up to where Lenny stood, partway between the parked vehicles. The toothpick clung to his lower lip as he spoke. He was, at close range, just as tall as Lenny. His girth was a full barrel that wrapped his torso from shoulders to hips. The man's thick chest and belly was the difference-maker. Lenny felt self-conscious about his own body; though growing into the strong, lean man's physique he would one day have, it was still youthful and narrow. A work in progress.

"Sure, no problem."

"My *Frü* dere, she didn't mean nothing by telling you her name, eh? I mean—like—you get it that we're engaged to be married. Like, for serious..."

"Yeah. You said." Lenny took a step back. Jake had pepperoni breath. A half-eaten *Hot Rod* stuck up from his shirt pocket like a pencil. Shifting the screwdriver to his opposite hand, Lenny pushed up his sleeves and leaned back towards Jake. He tapped the screwdriver against his own leg. "I heard you, Mr. Schmietum." Jake's body threw off heat like a coal furnace. He could feel Jake's pot belly touching him and while it repelled him and even frightened him a little, he resisted the urge to retreat.

"Okay, den, Denny. Jost wanted to make sure we was clear as day on that part." He lifted his hands into the tight space between them. With a light smacking sound, he patted a fleshy fist into the palm of its partner. "Right? She's nothing but a woman, and a young one yet too. She is a woman, but I sure ain't, if you know what I mean." His eyes flashed, though dull and heavy-lidded. "But... hey! I still want you to follow us, though, right? To the

Big Smoke?" He gestured once again, this time with a tilt of his head towards Winnipeg.

"*Seea goot*," Lenny said with a cold smile, employing some more of his limited *Plautdietsch* vocabulary. Starla, her face clouded and worried, watched as they spoke.

After pouring himself back into the old truck, Jake's door slammed with a tinny clang. Knobby rear tires spun up a skiff of gravel, scattering stones into the ditch.

As Jake pulled away, busy checking his mirror, revving the motor, and trying not to spin the tires too much, Starla Grieves' head was turned, looking without reservation at Lenny as they pulled away. There was no mistaking it.

Gaining speed now, the vehicle shrank from view. Before it was too far for him to see, Starla Grieves waved a white-gloved hand at him through the rear window, fingers fluttering like a distant bird on the wing.

Alone on the sloping margin of the highway, Lenny watched them go. He felt confused and was not unhappy to see them leave. He would not follow them right away. He'd wait. He turned to get back to his truck.

As Schmietum Jake reached the shift point for third, Lenny heard a familiar, grinding, steely squall. Schmietum Jake's truck slowed. The summer sun, as if in anticipation, emerged in its full glory to gild the prairie in golden-amber light.

Lenny stared at the truck as it crept back onto the side of the road. He could see Jake's head angled towards the mirror and Starla was twisted around, looking back. He felt like an actor on a movie set. He considered Starla. He recalled Jake's surly nature, his wet toothpick and pepperoni breath. His barrel chest. Lenny saw himself in a serial vignette, the hero of a melodrama with fists raised and eyes flashing, but the image flickered and blurred in his mind. He thought of Matt's Grandma Zehen on Barkman Avenue and his cousin Sarah. He imagined his sisters and his tireless, good-natured mother.

Lenny drove the truck ahead slowly along the edge of the highway, two wheels on the straight and narrow, two on the rutted gravel. He parked and pulled his screwdriver out from its scabbard and went to the waiting couple in the truck. The driver-side window wound down.

"Here, consider this a wedding gift. I can get another when I get to Winnipeg." He handed the yellow-handled tool to Schmietum Jake who took it with a smug, silent nod. Starla said nothing and resumed her post against the far door, hands in her lap, face forward.

Lenny hurried away. The heroic, cowboy daydream crept into his mind once again and he was tempted. He envisioned Starla's blue eyes, blonde hair, and her fair face adorned by the sun. But then the more familiar women's voices resumed in his head. He imagined his mother, pulling a rusted wagon packed with pillowcases and lamps and Rebecca when she was a toddler. A stoic entrusted with family treasure on her way to the next labour to be endured. Lenny took their ethereal advice. Their visions so sympathetic and symphonic and kind, assuring him he had done the right thing—leaving Starla to control her own destiny and make her way in the world without him; such as it was and in the way she alone chose.

Afterall, he said to himself, **if I stick my nose in uninvited, then I'm no better, or maybe I'm even worse than that Schmietum Jake.**

The Grittiness of Mango Chiffon

Oh, those squinty little eyes. I'll never forget the look of them. Like the night she found tobacco crumbs in my baseball jacket pocket. One night out of many when she "had the goods on me" and "lowered the boom." My mom loved her clichés and despite sounding like an episode of TV's "Mannix," her message was always clear. Crystal. She spread the brown tobacco flakes out on a white napkin under our dining room table's one-hundred-watt bulb.

"Matt, I thought you told me you did not smoke?" she said, her finger pointing at the damning evidence. Her voice was calm, level as wet cement. Justina was her name—Justy for short—and well-named she was. She was justice personified; relentless and forthright and five-foot-two.

The clock ticked on the mantle, sounding just as nervous as I was.

"Thought you were an abstainer," she added, breaking the near silence like a firm, light rap on the skim of ice topping a bucket of water. For this she used her secret weapon—a large

English vocabulary. A second lexical ordnance to complement her mastery of Low German.

"You mess with the bull," she'd say, ignoring the gender incongruence, but concentrating instead on her *film noir* delivery, "you get the horns."

She was rail thin, but each length of her was oddly punctuated with a jutting joint that reminded me of an ink blot on an otherwise smooth straight line. Wrists, elbows, hips, and narrow shoulders each clenched like a knot in a rope. She was slightly stooped, though not tall, and the shape of her back foretold of a hump that would appear in her last years. Her voice was gravelly from cigarettes, but the gruffness I heard could have been more a reflection of what she said—far more John Wayne and Tommy Douglas than the feminine icons of the day. She may have been quoting the Voice of Women movement, but it sounded like the voice of Bogart, Humphrey.

Mother wore modern, tight-fitting slacks and knit sweaters. Her hair was bobbed short, and she had an affection for hats. The shelves of our closets were bulging with *Kopptijch*— brimmed, knit, peaked, and proud. They rested in neat rows awaiting their day in the sun. Clothes and their meanings—implicit and explicit—were important to her. Her flamboyant style and by extension that of her children was her trademark and it stood out in contrast to the staid fashion sense in our conservative town.

Clothes not surprisingly were at the heart of another memorable incident—one of my favourites in a wardrobe holding many such misadventures—when my sister, Edith got in trouble at the high school. I recall it just so, partly witnessed and partly imagined. I remember the event as if I had been there filming the whole thing: "The Justy Zehen Story," a TV documentary. I suppose our school principal from that time remembers it too, but for him, more like watching *The Nature of Things*: "The Moray Eel—Dangerous when Provoked!"

The *Hartplatz Ministerial Association* had, way back in 1960, decreed that it was improper for girls to wear pants to high school—it was skirts or dresses, full stop. Now, while Americans walked on the Moon, in Hartplatz other matters took precedence.

When the Arctic air arrived in Manitoba that January and the mercury hunkered down at thirty below with a gusting wind that licked the frozen ground, my mom rebelled. She stood her ground, also frozen, and pushed back against the all-male HMA Board of Directors and their hatchet man, Principal Reimer.

"Foolishness!" she said, exhaling a bluish stream of smoke towards the kitchen ceiling. She peered out of the frosted window as snow devils wound curlicue trails on the ploughed field across the road from our house. The wind heaved with a grunt against our bungalow, managing only the slightest quiver, registered by a timorous cymbal in the cupboard where the once-a-year crystal dishes sat. "This will not stand!" she assured the whimpering dishes and the cutlery, cookware, and condiments.

I'm sure she saw the HMA board members in her mind's eye as she entered *Wiens Dress Shoppe* ("For the smart set!") later that day. She marched in with a purposeful stride, Edith in tow. In her agitated state Mom must have been mentally targeting them: their bleary staring eyes, their balding heads, and their jowly neck wattles overhanging starched shirt collars. She visualized their cocksure frowns of disapproval, using that image to hone her resolve.

Curtly and without a second thought, she blinked them away, took a portion of her summer vacation war chest money and bought Edith a proper lady's pantsuit in a pastel yellow. The suit jacket hung midthigh. "That is at least as long as those crazy miniskirts, and *those* are allowed!" Mom seethed. The pants had a tasteful loose fit and sharp dressy creases down the front and back of the leg. They sported modest bell-bottoms. "What's wrong with that?" she said to Edith with revolutionary zeal. Undergirded by a pair of double-thick leotards, Edith would be warm as bread from the oven on her half-mile trek to school and back.

But Edith resisted, protesting, "I'll just get in trouble. I'll get sent to Principal Reimer's office in my first class, guaranteed."

Mother was resolute. Like her defenseman husband, my father Hart, she took the body, not the puck. "Let them. Let the teacher send you to Reimer. You just tell that Principal Reimer, that miserable Red Penny Reimer to call here... tell him, 'Call my mom. Call Justy Zehen.' that's what," she told Edith. Then under her breath, "Who does he think he's dealing with? A high school girl?"

"Why do you always call him Red Penny, anyway?" Edith asked.

"Oh, yes. Red Penny. Well, pennies were once made out of copper, you know. They were fire-engine red like Reimer's hair and the enormous moustache he had when he first became Principal. Well Donald Reimer was so strict with laying down the law for some kids—but not all—that we called him Red Penny because the joke was he should have been a copper. You get it?"

"Yes, maybe. Like police, they're called cops, right? Coppers?"

"Right! It's not that funny but it felt good to say it anyway. It was our code, our way to feel like we had something on him. And some of us did. Hey! Do the kids still call him that?"

"Not much. I think I will start to though."

"Good! Just don't get caught. Like most insecure people, he's extremely sensitive."

The first day Edith wore her new mango chiffon pantsuit,

sure enough, it was off to the Administration Office before class began. Banished, Edith was, even before their daily singing of "God Save the Queen" and recitation of The Lord's Prayer.

I was home with my mom that day, sick with the flu. I sat at the oval table sipping flat *7-UP*, Mom's home remedy for a *buckweedoag* or "stomach hurts day" that I favour still. I saw those eyes—tattered blue—and how she looked, pacing the kitchen floor, awaiting the phone call from Principal Donald Reimer.

She had told me once about how she and Principal Reimer had crossed paths when she was in Grade Twelve. He was fresh out of Teacher's College. Young and affable, he was only a few years older than the graduating class. Reimer was handpicked by the HMA board, and was seen as the perfect choice; strict, popular with parents and teachers. Students did not like him even though he often tried to be a "buddy" but his rigid strictness and lack of respect for students from Hartplatz's lesser families belied his attempts at true détente. He was even-handed when it came to preachers' kids or big businessmen or those from Hartplatz's more elite families, but he seemed to take out any pent-up frustrations on the humble and the meek.

As Mom witnessed, he also had a temper that sometimes ran away from him. The instance she shared—after literally making me cross my heart—was a fleeting encounter between Reimer and a tall, contrary boy in her grade. He was a foster child raised by a local family, the Sukkaus. He did not always fit in and often skipped school to spend time at the local pool hall. The truancy officer had dragged him back to school on several occasions and the boy was definitely, "on Reimer's shitlist," as Mom declared. She described how on one occasion she approached the two who were arguing, voices raised and both very excited. They stood toe to toe at the top of the main staircase. The first class was in session and Mom was alone in the hallway, sent to fetch a box of chalk from the supply room. As she neared them, the Sukkau boy, Boris, swore a vile string of oaths and Reimer lost control, shoving the boy down the stairs.

Mom pulled in a deep breath as she told me, "Boris somersaulted backwards, instinctively curling into a ball as he tumbled. When he stopped at the bottom and scrambled to his feet, seemingly unhurt, I looked at Reimer. He was walking quickly towards me, his eyes locked on mine. I heard Boris's footsteps as he ran out the front door, cursing and promising, "You'll pay. Justy saw! You'll pay, you, *stinking Red Penny Kackkunta!*"

I can still see her stance as she awaited the telephone call from Reimer—jaw thrust forward, a cigarette squashed in her fingers as she lifted the jangling phone from its cradle. I imagined her recalling that long ago morning with Boris Sukkau and gathering her thoughts about the mango chiffon pant suit. I can almost hear the creak of the floor as she stood swaying in rapt concentration, the phone to her ear and her small eyes lasering two smoking black holes into the back wall of *Broesky's Autobody Shop*, behind the house. A sprig of dill, on parole from the deep freeze and chopped fine on the cutting board filled up the room with a clean and healthy tang—smelling salts' country cousin— confirming that this was a real event, not a dream.

"Yes, this is she. Hello, Donald. How are you? Fine here, too. Shirley is well? Good, uh-huh." It was as if she was circling him, looking for an opening, her breath coming out of her nose in short hard puffs. "*Nah joh*, then. To what do I owe the pleasure, Donald?" Her tone, burnished by a lifetime of this kind of weighty conversation, offered phrasing carefully chosen and sharply enunciated. "Oh yes, I recall. Edith brought home the note about girls only wearing skirts and dresses to school. Mmm hmm, that note was perfectly clear. Ministerial Association... Yep. Don't really know what jurisdiction they have in a public school, mind you, but no matter. So, she is wearing her new pantsuit today. It was seventeen dollars *plus* alterations at your sister's dress shop, by the way."

Mom butted out her cigarette after first lighting a new one. She nodded and said "uh-huh" every so often as Principal Reimer mounted his defence. To no avail, I suspected. As I watched her I could feel my body tense with hers. It was a certain kind of feral tightening, a tension that stood the hair on my neck and prickled up goose flesh. It was the animal tension of a cougar crouched motionless in a tree, riders approaching along the trail below.

Mom had grown up in Little Moscow, part of Hartplatz where many of the poorest Russian Mennonite emigrants congregated. The area was seen as a kind of stain by some, who might—in stinging "*spott*"—sing-song "*Mie hungat, mie schlungat, mie schlackat de Buck!*" A slurring schoolyard taunt, it meant: "I'm hungry, my tummy wants something that's yummy!"

The Sukkaus lived two doors down from my mom in Little Moscow and so Boris and her had a connection, having both been on the receiving end of those catty grade school provocations.

With this in her background, my mother had a simple attitude towards suffering. She did not seek to endure in silence, or to see it as a sacrifice or a purification. No, that was fool's gold. Her approach was more like a runner in a relay—she'd accept the burden and hurry to hand it off, usually with added dross and compounded pain of her own manufacture.

Plus, since high school both her and my dad had gone from a legacy of poverty and a humble presence in the town to one of rising social status. In a few more years, they might even become part of Red Penny Reimer's "untouchables," as she called it. The inner sanctum of students who, owing to their parents' high social standing, could do no wrong.

"I used to stand with my hat in my hands at those school board meetings," Mom would often rail at us when we got her on the subject. "There were times when only the men or maybe a few of the wives of the big shots got to speak their minds. We lesser lights from Little Moscow, well, we never got a chance. What good is that? So, I decided when Matt was just little, I decided I was gonna say what needed saying, no matter what. So now I'm Justy, not 'Mrs. Hart Zehen.' Just Justy."

Abruptly, she snapped me out of my thoughts, speaking loudly, swapping the phone from one hand to the other, and leaning into the corner and trying, unsuccessfully, to reduce the volume of her voice. "Now, EXCUSE ME, but you're just repeating yourself, so I'd like to say a few things. EXCUSE ME, SIR! Alright? Good then. Unlike you, I won't repeat myself so please listen carefully..." She paused with her palm over the phone for a few seconds, then pushed her hair back from her face and continued.

"Now, Donald, let me get this straight. My Edith is there... and is in your office... and she is wearing a nice warm pantsuit... and she is not supposed to do that—unlike you—despite the weather conditions. Is that right? It is? Okay, good. Donald... well, to me, it sure seems just as easy as pie... yes, it does. Those pants, Donald? Just tell her to take them off!"

There appeared to be a few seconds of confused silence. Suddenly, Mom yanked the phone away from her ear and I could hear Mr. Reimer's bass voice—not subdued, not polite, no longer on defence. Mom listened, the phone held a foot away. At first, her face radiated pleasure but then changed until it was like a clenched fist. Eyes narrow and lips pressed white. Reimer's voice continued in intensity.

"*NAY!*" she said, jumping in. "You're not going to do any of that stuff. You are not going to expel ANYONE, you are not going to review Edith's grades or her report card and you are not going to refuse to re-admit her unless she wears a dress. Those are the things you might do to someone else, but you are not going to do that to the Zehens. Do you hear me, you *stinking Red Penny Kackkunta? Am I communicating, Donald? Do you take my meaning?*"

She stopped there, a Little Moscow threat dangling but not yet hurled.

Not quite.

I stood at the table, facing her. She tucked the phone under her chin and after listening for a few seconds gave me a comically enthusiastic two-thumbs-up salute and a smile as bright as a silver dollar. In that instant, looking at my mother's often severe countenance and her small angular body, I felt safe and secure in her presence—no matter what threat might come. I saw her bravery and the utter dedication to her family, regardless of how she managed it and what people might think.

Fetch

I step on the gas and we clatter across the bridge with speed. Is this the time we crash through? Tires hammer out a double-time beat on the weathered planks, then quiet as we return to the pavement. We leave the old wooden bridge behind us.

Sarah speaks up just then and tells me about what happened with her and Dick Loewen. She tells me about the consequences and what she's decided to do. I keep driving, heading east towards the farm. I remember how Sarah's Dad stood by me when I broke my arm the summer I was fifteen. Riding horse and got bucked off. The hockey coach wanted to take back his offer for me to go to the try-out camp in fall. He said, "Lenny, you should have known better." He may have been right, but Uncle Cornie told him, "No, Lenny earned his try-out. He'll be ready before the ice is. You watch." I was, too.

I'll stick with Sarah, I decided. I'm all she's got, like her Dad was for me.

The highway runs parallel to the Canadian National main-line along here, in the swamp drained by Hazel Creek. Roadway and tracks cross the wetland like rocky welts, straight east-west, pin-marked with telephone poles that lean against the stretching wires. Tension is all that holds them up. Soil as thin as stew.

We carry on in silence for a while. I think about Sarah, just finished high school, graduation dinner in a week. Aunty Cath is baking for that weekend already; buns by the oven-full, and Sarah's Uncle Patrick is bringing fruit from B.C. I think of Loewen and their team, one of the best around. I had planned to play hockey with them this winter. Uncle Cornie will wonder why I don't.

There's a freight train beside us, also eastbound, the exhaust streaming out hot and clear from blackened pipes. Trailing the engine there's car after car of prairie grain, potash, and B.C. coal. The tonnage is pulled by twin diesels at the head-end. I run the old pick-up full-out until we're alongside. The truck motor rattles like nickels in a clothes dryer. Timing chain is loose again.

The engineer's grinning at us. No, mostly he's leering at Sarah, who sits with her hair blowy in the passenger seat. I feel the thrum of the train engine. Feel it in my fillings. Then I've had enough. Enough of the clatter. More than enough of the old hogger flexing his rolled-sleeve bicep at Sarah. My foot's off the pedal and we lag behind. Caboose lights blink goodbye.

Sarah straightens her hair with one hand and rolls up the window. My favourite cousin, at least that's what we've always called each other; cousins. The hot evening sun is sullen behind us, drowning golden in the swamp. Her head is backlit, wild honey shining in the horizontal glare. Dust motes swirl inside the cab and two noisy horseflies butt their heads against the back window.

"Have you told your Mom and Dad?"

The last of the warm summer light angles across her face. Her lips are glossy. They part as if to speak but she does not.

* * *

The borrowed car—my friend Rob's tiny little *Datsun*—rolls along the smooth concrete of the Interstate highway. Ours for this trip, which is too far for my old pick-up, the car takes us south to Minnesota. The morning sun is out after an early rain. We're flanked by sugar beet fields, leafy and full. Summer is beginning to fade and the scent of wet earth and the last of the wormwood growing in the road embankment comes through the window. Smells like liniment.

"How far now?" I ask Sarah.

She studies the map resting in her lap. "Just stay on the Interstate, I'd say fifteen minutes. Then take Exit 15 and cross over the bridge into Moorhead."

"Okay, Cuz. Fifteen in fifteen."

She looks down the deadset-straight highway like it's a long, dark mirror. "The clinic is across from a park. Wait for me there, that's what Eileen said."

"Eileen? From the drug store? She's been there, eh? I mean, where we're going?" Shit, I thought. Watch what you say.

Sarah is quiet. She fusses with the map, thinning the fold between her fingernails, red. "The doctor is a woman," she says, almost a whisper.

I nod. "What time is the, you know... we can still go back."

She studies the map for a second, not moving. "You just get us there, Lenny. I'll do the rest." She tugs on the seatbelt at her waist, then loosens it. "We're almost at the turnoff."

No going back. She's scared, and so am I. Fifteen in fifteen. Park at the park. Wait in the car and then drive back home. Border closes at nine.

We carry on in silence, parting the ripe fields. The land here is like home, but no swamps like Hazel Creek—they've all been filled in. Every acre is farmed. It's intersected with parallel lines—roads, fences, and shelterbelts—that end at the horizon. There's an overpass every few miles, each one held up by nine concrete pillars as wide around as a tractor tire. Their shaded undersides are dotted with swallow nests, mud-glued into the corners. Out on the prairie, solitary hawks perch on telephone poles, scanning for prey.

"You playing hockey with them—with Dick Loewen and them?" she says.

Her head is down. "They want me to." I turn off the radio. "Your Dad too, but of course, he doesn't know everything. He says that playing with them is a stepping stone. Says if I do well I might get a try-out in Winnipeg, with the *Whirlaways*. I haven't given Loewen an answer."

She picks at a loose thread on the seam of her jeans. "I know you're on my side, Lenny. I'm just... I'm in over my head."

"I could easy play somewhere else. Ste. Anne or La Broquerie. Just say the word, Sarah. I mean it."

"No, no. Never mind that. I'll be fine. You should just do what's best for you."

* * *

Dick Loewen taps the brakes. The hulking *Packard* shudders on a section of washboard in the night road. I sit in the back, shoulders pinched between two others. It's cool out tonight for September but warm in the old car, jammed full like the penalty box after a big fight. A donnybrook, like they say on TV.

"Hey, Lenny," Dick says. "So... how was your summer? Work up at Hazel Creek on the farm, or what?"

"Nah, construction. Basements and framing in Hartplatz. I made good money." I suck in air and rub my palms on my thighs.

This is the first time I've met Dick Loewen in person. Talked to him on the phone a few times. He figures I'm going to sign with them—Uncle Cornie's as much as told him so.

Dick watches me in the mirror and shifts in his seat. "So, anyway, about this thing we're doing tonight...What you do is, you pick out one of the guys on the Ste. Anne hockey team when they come out of the theatre. They'll be together, wearing team jackets. So, you pick a guy, like, 'the guy with the blue ball cap,' or whatever, and then you huck your stick at him. If you hit him, fine. If you miss, you gotta go fetch the stick." He sips at his beer. "That's why it's called fetch."

The guy beside him in the front laughs as if he hadn't thought of that before. His name is Penner. The two guys flanking me in the back seat chuckle. Everyone is drinking beer, mine sits untouched between my legs. Dick takes another swig to finish his bottle and sends it whistling over the top of the car. It lands in the ditch and with one bounce disappears into our cottony dust-wake.

"What time's the show let out?" I ask.

"Soon. We'll be there in a few minutes. You scared?"

He slows for an intersection, then peels the car through the curve, skidding the back end around. The corner is dug out and smoothly banked from the trucks lumbering by on this stretch, fully-loaded from the gravel pit at the top of the ridge. I taste the dust that filters up through the car's rusted floorboards. Like sucking on a coin.

"Nope. I'm gonna give as good as I get, I figure. You sure the Ste. Anne guys are at the movie?"

"Yep, they'll be there. A bunch of 'em, for sure."

My mind is made up. All the same, I'm starting to feel nervous.

"It's a violent world," Penner says, looking back at me. He's the team yes-man. The equipment manager, his dad's implement business is the sponsor. Penner's face is narrow and his eyes are too close together. It bothers me and I always stare, glancing away when he notices.

"Takes guts to play for us guys," Dick says.

"Sure, I get it. But what if I miss with my throw and there's too many of them for me?"

Penner looks sideways at Dick and says, "We'll help you out if it gets ugly. Besides, Lenny... they know it's just our initiation."

I start to speak but he holds a finger up to continue, "If you do miss with your throw, do what Dick did, back when he done it..."

"What's that?" I ask, knowing there's no way I'll miss.

Penner's face is greenish in the glow from the dashboard. Rodent eyes glisten like black gemstones. "Well, Dick, he got out and just sucker punched the biggest guy, without no warning." Penner grins at Dick who stares ahead.

We drive under the first streetlights on the Ste. Anne main drag.

"I ran up to him," Dick says, holding up his fist. "And nailed him right in the throat."

"Christ," I say in spite of myself, thinking this whole thing is stupid, including my plan. "It's a violent world alright"

Dick holds out his hand. "Gimme a beer. And if you don't mind, Lenny, no taking the Lord's name in vain."

Arriving, we circle the block once, tires crunching yellow poplar leaves, and then Dick stops the car on the deserted street near the theatre. I take the "fetch" stick out with me and back off a step or two for a better angle. Nervous laughter spills from the open car windows as we wait. My weapon is a sawn-off hockey stick with something heavy taped to one end. I heft the short, blunt thing to get the poleaxe weighting of it. It feels purpose-made and lethal. I make up my mind to go ahead—no turning back. Don't care what Aunty Cath says about the Sermon on the Mount.

The doors open, and the crowd spills out. Smell of popcorn, the sound of many voices at once, like radio static.

"So, Lenny," Dick says with a smirk. "Who ya gonna pick?"

"Big guy with a stupid grin on his face."

Penner twists around, squinting, "Which one is that?"

I ignore him and glare at Dick who sits with one arm hanging out of the car window.

Reaching as far back as I can, I pop open a snap on my jacket front as I draw the stick behind me. But instead of heaving it point-blank at Dick, as I had planned, I stop. My raised arm drops like a semaphore signal. There's silence from the car; they're confused—*why hasn't he thrown the stick?* I notice the moon, a motionless spotlight in the empty sky.

"Screw this," I say. "Screw all of it." The heavy stick clatters on the pavement at my feet, out of the fight. The sound is like the timing chain on the pick-up truck and I think of Sarah's blonde hair tossing in the wind, bright shining in the sun beside Hazel Creek.

The Ste. Anne players gawk, pointing at us. They stand under the marquee, faces pale in the fluorescence. Seeing them in their matching jackets I think of mallards, clustered together, circling and butting drake green chests. Or like the pigeons in the park that day in Moorhead, strutting sequin eyed as I waited and waited for Sarah.

Dick jerks forward, cursing loudly. He butts his shoulder

against the door and it flies open and his beer spills as he struggles to get out.

I make a fist and want to hit Dick in the throat, just like he said in his bullshit story. Instead, I push against the door to pin his leg—paw in a trap. And then, driven by a storm of half-formed thoughts—venal, indulgent, overpowering—it all comes flooding out.

"This is from Sarah!" I roar in his face, then pull back suddenly on the door and batter his shin with it, a cross-check... and then another. The second time there's a crunch like a stick in a dog's back teeth.

A half-dozen of the Ste. Anne guys charge towards us. Penner scrambles around to the driver's side and gets in, pushing Dick across the seat. The car peels off, Dick Loewen screaming he'll get me, he'll get me. I don't care. I run through neighbourhood backyards and then across a school playground, the teeter-totters at rest after a day of contradiction and discord.

The Ste. Anne guys quit chasing me and I slow to a fast walk. I cut across an alfalfa field to get to the highway and hitch a ride home. The crop's bouquet is strong, earthy and rich. It's sickly sweet too and Uncle Cornie says that's how the plants tell the bees they're ready for pollination. There are some late season grasshoppers left and I can hear them clicking and whirring off into the dark as I stumble through the rows.

Sarah's folks sold off one of their alfalfa fields. It was land Cornie's father had cleared forty years ago. I was surprised. They used the money to pay for tuition for Sarah. She went off to Caronport, to Bible school the next province over. Got away and her Mom and Dad were happy for her to go. "She'll find her way," they said, confused by how she changed over the summer.

Maybe, I thought. But it'll take more than the school. In fact, that might make things worse. Still, it's Sarah's decision and not my place to second-guess, though the whole thing made me feel like shit and what I did today did not help.

I think back to Sarah and me at Hazel Creek that day in June. The day she told me about Loewen and what went on. She told me and no one else. We had always been close, me and her. Two horseflies turning circles until they drop.

I'm almost to the highway now. Hot, I pull off my jacket and wipe sweat from my face. I look up into the glare of the oncoming headlights and hold out my thumb, squinting.

I remember the heat that day back at the Hazel Creek bridge and the drumming sound of the big locomotive stretched out for Toronto, churning past us and then up to South Cross and Longpine and on. The train engineer didn't deserve to be on that trip, to see all that pretty country. I wish we could have gone, Sarah and me. Jumped that train somehow, like in the Lightfoot song, two secret stowaways swept up and taken far away. Taken to a place where she'd get a job, meet someone nice, have children— maybe I could coach their hockey team?

I can see the train and how it would look racing through the forest at night, headlight cutting a clean bright tunnel through the winding blackness, shining on the tamaracks and Jack pines crowded on either side, leaving them behind in the dark. And the crossing lights blinking cherry red in the blackness. I'm sure it would look wonderful, all of it. If only we could be there now to see it.

Breezy

Hart Zehen was an intimidating man. If you didn't know him, he gave the impression of violence—it seeped from him like red from a beet. Worst of all, it was like he was possessed if he sensed you were bullshitting him. Relentless questions: scornful laughter when your story fell apart; and then suddenly he'd go dead-eyed and silent as if he had entered a private fury beyond all understanding. His employees, in particular, learned to avoid the experience.

"This mixer goes on at 4:30 AM and it had better be full," he would say to new employees on their first day of work in his bakery. "And if it's not, then you go home and stay home," he'd add with finality as he shook the last of a one-hundred-pound bag of flour into the stainless-steel bin. Then with a slap on the back, he'd offer the terrified worker a stick of gum and a smile so bright they had no idea if he was kidding or serious. They generally erred on the side of caution and were smart to do so. Being on time and pulling your weight were, as Hart put it, "Serious. Serious as *two* heart attacks."

161

He was very much a "talk slow, talk low, and don't say much," kind of guy, and even though he had such a threatening demeanour, there were many who insisted he was a kind and thoughtful person. Without question, dutiful employees were treated exceptionally well and generously. They adored him, even those of a devout nature who managed to find ways to forgive him his habitual absence at church on Sundays. Hart was also known to be a patron saint for local down-and-outers, a social class rare in the progressive little town, but a few existed and he was kind to them.

Hart was stuffed into his white baker's tee-shirt like a sausage left in the sun. He had scars on his chin and his lips, and his front teeth were clipped off at an angle and capped with a thin sliver of gold. He would sweat profusely in the heat of the bakery, with the ovens creaking as they slowly rotated their load of loaves. Hart would pause in his work to wipe his forehead with a thick finger and flick the sweat off to float through the air like viscous strands of liquid mercury. When the drudgery of a dreary predawn work-day caused spirits to sink, he would cough his throat clear and begin singing in an unexpected and beautiful tenor voice, leading the other bakers in familiar hymns or popular songs.

His given names—Norman James—were seldom used; everyone except his mother called him Hart. He earned the name in a hockey game, playing with the men's team when he was 14. The game was a desperate one, in the spring, with the ice threatening to rot in the La Broquerie rink. Hart famously took on a tough player on the Habs and managed to hold his own, suffering only a cut lip and a ripped sweater. The "platz" portion of the embroidered "Hartplatz" insignia on his chest was torn and dangling. As Hart skated off, stiff-legged and wiping the blood from his face after the fight, he noticed the ripped crest on his hockey sweater. He pulled off the loose piece and tossed it angrily into the Habs bench, unleashing a further ten minutes of scrum on the ice and scuffles in the stands.

He played the remainder of the game without leaving the ice and scored a perfect goal—the Habs' goalie deked out of position and left sprawling—to deliver the season-ending win. The local paper carried a memorable picture of him, gliding on one skate with his stick held high, illuminated in the white glare of the bursting flashbulb. The torn, blood-stained "Hart" insignia was centred in the image and from then on, he was known as Hart.

Hart Zehen would often hire a bust-up fellow called "Breezy." Breezy was an alcoholic on his last legs, and sometimes disappeared inexplicably and for days at a time. He lived in a shack behind the *Tourister Hotel* in Hartplatz. The beer parlour had a low arch-rib storage structure behind the men's-only pub and Breezy squatted there. The roof was rotten and he patched it with comically inappropriate and insufficient materials like newspapers and plaid woollen jackets and any number of other goods that could be had for free and within easy reach. His living space was crowded with spider-webbed stacks of beer bottle empties, and a dim jingling sound could be heard at odd hours as he rearranged his furniture.

Breezy was hired to sweep the sidewalk in front of *Hartplatz Bakery*, wash the delivery trucks, carry bags of flour from the storage bunks in the back to the mixers near the front and other menial chores. He would breeze into work—hence the name—anytime from 4:00 am to ten in the morning, more often the latter. Then he'd pick up his broom or shovel and act as though he had been there all day. Hart paid him the going rate for a full shift regardless of his habitual tardiness. That income was reinvested by Breezy, Mon-Sat at 11:00 am sharp, in the *White*

Seal Brewing firm of Winnipeg, Manitoba by way of the *Tourister Hotel*.

"What good is giving him money? He just puts it all into drink!" This was the talk of the coffee shops and church basements and around the Arborite tables in the curling rink. The people in the little town were mostly descendants of "Kanadier" Mennonites—the first to leave Russia in 1874. This was the ill-prepared vanguard that withstood the first Canadian prairie winters, surviving in crowded sod huts with wolves literally at the door. The community had little patience for the idle and the unrepentant *aufefollne* and they were shunned for their backsliding ways.

"Breezy can't handle his liquor," the men would say. "I think he has Indian blood or something."

"Yeah, he's from Calcutta," Hart would reply with disdain, snapping his Winnipeg Tribune to attention.

"Look," Hart would say when he got wound up, a puff of smoke from a cigarette accenting every syllable. "Breezy is a grown man. He can think not half-bad when he's sober. I have no right to tell him how to live. Nor does anyone else have the right to tell me what to do with my own money. End of story."

On one occasion, Hart met a thumpingly-stern town leader, just before the pub closed down on a stormy Monday night. The red-handed man carried a dainty six-pack of *Labatt's Blue* out of the beer vendor's back door, making his way back to the brand new 1972 *Plymouth Valiant* demo idling in the parking lot, pointed in the getaway position. Recovering his nerve with a bullshitter's aplomb, he explained that he was just getting some beer, "for those Kinsmen," who were coming over that week for a company event at his house. Kinsmen, of course, being a kind of code for those with non-Mennonite names—the Mc and

Mac of the English world who had seeped in along the edges of Hartplatz's brethrenly Mennonite Main Street. These misfit round pegs were bankers and pharmacists and other secular necessities.

The six-pack man was flustered and embarrassed, but as is the case when recovering from the high-speed wobblies on a motorcycle, he figured the best thing to do was "give it more gas." So, he did.

Pushing his Kinsmen beer up under his arm, he invited Hart to look back inside the pub. He held the door open to show the baker a passed-out Breezy, front and centre, his khaki pants stained dark where he had peed himself as he sat. Chiding Hart for funding the debauch, he urged him to give the same amount of money, but re-route the cash to his church, "where it can do some real good," he told Hart.

"No chance," Hart said, looking at Breezy. "It's better here, where I can see where my money is going." Then he sniffed and spat, eyes baleful and fixed hard on the six-pack sneaker.

The bartender, Cornie, had wandered over to the two men at the back door and heard the last few comments. He chuckled and Hart threw him a wink.

The six-pack sneaker was a big man of about six-four and maybe 260 pounds of loose packed cottage cheese. He looked at Cornie, the skinny little *Meksikaunischa* bartender and then he looked at Hart Zehen. He felt belittled by Hart's flippant "see where my money is going" comment. He was after all a serious person. He was a businessman; a member of the Chamber of Commerce; a Toast Master; and center-aisle usher for Sundays and weddings at the Landmark Gospel Bethel Tabernacle.

Slowly, with Hart and Cornie watching, he walked out towards his waiting car. He looked in both directions, leaned in to put the six-pack on the front seat and then glanced back to the pub where Hart and Cornie stood in the dim glow of a sixty-watt bulb near the back door. Seeing them in the light, he called back, "You don't do that drunk any favours, you know. He'd be better off with some tough love!"

Hart's eyes flashed and he took a short step forward. Cornie reached out to touch his arm. "Hold on. Let me. Hey, what's that guy's name, anyway?"

"He's a Wiebe," Hart said.

"Ok, thanks," Cornie replied. Then he trotted a few steps into the pot-holed gravel lot and called, "Hey, Wiebe! Come here once."

Wiebe paused, his car door open, then closed it and walked back towards the two men. As he drew close to them he said, "Look, there's no need to apologize, you guys. No hard feelings."

"Listen, there are some things you need to know," Cornie said, interjecting. Wiebe looked down at the short bartender. Cornie had a *Fu-Manchu* moustache and his teeth were completely rotten—black stubs. He had Paul Newman blue eyes and a small gold ring in one earlobe.

"Breezy's real name is Arnold Plett," Cornie said, hitching up his pants and rising to his full height. "He came up from Mexico the same time my parents did. He's a few years younger than my dad. Arnold got a job at an implement dealership in Winnipeg. Back then, he weren't no *Schinda*! The opposite. I'm telling you, that guy was a genius with motors! He made good money and had a nice house in the city. He only came out here to Hartplatz once in a while. Mostly to see my dad and sometimes a brother, who lived on a farm south of town."

Wiebe's confused face cleared as he listened. He knew the man only as "Breezy," like most people in Hartplatz and he knew few Mexican Mennonites. They attended a different church than his. Cornie continued with the story.

"Arnold loved fishing. He bought a nice boat and him and his wife were out at Big Whiteshell Lake this one time," he said. "She was four-months pregnant and Arnie had just been made a manager at the *Case* tractor dealership on Panet Road. Life was good, y'know?"

Wiebe nodded, looking through the smudged glass in the pub door, where he could see Breezy—Arnold—sleeping in his chair.

"So, it starts to rain," Cornie said, carrying on with the story of Arnold Plett. "the *Midje* are buzzing and biting like the devil and his wife says they should go. Arnie says goodbye to some guys he knows who are fishing near them and goes to start the boat, but he can't get it running. The battery is dead. He pulls the cover off of the outboard and winds a rope around the flywheel and is gonna pull-start it. It was a *Johnson* forty-horse, so he has to really give it a tug, y'know?"

"Yeah, I have a forty *Evinrude*," Wiebe said, looking at Breezy as he spoke.

Cornie glanced at Hart, took a deep breath and continued. "So, Arnold gives it about three good pulls and it almost starts. Then he gives it a super hard yank and he slips and falls back. His wife Tina is just then standing up to stretch and he stumbles backwards, right into her. She gets knocked over and falls out of the boat. Arnold is down in the bottom of the boat and he scrambles up and looks over the side, but she is already under. He could see her yet, under the water. Sinking."

Wiebe exhaled loudly. "Oh, but nevers not!" He stared at Cornie who put his hands down into the front pockets of his jeans before continuing. Wiebe shifted uneasily.

"Arnold kicked off his boots and dove into the water. He was a shitty swimmer though and he came up again almost right away. Plus, it was only a few weeks after ice-out. The guys from the other boat came over too, but by then Arnold had gone down a bunch of times and he did not get her."

Wiebe shook his head. His eyes were watery.

"Arnold stayed there in the boat with some of the Hartplatz guys and the other boat went to get the cops and the Conservation officers. They got her body the next morning and a snapping turtle had worked on her some already. The cops said her nose was busted and she probably got hit in the face with the back of Arnold's head. She was out cold when she hit the water, the cop figured. That's why she went under so fast. Arnold could not forgive himself for taking off his boots. He said he did it without thinking and it only took a few seconds, but maybe that was the difference. That's all he could talk about. It drove him crazy— that and why he couldn't get the motor running and why he was so clumsy."

"I knew Arnie from hockey," Hart said, picking up the tale as Cornie stood quietly staring down at the ground. "He was the equipment manager for the *Winnipeg Clubs* when I played there. We hit it off. After that happened with his wife, he quit his job, sold his house and disappeared. Word is, he went back to the Manitoba Colony in Mexico after the accident. About three years later he came back here and he was Breezy. It was like the old Arnold Plett we knew stayed in the boat at Big Whiteshell."

It was still for a while. The moon came out, shining on the puddles in the parking lot. Dozens of miniature moons shone back up at the night sky.

Wiebe nodded his head slowly. He patted Cornie on the shoulder and said, "Thanks, you guys."

"Just keep it to yourself, Wiebe," Hart said, his voice low. "Arnold Plett don't need no sob story. Just mind your business. Your cars and your Kinsmen."

Wiebe looked stonily at Hart, then pulled his coat tight and walked to his car.

"Time to clean *Arnold* up," Cornie said, swinging the door open and holding it for Hart. "We shoulda invited Wiebe to stick around for that."

"Ha! Tough love, right?" Hart said, adding, "Nice touch with the boots, Cornie. If we keep this up long enough, people are gonna genuflect when Breezy walks by. But I think the snapping turtle part was a bit too much."

"Yeah, maybe," said Cornie, with a black-toothed smile. "Wiebe seemed to buy it though!"

Rommdriewe

The bright red rental had that new car smell. It was fitted with the latest gadgets and the radio even had satellite stations. This modest modernity seemed odd in the context of the prairie landscape, which looked to me worn and old-fashioned. A monochromatic tableau, reminiscent of the dog-eared pictures in our family photo album. The flat, snow-covered fields were dotted here and there with granaries and delineated by loosely strung barbed wire and the steady redundancy of mile roads—wind-swept gravel straightaways flanked by telephone poles. This was Mennonite country.

Mom had called a few days earlier.

"Dad's in the hospital," she said.

Characteristically, there was no "hello," no "how are you?" Her voice came through a few octaves lower than I remembered from our last call, Christmas, I think. No. Two Christmases ago.

I responded only after a momentary stunned silence. "What? What's up? Dad? He's alright, though, eh?"

"Yeah, yeah. Dad's okay. But you remember, Abe? *Darschtijch*

Abe, like, ahh, "Thirsty" Abe?"

She sounded about half-lit. "Of course, sure. Uncle Abe," I said. "Dad's old hockey buddy. I thought he was in the hospital... in a wheelchair?" I had a sudden flashback of Abe crouched behind a police cruiser on Main Street, a screwdriver in hand, the cop car's licence plate about half-off. I remember his bright grin, the irreverent sense of fun, but fun that often went too far.

"Well, whatever. Abe was in hospital but he was in awful shape, acting up, so they let him out a few months ago. That was a mistake. He went right back to his regular routine."

"Every day at the pub, right? Him and Dad..."

"Oh, Matthew, I wish you wouldn't say such about Dad. He isn't as bad as Abe. He never was, not anything like Abe!"

I didn't answer but listened instead to her breathing. She exhaled and I imagined her smoking, a drink sitting on the shelf by the phone. It's mid-morning in Manitoba, so probably a Bloody Mary—beer and tomato juice. Vile. I had stumbled so quickly onto an old battleground; a skirmish we'd had so often before. I asked her to go on, ignoring my rising anger.

"Anyway. Abe. Abe, he died, Matt. And he just about took Dad with him."

"*What*? My God, Mom... how? But what about Dad? What the hell?" I felt the old helplessness coming back, the frustration at the unending boozing and denial. The endless cycle of dysfunction. This was the reason I finally left, pulled my link out of the chain. Found a girl. Married and stayed away.

She continued, the sound quality going tinny on my phone. "Dad is okay. Abe and your dad were playing cribbage in the shed out back. They must have fallen asleep..."

Passed out, more like, I thought.

"And Abe, he maybe had a seizure? They're not certain. I

found the two of them at about midnight."

"You were home the whole time?"

"Yes, I went to bed early. I got up at night and wondered where Dad was. I found them in there with the fire out, the door open and the place was cold as hell and I couldn't wake either of them up. I called the neighbour, Koop, she's a nurse and she took care of them until the ambulance came. It came almost right away." She paused and I heard her puff on her cigarette. "Abe looked pretty bad. He was alive, but—... but not good. We still couldn't wake Dad up. They gave him some stuff in the ambulance already, you know, through a tube?"

"Yeah, intravenous."

"That's it. He woke up by himself in the night."

"How is he now?" She took a slug of her drink. I heard an ice cube tap against the glass.

"Dad had something bad; they think maybe a stroke. Maybe not. His heart? It was hard to get it all. They say he was unconscious for a long time before I found him. Too long—more than an hour. They did lots of tests." Her breath caught and she paused for a minute. "He woke up maybe three hours ago. I just got home. Dad can talk, but he slurs and he's not himself." She quieted for a few seconds, then continued. "There was soot in his nostrils, Matt. You know, I think the chimney backed up and with them both asleep... it's bad."

I had all I needed to put it together. Abe and Dad pounding drinks and bullshitting in the shed. Her drinking alone up in the house. She was drunk when she found them. Drunk in the hospital and making a scene. She sobered up as she waited for Dad to recover. Her better angels arrived then, together with remorse, shame, and guilt. Then a bout of denial, and a trip home to get a drink. Just one.

I paused, calculating. "I'll come right out there. Two days, or should I come sooner?"

"Sooner if you can. You're so smart about doctors and such. I don't know what to ask. And, Dad wants to see you. It's almost the first thing he said. After he asked for a cigarette, the bugger." She laughed without humour, low and guttural.

"Yeah? Sure, Mom. No problem. It'll... it will take a day to set things up at work and get a flight out. Do you need me to bring anything? Should Trudy come out too? And the kids? Are *you* okay? Tell me more about Dad... he's alright now, eh? For sure?"

"I think he'll be okay, he'll survive, Matt. I'm gonna sleep now here at home and go back in a few hours when they know more. I'll phone again from the hospital, later."

I did not press, did not say, "No driving, Mom," although I wanted to. But I didn't...picking my battles. Besides, she might not have a driver's license right now.

"Trudy should stay home with the kids, Matt. You can all come out when Dad's back home."

I was quiet, plotting my steps.

"And don't worry about your dad, Matthew. We're like weeds, him and me, you know. We don't easily perish."

That gave me some comfort for her, but I wasn't sure about Dad. She is a shell of the old Mom I knew so well, loved so dear. She is bitter and broken by drink and something else that I think I might have avoided, maybe not. I think of her when I was a kid— vibrant, alive, and always wise-cracking. Quick with a joke.

We talked a bit more, she said to say hello to Trudy and the kids and we hung up.

"Dad wants to see you," she had said. I listened to the dial tone. *That's a first.*

* * *

He was hollowed out. Eyes yellow, fingers trembling. A five-day beard, grey and just starting to curl framed his once-round face. Crusted pus traced the slope of his cheeks from his tear ducts down. After a shambolic fashion, he could walk and insisted on doing so with me hovering beside him. He took inch-long sliding steps, swaying as though listening to music, and it seemed like the sound from a slammed door could topple him. Tubes hung from him like vines. Seeing him thin and sunken-chested, I thought back to my most familiar image of him—speeding by with his thick forearm dangling out of the delivery truck like the peeled limb of a tree.

He had not had a drink since his "incident"—the name of choice for what happened. He was shaky, fighting through his withdrawal, although the doctor said they had medicated him for that too. Dad downed as much *Pepsi* and *Orange Crush* as he could get his hands on, craving the sugar. His breath smelled like cotton candy.

He slept 20 hours out of 24 and sweat stained his pillowcase a dirty gouache yellow. The nervous young doctor told me Dad had shat himself the night it happened, surprising me by saying this so bluntly. It seemed unprofessional. Magnifying my unease, he added, "That's usually a really bad sign, and we found markers in his blood for heart stress." As we spoke, he went on to say that Dad was "tough as his reputation" and that he had a "window for recovery," but would not add to that vague prognosis.

"We know he's a drinker, so that complicates things. Your mom said he was on the wagon, but his blood alcohol was sky high when he came in, so..."

He stopped talking at that point and it didn't matter, I did not need to hear the rest. I took a deep breath and tried to slow everything down. Regroup.

As time went by, there was no change and he could barely manage to write his name, a task his nurse asked him to do four times a day. A kind of barometer, I supposed. I knew the nurse's sister from high school, and she pulled me aside. "Be prepared, you and your mom, okay? Be ready."

I took her meaning—more vagueness—but did not know how to tell Mom or if I even should.

* * *

My routine was to stay late each evening, hating the cubical dinge of my "suite" at the local motel more than the silent desperation of Dad's hospital room. I did not stay with Mom. Late one night, I woke up in Dad's room with a start. Cold, my neck hurting, I rose to gather my things.

"Hey, kiddo," he said, his voice a muffled kettle drum, rumbling out of the darkness. He tugged the string that turned on the fluorescent light above him, then shaded his eyes. A mickey of rye, near empty, sat on the bedside table in the flickering light. His lop-sided grin showed where the contents had gone.

"Mom bring you that?" I rubbed my neck.

"I blackmailed her. She held out, damn her." He shook his head, burped and looked down at his feet. "I said I wouldn't tell you what I knew if she dint bring me the booze. She only brought this," he gestured, his hand almost knocking the bottle over. "But it's enough... Sit down. Let's talk."

The typical speech at these times—the same one I used to hear as a teen—was a garbled monologue. Heard it before, I thought with a mental grimace.

"*Rommdriewe!*" he said forcefully when I was seated next to his bed. He said the word with a German flourish. Chuckling quietly, he glanced up, and refocused on me with effort. His head nodded, drunkenly. He touched my shoulder and then pointed to a sketch he had drawn on his name-writing paper. "Hart" was written in slanting, child-like cursive, the pen having run off the paper on several attempts. Beneath these scrawls were darker, much more deliberate lines, including "Matt" in a botched scrawl. Alongside our names, were what I first thought to be blotted scribbles, but then determined that they were lines drawn with halting care and some precision. The lines resembled stiff entwined wire, weaving and twisting across the page, criss-crossed and pressed deep into the starchy paper.

"See that?" he asked, his voice gravel in a bucket. "See those twisty lines? Thas you an me. That's us, son. On the snowmo-biles! That's *Rommdriewe*! You know? *Rommdriewe*! It means, you know, driving around, but—like, wandering or aimless, but in a good way. Seeking, maybe... Understand?"

I was used to the rambling, maudlin routine, the melodra-matic "the earth circles the sun" profundity that washed away like spit in the sink the next morning. A tedious, histrionic repetition, with himself as a fallen champion. But this sounded like a differ-ent refrain. "Yeah. So? '*Rum-Dreeve*,' is that right?"

"It is, yes, that's how you say it. And that's us," he said, his index finger following unsteadily along one of the winding trails of black ink. "*Rommdriewe*! Like when we would ride the snow-mobiles out there on the fields. Like a couple of fighter planes! Roaring along. These lines are like the lines in the snow, our tracks, weaving in and out, over and under. These lines... that, that's what God saw, that's what it looked like to Him. You and me far out in the cold, together. Father and son. It's beautiful. It was to me, anyway."

I took his pen and without planning to, began sketching the homemade sled Dad built—a copy of the factory-built one he swapped for an industrial-sized welding unit when I was eight.

I tried to draw the mechanical energy of it, the reckless, boxy might of the thing. Dad's gaze, baleful and sad, rested on me as I drew.

I loved it too, I admitted to myself after a moment. Riding those snowmobiles. The excitement of being almost an equal to my powerful father. Each of us on our own sled. The speed; an intoxicant we shared.

"You think I'm fulla shit. I know," he said with a lurch. "That's fine. I confess. Guilty as charged. I have been for a while now." His head slumped and I thought he had fainted, but he continued.

"*Rommdriewe,*" he said as if it was a magic incantation. "*Rommdriewe,* Matt."

I nodded, then touched his arm, the way you reassure someone at a funeral. It felt papery, the skin uncomfortably thin, worn out and no bulge of muscle beneath.

He smiled, breathed in unsteadily, and pointed again to the twisting lines on the paper. "We were just missing each other, you and me. We kept missing until that bad day. The day you fell asleep. You remember? Wait! Don't answer, that's a stupid question! I know you remember. You and me, that's *all* we remember. Goddamn it. That's our problem, son."

He burped again, making a face, then struggled to sit upright. I fixed his pillow and helped him hike himself up.

"But here's the thing. Here it is..." The room was quiet except for the regular click of the monitor he was attached to. Lights blinked green as he gathered his thoughts, and the machine made a soft digital ping, reminding us of the passage of time.

"See, Matt, I was talking to old Abe that last night. He used to be a pretty good mechanic—did you know that? Used to work with Mom's brother Dan at the Dodge garage. Well, we were talking about that snowmobile I built. He helped me with it, eh? I reminded him about what happened—you and the big crash we had on Verwandlung Road. How you fell asleep and ran into me when I was stopped on the trail. And I told him how, after that, you got in trouble all the time. And you turned into a real handful in your teens... and that's no shit. I used to think that the worse you got, the more I drank." He paused, filled his lungs and squeezed my hand. "But truth is the more I drank... the worse you got. I forced you, not the other way 'round."

I felt the muscles on my temples tighten and my heart suddenly beat hard like I was out on a run.

"You know, it's funny about the drinking. Used to be Mom and me, we drank just to piss people off. Church people. To be rebellious. Then it changed. We drank at the end of our long days, it was a reward. Kept us going. Then, I don't know—it took over, I suppose. We drank because we couldn't not drink." He looked away and sucked in his breath, sniffing loudly.

"Anyway, anyway... here's what old Abe tol' me. See, Abe, he reckons you didn't just *fall asleep*, while you were driving like we all thought. He says one-hundred percent, no doubt..." And then he sobbed, pushed my hand away and reached for the rye. But he stopped and looked me full in the face.

"Abe says, see, he says you were poisoned. You had carbon-monoxide poisoning! You didn't fall asleep at the wheel, my darling boy, you got fuckin' gassed by that snow machine I built and it was all for my bloody pride anyway. To show how I could build something as good as some factory, but from scratch. Show the town what Mom and I could do—what no one else could do. And then, after I built it, I realized I wanted nothing more than just to be out there on the fields with you. *Rommdriewe.* Our perfect thing. Racing along, just us two, under that sky..."

Dad stared at me, his dim eyes up close in the harsh hospital light, hazel and a little bloodshot. Eyes that pleaded with me. I rejoiced in the look of them and the truth he and Abe—Uncle Abe—had discovered. At last, all these years later.

"*Rommdriewe*," I said back to him and it was my turn to soften my gaze. And my heart too.

We hugged and I felt the room was turning slowly counter-clockwise—lefty-loosey, and with each turn the weight on me lessened. My heart slowed and I felt dizzy, my mouth dry. I thought back to the accident, Dad ahead of me on the forever awful, frigid day, night coming on. Him leading, solid and resolute. Me following, doing what I could to keep up. The heat pouring out of the engine cowling in front of me. Then nothing, blackness, unconscious. Plowing into Dad. Flying through the air, engine roaring. The crash landing on the packed snow. A rib broken, snowmobiles destroyed. *Smashed to cat shit,* he said back then.

I pushed the old familiar sequence away. Shed it. I saw it all anew. And I saw more in it, too. A lot more.

"Thank you," I whispered. His shoulders moved up and down as he wept. A drunkard's weeping—sloppy and shuddering, with everything in it. All the pain, nothing held back.

I had more to say but chose my words with care, picking my way on a dangerous trail.

"See, Dad, I got poisoned and it was hard for *you* to see it. Hard to accept it as anything less than a failure of strength—no, of *character.* You felt I had failed and that meant that you had failed as a father. See?"

He nodded; his face worn from a life lived hard, his thumb always on the throttle. He looked as broken as I'd ever seen him. *Smashed to cat shit,* came to me with no pleasure in the repetition.

"But listen, Dad, there's more. Listen, please." I took a tissue and wiped his face dry, then blew my nose. He smiled weakly. "We *are* the same, Dad. See, it wasn't just me poisoned by the exhaust, you got poisoned too." I reached across and held up the mickey, the heel of it an ugly amber smear in the bottom of the bottle.

He focused on it, at first quizzically, and then as if a great understanding had been passed to him. With a quiet sigh, he shook his head gently and smoothed some wrinkles in the blanket. His breath came out in faint wheezes, eyes blinking slowly. He stared some more at the bottle in my hand. He took it from me and set it on the bedside tabletop. Motioning me to come closer, he murmured, "*Rommdriewe*," a last time. Then he crooked his arm around my neck, drawing me close, his bare skin once again feeling strong like a peeled tree limb, heavy and full of life.

A Heckuva Thing

It was late. Matt blew a soft puff of air out, cheeks rounded. He sat on a chair in his motorhome, parked on his daughter's driveway in Aldergrove. He could hear his wife Trudy's steady breathing. Their granddaughter Isabel slept soundly under a homemade comforter on the fold-out bed. A warm B.C. night, beads of sweat stood out on Isabel's upper lip and the hair was damp on her temples. She looked like his mom, kind of, petite and animated like "*Oma*" as Izzy called her great-grandmother Justy. The two of them would sit for hours and read books or do a puzzle, chattering away agreeably until one or the other flared up over some insignificant disputed point, neither one giving an inch.

Mom's still back there in Hartplatz, he thought. **Still ploughing up a big furrow wherever she goes in that *kuhscheißende Darp*, half the town scared to death of her, the other half treating her like she rode a donkey side-saddle and they held the palm fronds.**

Maybe I shoulda been more like my mom. Maybe Trudy

and I shoulda stuck it out, instead of scooting out of town, he thought, almost saying it aloud but not wanting to awaken Izzy. He shoved the Hartplatz memories from his mind—his parents' drinking, the accompanying irrational behaviour, the shame and isolation that was the town's reply. He recalled the roaring echo of his motorcycle on the deserted main street, him gunning through the lone red light, flipping a final baritone bird to the churchy little town as Trudy and he lit out for the West Coast; Vancouver and all of its worldly delights.

Disturbed by his presence, Isabel shifted, murmuring in her sleep. **Tomorrow will be a big day for her,** he thought. He was eager to share the morning with her at the Vancouver Zoo in Aldergrove. A place he knew well.

He began to open the envelope he held, taking care not to let the brittle paper crunch too loudly. Pausing, not fully committed to opening it right then, he gazed up instead at the framed scripture hung on the wall above the bed.

"Many waters cannot quench love; rivers cannot sweep it away." Song of Solomon 8:7.

He reached up to straighten the picture, then remembered it was screwed tight to the wall in the RV. **Means the same even when it's crooked,** he thought, returning his attention to the envelope in his hands.

Matt had received the letter decades ago, not long after their daughter Rosie was born. He worked at the zoo in Aldergrove back then, the same place he and Izzy would be visiting tomorrow. It was spread out on a few acres near the ticky-tack rental house Trudy and he had settled into all those years ago. They had sought the secular humanism of Vancouver but had landed just short—in the quilted familiarity of the Fraser Valley.

"Aldergrove's just Hartplatz with a view," the wise-asses back home told him. Matt and Trudy were married here and found they could play *Tjnippsbrat*—crokinole—with their relatives any night of the week because cousins and uncles and aunts—*Frindschauft*—lived all around them. Family could be found in dreary-cozy little places like Clearbrook and Yarrow and half a dozen other replicas of Hartplatz, there in the rainy delta just east of VanCity.

The letter he held tonight in his hands had come from Human Resources back then. A formal written reprimand from his employers. It concerned a work-related dispute he had with his boss. The bolded subject line read: "RE: Lead Hand Complaint—Disobeying Direct Orders. One (1) Demerit."

The paper smelled mousy. He saw the notes Trudy had scrawled in the margin, "Romans! How dare they use the Bible?" in angry block letters, her pencil debossing the paper. "The gospel according to H.R." he remembered her saying with contempt and fear. And the two of them so new to everything and a baby to feed and rent to pay. Besides this trouble with his boss, their new life then was filled with bliss. Little Rosie and talk of another. It was simple and joyous though the financial side was tough.

Trudy could have been a minister, easy! No one knew the Bible better. But all they let the women do is make tea, wash dishes, and sing in the choir. Especially once our hometown church Deacons did the math—and discovered that Rosie was in fact, born out of wedlock.

He read the letter again, the first time in years, but he still knew it line-for-line. **Still don't think a man should get a demerit just for disagreeing with his boss,** he thought with a glower. **I didn't cuss or get lippy. But this letter makes it sound like I led a workers' rebellion. Sure, I was new and an outsider, but I thought we escaped petty tyranny when we left Hartplatz.**

Man... we needed that paycheque so bad.

He read the portion that had bothered him so much, for so long:

"Matt, I know our organization isn't perfect. My encouragement is to pray daily for our leadership to be guided by the Lord. This is my prayer, and I also pray that I will support your supervisor's efforts in a way that honours God. Furthermore, I believe that George wouldn't hold his Lead Hand position if not appointed and allowed by the Lord..."

* * *

Isabel and Matt's day together at the zoo was almost over, and it had been a rainy one. Matt felt broken down and his bad knee was close to locking up, but he still wanted to show Isabel the footbridge—one of the projects he had worked on at the zoo. He mulled on how his daughter Rosie's small family now lived here, in the same Fraser Valley town he and Trudy had once settled into all those years earlier.

"Hey, Gramps!" Isabel hollered from the far end of the wooden foot bridge. "Is this the thing you wanted me to see?"

"Yeah! Wait up, eh? I'll be right there." He walked across to Izzy, his boots clumping on the wet wooden deck

"Well, you know, Gramps, this stinkin' ol' bridge is crooked!"

"Yeah, an' you better get used to it Izzy, 'cuz that's about par for the course in this stinkin' ol' world..."

"WHAT are you talkin' about?" she shrilled as he came closer. She dropped her voice to a conspiratorial tone. "I'm telling you this thing's as curvy as *Opa's* hockey stick!" She crouched bug-low, like only a small child can. Pointing at the depression in the deck boards, her chin jutting out, she singsonged, "If you built this bridge back in the day, you didn't do a very good job. See?"

"What the heck! Are you five-years-old goin' on Building Inspector?" he asked with only partly faux indignation.

The Aldergrove rain, omnipresent from November to May, ticked on her glossy jacket hood. She hunched her shoulders up in a precocious shrug, like an elfin Bronx cabbie, "Hey, I'm just sayin'…"

"Okay, okay. Let's get down underneath this thing and check for—heaven forbid—shoddy work."

Hands held, they slid down the embankment. Damp ostrich ferns feathered dewy strips on their pants like leafy paint brushes. A steady stream of water ran in the bottom of the creek bed. "*Drepple, drepple, dreppekend—drizzle, drizzle, peppermint candy,*" he said to himself, thinking of his mother's love of *Plautdietsch*.

"Look there, Izz…" He pointed up at a broken cross-brace. "See that there? This bridge has one cross-brace beam that broke. The board had a big loose knot in the middle and cracked 'cause of it. Mystery solved. I'm surprised ol' George missed that."

"Who's ol' George?"

"Oh, George was the lead hand. He was my boss."

Matt remembered the day he had tussled with George, verbally. Twice in one day, in fact. At noon, they had been in the zoo's one-ton, rain drumming on the roof. George Dueck and his buddy Art Kroeker had been grumbling about "secular politicians" and various other common topics. Art, Matt recalled, was the worst carpenter on the crew. "Artless," his co-workers called him in secret.

Both Art and George had relatives in Manitoba, back in Hartplatz. They seemed to resent them, and Matt as well, as if there was some kind of competition between the communities. He felt as though he knew these two *joh-Brooda* better than they could ever guess. He knew them like he knew all yes-men; like he knew the hump of Hartplatz Main Street or the wail of the town's noon siren.

Matt tried to zone out George and Art's monotonous conversation. He bit into his sandwich, despite the fine metal filings his fingers left on the white bread. Baloney and hot mustard and the residue from his morning spent on the workshop lathe. Trudy had brought his lunch one day and couldn't believe it when he ate his sandwiches like this, inky black fingerprints and all.

"It just looks bad, is all. No harm. All the guys do it," he told her when she protested, dismayed. It took too long to wash off their hands and so the men just ignored it, joking, "Carbon in, carbon out."

"Well, Matt, I'm glad you don't do everything 'all the guys do...'" Trudy had cajoled in a scolding falsetto. He grinned and took a big bite.

* * *

It never failed. George and Artless spoke in loud voices, their faces angry when the topic of abortion came up. Matt wished lunch would end. He looked out through the fogged windshield at the passing traffic. George nudged his arm and twisted sideways in the crowded cab to face him. "What about you, Zehen? What do you think of abortion and all that stuff? Think we should hafta pay for that? Think it's right in the first place?" He scowled and breathed heavily into Matt's face.

"Why you askin' me?" Matt shot back at George, irritable from the smell of dried sweat and the too-rich indignation of their daily conversation. He felt his eyes narrowing. "I'm not a pregnant fifteen-year-old on Hastings with no place to sleep tonight. Or maybe a girl, still a child herself, raped by her damn uncle. Go ask someone like that. Who's gonna help her, eh? You guys?"

I'm a man, Matt thought. I eat razor-sharp carbon filings for lunch, so what the hell do I know about babies, and pregnancy and how a woman feels in every case? How can I know? Why should I—a man—be asked to decide? How the hell can a man presume to decide? Matt did not know how to express this or why he had let himself get roped into the conversation. Face reddening, he put his attention back on the sandwich, but his appetite was gone.

He thought—too late by only seconds—of his wife's almost-daily admonishments...

"It's a great job," she kept reminding him. "Dental plan! Just keep your head down and don't take the bait! They're just hazing you because you're young, and new, and from Hartplatz!"

He wondered what Trudy would think of what he had just said. Would she have given him a pass or was this too just something he needed to shut up about? Too late, but still he wondered. At least his snappish comment had shut them up. For now.

It didn't take long for Trudy's warning to come true. Late that afternoon, George suggested they bolt together a cracked blade mount on a grader, so the machine could go out the next morning. It was a risky plan and Matt told George as much, arguing in favour of taking some time to grind it down and weld it, rather than doing a half-assed patch job. After some skirmishing back and forth, George got huffy, despite how illogical his solution seemed. Even Artless had sided, via his uncharacteristic silence, with Matt.

"It'll just break again, unless we fix it proper," Matt said aloud, lost in the memory and reliving his frustration. He recalled George's angry look and how he had suddenly nodded and replied, "That's not a bad idea, Zehen, come to think of it. Not bad at all... Fix things proper and for good."

"What are you talkin' about, Gramps?" Isabel said in a tinkling voice, scrunching her nose and staring up at him.

"Oh, shoot! I'm sorry, honey. Never mind me!"

"Okay," she said, her hand on the wet wood of the bridge. "But what were you talkin' about? What's 'gonna break? The bridge?"

"No-no. I was just thinking about something that happened to me when I was a young guy and Nana Trudy and I lived around here. Thinking out loud, eh, kiddo."

Izzy continued to explore the ditch under the bridge and Matt's thoughts returned inexorably to the altercation with George: How none of his co-workers would look him in the eye after that. How he knew something was up although nothing had been said. It became undeniable—flood water topping a dike—when George's boss approached him some time later and suggested they speak privately.

"Sorry, Matt," the manager said. He was a guy named Barkman and his family was from Alberta. Closing the door, he explained. "Budget cuts. We have to let two guys go and you're one of 'em. We'll give you a good reference, eh?"

"*Jauma...*" Matt had said. At a loss for words, he instinctively sputtered out the first word of a German phrase his mother often used. The demerit letter he'd received, just a few days earlier, now seemed like clumsy foreshadowing. More than that, it was a way for George to "fix things proper." He should have seen the axe falling. He paused, his mouth gone dry and his head searching, trying to think of the smart thing to say or do. The way to push back, to save his job. What would his mom do? Instead of something useful, all he said was "So, who's the other guy? Jared, eh? He's only been on the crew for a few months... less than me."

"Well, kinda... See, Jared's been given his own crew in

Queen Elizabeth Park, so he's off our payroll—City of Vancouver employs him now—but we gotta cut one more guy. With Jared promoted, that leaves you with the least seniority. Sorry, Matt. Union job, union rules. There's a cash severance…"

He could taste the blood in his mouth, like copper, after a long shift in hockey. His thoughts reeled: **Had nothing to do with that stuff with George and Artless, eh? Didn't have a thing to do with the Mennonite mafia and their exclusive insider's club, did it, Barkman? George is Jared's uncle, for shit's sake!**

A Steller's jay squawked and Matt lurched back into the now, standing in the tall saltgrass with his granddaughter. He was in the present, but still at the zoo, as if transported by Jules Verne's time machine.

"Gramps?" Isabel asked.

"What now Princess Isabel?"

"If the bridge is broken, how come it doesn't fall down?"

"Darned if I know. Oh, see here? See these long pieces that go from end to end? They hold it up and all these other little cross-braces, like the one that's cracked, they are all still holding on. The bridge bent, but it didn't break. It'd take a heckuva thing to bust 'er, eh?

"A heckuva thing," Isabel agreed.

"C'mon, Izz," he said, shaking free of the old thoughts in his head. "Let's get outta this drizzle and get a hot dog or something."

A motorcycle rumbled by on the highway nearby and both he and Izzy looked in that direction. The little girl was fascinated at the thought of her grandparents being young and moving across the country. She loved the stories about her mother as a child, too.

"Is that like the motorcycle you and Nana had, Gramps?"

"Pretty close, I'd say."

"An' you guys came here on your motorcycle, and Nana just

haaanging on to you, an' you had long hair and everything..."

"Yep." He saw the *Triumph* in his memory, low and wide, almost new and Trudy sitting on it, her eyes cornflower blue, her belly already swollen and rounded. "And your momma was there too, Izz, but she was hitchhikin' but like, *inside* Nana," he said, sticking his belly out and patting it gently.

Nothing could have been better, he thought, feeling it warm him. **Nothing happier or more satisfying than those days. Nothing ever, except maybe Izzy, right now, but that's its own special thing. One thing built on the other.** He felt the pride and the richness of the years. So too, he still felt the old resentment, as stinging as tears, being in this place and reliving the old thoughts again.

Isabel beamed. "Yeah, an'... an' like you said, my mom wasn't borned yet," Then, suddenly serious, "And my mom says Nana had got in trouble," she added, her face inquiring, uncertain. "And you and Nana got out of Dodge? Or something like that? What kind of trouble? What's, ahh, 'Dodge?'"

"Oh, those are just funny ways to talk about it. The important thing is how much we love your mom and dad, and Aunty Tess and Uncle James, and all you grandkids. That's what really counts."

"Yep, that's what counts..." she repeated, cheeks dimpled, head cocked sideways as they climbed up out of the damp creek bed. "That's what my mom always says too. And after you worked here at the zoo, you and Nana took my mom when she was just a baby and moved back to Winnipeg?"

"You got it, Izzy."

"How come you and Nana did all that movin' around? How come you guys didn't just stay in Hartplatz like *Oma*? Or stay here in Aldergrove?"

"Good question, smarty-pants. Maybe we shoulda stayed in Hartplatz and maybe we should have stayed here in B.C. too, instead of moving to Winnipeg. It was a heckuva thing that made us move, each time."

"Yeah, a heckuva thing. Like the bridge," she replied, her large eyes looking past the knotted blackberry vines, past the red-leafed maples and into the dark cathedral of hemlock beyond.

The Worth of Sparrows

The man was broad across the chest and shoulders. He wore an ironed plaid shirt and his salt and pepper hair was trimmed neatly. His expensive eyeglasses suggested he had exercised some preference—no grocery store cheapies for him.

He sat in the school library on a metal folding chair. His seat was one of a dozen or so arranged in a circle. It was a men's group and was made up of fellows his age and older. They sat with their heads down and eyes closed. Most of them held Bibles, resting on blue jean laps in their large hands—the hands of older men. All of them were white, save for one man of Asian descent. A row of ball hats and similar lightweight jackets hung on hooks near the door.

"Amen," a grey-bearded man said, drawing his feet under him and taking a breath to speak.

"Welcome here. I am Aaron Vogelaar. Today, we are honoured to have two new members. Art and Diedrich. Guys, please stand up and tell us just a bit about who you are and what brings you here. Art, will you please begin?"

Art wore a new golf shirt, faint fold marks still visible in the shiny fabric. He was the lone Asian man in the group and Diedrich remembered him from high school, a few years behind him. His adoptive father was a Mennonite of Dutch-Prussian-Russian origin, a minister, whose name was also Art. His friends had called the young Art "Thou," taking a poke at him and his preacher father. The nickname came from his father's bombastic preaching style. "THOU ART..." Pastor Von Ast would roar from the pulpit and the kids started calling Art, "Thou Art" which eventually shortened down to "Thou."

"I am Art Von Ast. I'm from Bethel Christ Mennonite Church and my wife Mary and I are retired. I have throat cancer." He sat down and crossed his arms across his chest.

Diedrich stood and took off his expensive glasses. "I'm Diedrich Deutsch."

"Why are you here, Diedrich?" Vogelaar asked, just as Diedrich began to sit and was putting his glasses back on. He stood again, awkwardly, dropping the glasses with a clatter.

"Cancer. Just plain cancer," he stammered. He retrieved his glasses and inspected them carefully before he sat. He was not yet comfortable describing the specific type of cancer—his personal variety. **Would he ever become as glib and off-handed as these men appeared,** he wondered?

They took turns going around the circle, sharing other thoughts or asking questions. When it was Diedrich's turn, he politely deferred, suggesting he would prefer to listen because it was his first time. He blushed as he spoke these few words, his fingers punctuating the syllables with a simultaneous clasp and release of his glasses. **Since when have I become *this* shy?** he asked himself, unhappy with his meekness.

After coffee and some of the same Saskatoon berry *Plautz*

that Diedrich had so loved as a child—a sugary flat pastry first made for him by his Aunts when he was a boy—the leader rose and read a Bible verse. He held the book confidently in one hand in front of him, the soft-from-use cover flopping open like a rabbit pelt.

> "Isaiah 41:10 So do not fear, for I am with you; do not be dismayed, for I am your God. I will strengthen you and help you; I will uphold you with my righteous right hand.

When he finished reading the verse, Vogelaar unfolded a photocopied sheet of paper and read the story of a cancer patient. The article described how a retirement-age fellow named Klaas with stage IV cancer had, with the support of his church and a massive online call for prayer, defeated the disease. This anonymous Klaas went into a completely unexpected remission and had been cancer-free for two years. Benefiting from a strict diet, an exercise routine and the unflagging underpinning of his family and church, he had met his third cancer objective. The third of four for Klaas—the last being to remain cancer-free.

The group was then led in a collaborative encounter session. Following Vogelaar, the group read responsively from the printed text. "You will not give up hope... " "I will not give up hope," and so on through a litany of positive call-and-responses.

Canned empathy, Diedrich opined to himself. **Like the Bible verse, platitudes but no action. Shouldn't we be going on a full-court press here? Like, fall-down bawling prayer? This routine is like at a funeral when people manage to touch you on the arm without actually touching you on the arm...**

After twenty minutes or so of this tedious group session,

Diedrich was tense and upset, He was ready to unravel. He texted his daughter, "Call me NOW!" She did and he used the phone call as an excuse to beg off. Leaving the meeting, he plucked his jacket from the Shaker-neat row on the wall. He pushed open the glass door and skipped down the concrete steps. His minty 1968 *Chevy* C/10 waited in the parking lot.

He loved that old truck. Had it just the way he wanted it. His one prideful excess—Lord knows he could afford it—was the set of retro *Cragar* chrome mag wheels, which he kept sparkling clean at all times. There was one other customization: the kids had given him a Reggie Jackson autographed number 44 *Louisville Slugger* bat. He mounted a custom-painted gun rack in the rear window for the lovely wood bat to reside, riding shotgun with him on the leafy streets of the town.

Diedrich stood looking over the old pick-up as a light rain fell on him and the truck. "God causes the rain to fall on *Chevs* and *Fords* alike," he said quietly. He walked to the front of the truck and wondered how he could mount some fog lights without changing the look of the grill. Stuck there, crushed and mangled was a dead sparrow. He picked the bird free and collected the loose feathers in his free hand. He wrapped the tiny corpse in a tissue and gently laid the remains in a paper sack in the cab.

Light rain spotted the hood. He sat slumped in the truck listening to the sound of the engine idling, as it warmed. He let his mind range in ways he had not permitted during the meeting. **How could they say that Klaas—the Klaas in the story—had received a blessing? A *blessing*,_meaning that God had singled Klaas out. Why him? Why some anonymous guy named Klaas and not any of them, the fellows in this group? Why not Art? Art, "Thou," the guy with the fresh-from-the-package golf shirt** who was scared shitless, but trying so hard not to show it? How come he didn't make the cut?

Diedrich rolled the window down, a few revolutions on the crank handle.

The fellows in this little group were surely no less devout; no less confident in their individual walks with their personal Lord and Saviour. And, not to change the subject but, seeing as He is in the Saviour business, how about it? How about me? Diedrich, thought with rancour. "I could use a little saving right about now," he mumbled out loud. "Why does Klaas the Louse get a goody bag, an 'existential *Tütje*,' like us kids used to get at church on Christmas Eve, and I don't? Do I not deserve a blessing?"

He inhaled, then blew the air out slowly. With a lurch he wound the window back up, shut off the engine and jumped out.

"That Vogelaar guy wants participation, he's going to get it." Diedrich said, walking briskly back towards the school entrance.

He entered quietly and left his jacket on, reclaiming his seat.

"Welcome back, Diedrich," Aaron Vogelaar said.

"Sure. Thanks. Not to ruin the conversation or anything, but I have some stuff to get off my chest or whatever. Have a discussion, maybe? I'm sorry to bust in like this, my first time and all."

One of the other men spoke up, "Fine with me, we're kinda going in circles a little. No offence, Aaron." Diedrich thought, **How Menno of him. Blunt as a square-toed boot. Reminds me of Aunty Rosalyn.**

Vogelaar gestured for Diedrich to carry on.

He tapped his fingers rapidly on his thigh and wondered whether he should sit down or not. Before he could decide, words tumbled out, the things he had been thinking in the truck.

"Look, guys. I'm asking, like everyone here does I guess,

'Why me? Why now?' Stuff like that. I have faith and such, but it just doesn't seem to fill the gap. I mean, like I was just thinking, how are the choices made? Seems kind of arbitrary, if you don't mind me saying so." He paused wishing he had some water. Some of the men shifted in their seats to face him. A few nodded and one fellow smiled encouragement. Diedrich pushed on.

"Like, I was never perfect, but, I mean, no big sins, I don't think. A few petty things, some taxes I chose to hang on to, but no biggie..." A few men chuckled. "Thing is: why me, why Art over there, why that Klaas guy?"

Aaron Vogelaar uncrossed his legs and then recrossed them. He checked his watch.

"Sorry, Aaron, but I came here to share, looks like." He felt out of control, like he had swam too far out and now might not make it back. He opened his hands in front of him. "To tell you the truth, it feels like I'm being punished. Or is it that I have already received too many blessings? Have I used up my quota? Is there an accounting system or is it random selection? Is there a lottery, like the U.S. had for Vietnam? If so, I hope Nixon is not running this one." Art Von Ast and Aaron Vogelaar both smiled. Having raised the issue of Vietnam, Diedrich remembered the oft-retold story he had shared with his old ballplayer friend Ernie—the last time just a few nights ago at their grandkids' T-ball game. Ernie and he had reminisced about that long-ago American guy, the smooth-fielding shortstop from one of those Fair Day baseball tournaments, down by the Minnesota border. The guy was a Vietnam war draftee, as they found out at the beer gardens.

Diedrich sat down, drained and blank-minded. He listened to the others' responses and tried to concentrate but he had lost the thread, thinking now of old times, baseball, and youth. The meeting adjourned soon after and Aaron was particularly kind. Several of the other fellows patted him on the back and offered their hands. Their actions felt sincere but his questions lingered. He walked out with them, his mind absent, still fretting and trying to solve the puzzle of his mortality.

Wonder if he made it? he thought. That draftee short-stop from the States. His name was Marty and we called him "Martin Luther," joking that he played for the "Reformists;" a team that nailed their lineup card to the dugout door. Bible school humour.

Diedrich considered all he had been led to; the prosperity and his peaceful, fulfilling life. Things from which he had been spared, things he had faced and overcome. He thought of Doctor Rempel and missed him. Missed his gruff manner and big heart. He freed his mind again. What if he had just stumbled ass-backwards into it all, tumbling out of control through a vast and incomprehensible universe? The impermanence of his father. The saving grace of his Aunts, Myrtle and Rosalyn. The bottomless caring of Doctor Rempel. Which was he, anyway: a castaway boy blessed by the kindness of others or just another victim like Art: scared and lost, bereft of grace? Or was he simply one of those among all the creatures who somehow did not receive a blessing, like the sparrow he'd found crushed on the front of his pick-up.

Now, when he needed his faith most, he was not sure. He felt abandoned. Alone, because the faith he had always counted on for times like this seemed weak and diluted. Were the beliefs he'd held for so long now at last revealed as a falsehood? A silent void from which no mighty voice issued. How might Doctor Rempel explain it?

Forgetting where he was, standing with the a few remaining

men under the overhang outside of the school he spoke out, catching them and himself off guard, "Did he make it? The big American shortstop? Surely, You saved *him*, Lord?" he prayed aloud, demanding, then pleading with his eyes squeezed shut.

Did he make it home? Was he worth enough to be saved? How about those people—the ones in Vietnam—those he killed to stay alive? What about their grace? And did their deaths count against Marty? What kind of a choice is that? If I make it to heaven, should I expect him to be there as well? Or will I just be one who died rich and that's all?

He felt his legs shaking as the small group stared at him with unhidden concern.

"Sorry, guys..."

Art touched his shoulder. "You want to head over to *Chicken Chef* for a coffee? A few of the guys are going. C'mon along."

"No, no. It's getting late." I'm just going to go back and talk to Aaron, apologize for busting in there. See you next meeting. I'm good."

"Take care, buddy," Art said, his eyes glistening in the dusky light.

Diedrich watched them walk towards their cars and went back inside.

"Hi, Aaron. Need any help straightening up?"

"No," he said, looking up. He paused, "What's up?"

"Well, this feels totally wrong, but if you don't mind, can I tell you two short stories?

"Of course. Go ahead. That's exactly what this is all about." He swung a chair towards Diedrich and sat down himself.

"I am doubting my own faith, wrestling with that and I would like to be honest and also to hear your honest thoughts. I need to get this out, I suppose."

Aaron reached for his Bible and folded his hands on top of it in his lap and waited.

"I'll tell these fast, so just ask if anything is unclear."

He cleared his throat and began. "The first is about an old friend. Call him Phil. We lived far apart and he called once to ask for a get together. We arranged to meet at a golf course and had a long talk. Old times, mutual friends, kids, all that. After a while he changed the topic and told me about his health problem. It was a truly serious condition and he was on strong medications. He told me he could not cope and prayer seemed to do no good; maybe even made things worse."

"How's that?" Aaron asked.

"Because he expected to be heard and he thought the Lord might heal him. But no healing was coming. Anyway, he asked me for advice. He shared that his thoughts were sometimes frightening him and he was desperate for an answer."

"But no answer came?"

"That's right and not only that, but I had no answer for him either. Knowing Phil, and respecting him as I did, I would have thought that God would not deny such a person as him. He was, is, among the finest men I have ever known. I only mumbled something about God testing him and tried to think of a Bible verse, but came up empty."

"What happened to him?"

"He carries on and has his family and other nearby friends to depend on. The church is his rock, but as he told me, his questions still go unanswered and that, I'm sure, is a big part of his burden."

Aaron looked troubled and looked down as he considered the story.

"Look, I don't want to keep you here too long, let me move on to the next one."

Aaron nodded.

"Another person I knew through work and mutual friends had an extremely sad situation. I know our Mennonite ancestors, especially during the times back in Russia, suffered the loss of many women and children at childbirth. But today, we almost take it for granted that both mother and child will survive. This friend, call him Herman, was the exception. His daughter and her child both passed away during a horribly difficult labour and complications. The baby was stillborn. The mother clung to life for about a day. Herman was pious and a staunch follower of Jesus. Herman spent all of his time near his daughter and deep in prayer as she lay in the hospital."

A custodian poked her head in, saw the two men seated and waved before going back out.

"Herman told me that when the doctor came out of her room the last time, that he was certain that his prayers would be answered and at least his daughter would be spared. He explained to me that when the doctor told him she had died, he did not grasp it. He ignored the doctor and in confusion, blurted, 'Praise God!' but then knew from the response of his family and the doctor that it was true. That she had died. 'Yes, praise God for she is with our Lord now,' the doctor said, perhaps knowing from experience how disbelief and denial, during impossible times, can cloud a person's mind."

Diedrich paused to rest, his eyes cast down, hands limp at his sides.

"And now? How is he now, your friend Herman?" Aaron asked in a whisper.

"I'm afraid he has left the church. He feels betrayed by God and cannot forgive Him. He denies God exists, for no God could take his daughter and grandchild. He is stuck in time, suffering endlessly in that hospital on that evil day and I fear that nothing or no one on Earth can change things for Herman."

Diedrich was quiet. Aaron flipped his bible open, thumbed a few pages and then read, his forehead wrinkled, his hand holding his chin. After a few minutes he closed the book and spoke.

"I have a story too." He stood and stretched his legs. "May I, Diedrich? I think it relates."

"Please do."

"Before my own cancer, a few years back, I had a heart attack. It was not severe and I suffered no permanent damage, but on that day, it seemed pretty bad. I mean, I didn't really know. I was out for an early morning walk on a deserted road near the house and all of a sudden, bang! No energy. I almost fainted and could not get up after falling to my knees. I felt so sleepy and I was sure if I lay down on that country road, I would have been asleep in a few seconds. I feared that would be a long sleep..." He smiled weakly before continuing. "Anyway, I had about a quarter mile to get home and so I just crawled. When I got too pooped, I rested. Eventually, I got to our driveway and because that was downhill, I could stand up and I made it in. I took some aspirin and Edna called her nurse friend and then the ambulance. While she was on the phone, the *real* attack came and for about 10 minutes—neither Edna or I really know how long—all I could do was concentrate on relaxing and breathing. It was kind of mechanical. I was scared shitless, pardon my French, but I had a lot of things to concentrate on and I could not be distracted with any other stuff. It was kind of like fixing a stalled engine. You almost get it running and, I mean, this sounds stupid but it's true—that's not the time to stop and pray! You keep wrenching or whatever until you get it going again."

"And so, Aaron where was God, do you think, for you? In all of that?"

"Well, that's the funny part. I am baptized, I gave my earnest and truthful pledge and covenant to God, standing before the church when I was 18. I was washed from sin then and have led a good life; I have always walked with the Lord my God. But, I must tell you the truth and say that from the time I first fell down on that road until I had recovered and was safely in the ambulance, I did not think of God or feel His presence. Not at all."

Aaron was quiet for a moment after this, and then resumed.

"Nope. God may have been there—I'd like to think He was—but as for me, I was all business. My job was to stay awake, crawl home, chew some aspirin and stay alive. I was all about the nuts and bolts and all the beliefs I had, my whole life, all that religious stuff was secondary. I didn't stop believing or hold God accountable or to blame—I just was too busy staying alive to bother with any of that..."

* * *

Driving slowly, the truck's oversized exhaust rumbling and echoing on the tree-lined residential street, Diedrich drove around town. He thought of the tiny dead sparrow he had held in his own hand, of Marty the shortstop, and of Aaron, smiling when he thought of his off-handed "Pardon my French," comment.

He thought too of the old friends he had talked about and of Aaron crawling up the gravel road, focused on survival. He thought of his own baptism and the things he had promised. He felt a twinge of guilt for his doubtfulness, but knew that he was not alone in this. The men in the library each had their own doubts and he could not condemn them or himself.

Feeling relieved and eased from the tension of the meeting and his own tribulations, he thought of the great good his life had always been: of children, family, sports, work, his wife and the church. He thought of his many great friends, of Morton, back in high school, of Doctor Rempel and his smelly cigars. He thought of his Aunts, who took him in. He recalled distinctly the crochet Bible verse on their kitchen wall "So do not fear, for I am with you, do not be dismayed for I am your God..."

"Okay," he said aloud, deciding in that moment. "It's time to be good at being brave again. Fair enough. Let's go with that," and he set aside his worry and thought about his granddaughter's next baseball game instead.

The Narrowing

Matt walked the train track in the late morning, enjoying the crunch of the rubble under his boots. He waved away a blackfly and looked up and through the Narrowing. Frequented by freight trains and little else, its walls slanted in from the top down, until at the bottom it was barely wider than the tracks that ran its length. In places, the sheer stone faces seemed to close in overhead, as if forming an arch to thwart even the sky.

It had been blasted through the rock ridge here in the eastern forests of Manitoba before Matt was born. He had journeyed down its daunting length many times and returned as often as he could. Matt had planned to hike it with his grandson for a year now. He had run this gauntlet, and now it was Tim's turn. A rite of passage; a test of faith and of courage. Many risks he no longer took—he knew better now—but this one was codified, a part of his self-image and something he wanted to share with the grandkids, each in their turn. But from last summer into this one, Tim's mother had resisted.

The blackfly was joined now by others, buzzing and diving as

Matt reached the end of the rock trench and the swampy woodland beyond its western terminus. He stopped and turned around. Heading back the way he had come, he matched his stride to the creosote cross-ties. Every footfall was a hollow wooden tap followed by a faint echo from the nearby rock walls. "Tap-tap. Tap-tap."

Maybe today's the day for our hike, he mused, quickening his pace as he returned home.

* * *

"How do we get through the Narrowing?" Tim asked. The boy's gaze came up from the scattering of Lego blocks on the floor of the little cottage. He looked at his grandfather in the characteristic way he had inherited, eyes quartered, cocking his head and not quite facing him squarely.

"Well, I like to just walk along the ridge until you get to the beginning of the real skinny part—I was there today. Then, if it's not too windy and the squirrels aren't chattering too loud or the crows complaining too much, I'll lay down with my good ear on the rail and have a listen." Matt wagged a finger. "A long, careful listen."

Stretched out on the floor like a manic willow switch, Tim joined in his grandfather's enthusiasm. He listened in exaggerated pantomime as if keening to hear the hum of a distant train.

"Then I usually like to take a sip of water—but not too much because I don't want to get bloated in case a train comes barrelling through the gap there..."

Tim smiled warily at that, his body stiffening.

"So anyhow, if we don't hear a train when we listen to the rails, then we just hustle our butts down through the Narrowing until we come out on the far side. It's less than a kilometre long. There are a few spots where it's just wide enough for the train and no more. Not a bear or a moose, not a deer, and maybe not even a grandpa!" Matt held his palms apart in ever-lessening amounts and winked.

The boy's face clouded. "But really Gramps, there's no trains there, right? Not real trains that could hurt us, right?"

"We should be okay, I suppose."

"I suppose too," Tim said, returning to his Lego. He had been building something—a spaceship, impressive in its complexity. Now he tore it apart, tossing the bricks into the bin.

"Here's the thing, Tim," Matt's daughter—Tim's mother, Rose—said, coming into the room. "The trains only run that line in the morning. I went there with Gramps when I was a little girl, you know. Afternoons are safe." She spoke as if to reassure herself along with him.

Matt went to the kitchen for coffee. Rosie followed him, leaving Tim rocking quietly on the living room floor.

"Dad," she said, quiet enough that Tim would not hear. "It's great that you want to take Tim on that hike, but don't forget how he can be…"

"Upset, you mean? About scary things. The whole anxiety business?"

"It's gotten worse. He latches onto things that concern him and he won't let them rest. He can't sleep and he gets out of bed really early. He can become unreasonable if something bugs him. The Narrowing is just the kind of thing that can set him off. The unknown, you understand? He likes routine and certainty."

"Don't we all," Matt said. "Remember when I took you there? You were ten, right?"

"Yep. I remember being a little afraid, yes. But, no… I'm built differently than Tim. And yet, I still think of that place anytime I ride a subway on one of my trips. I imagine how the air must get pushed out in front of the train at the Narrowing—just like it does for subway train tunnels. Whoosh! That still gives me the willies."

They stood quietly for a time until Matt said, "Could be you're different than him," then sipped from his coffee cup, and looked at her over the rim. "Or not."

"Are you saying I was that way too when I was his age—about the anxiety, I mean?"

"No. All I know for sure is that place is unique and just as I wanted you to see it, I want him to as well. It's a wonder of nature. A wonder of engineering and ingenuity and all that. Determination—you know? Because of his issues…" He looked at her frankly, "I kinda want him to have to face the fear. Right? We could go today so he won't be fretting tonight at bedtime…"

"Instead, he'll be congratulating himself for doing it," Rosie said, completing her father's thought. "It could work. Or it could backfire on you and he could be a terror. You saw him rocking, eh? That's a tell-tale. Sometimes he comes unglued, sometimes it passes."

"It's worth a try," Matt said, pulling her shoulders into a quick hug. "When is it ever wrong to confront your fears?"

"Whatever." Gently, she shrugged free of him. "He's been bad lately. Meltdowns over everything. Brushing his teeth, not being able to watch *Survivor*. If we run out of milk, he goes ballistic. But not every time—sometimes he's fine. When he does erupt, he takes it out on me the most, hitting and screaming. We've upped his meds twice in the last couple of months."

Matt grimaced. He hated the thought of the medication, but what else could they do? "Look, if it starts going sideways, we'll just turn around and come home. I can still out-wrestle him," he said, hoping to get a smile.

"You can't outrun him though, and he's likely to take off on you—for no apparent reason. Just make sure you have lots of water. He can get funny about drinking. Always thirsty, you know?"

Rosie stopped talking, her face a bit grim. She looked at him hard across the small kitchen, her eyes brimming. He was a little older now, stooped just enough that it bothered her to see him so, but still the same man she had known and loved as a child. She started to pick at her nails—a habit she got from him—but pulled her hands apart as soon as she noticed. Crossing over to the window, she swung it shut. The sound of fussing blue jays outside stopped abruptly as the glass rattled. For a second she thought she'd cracked a windowpane. She went to the table and twirled a bag of bread, watching it spin before cinching it with the plastic tab.

She was about to speak when her father broke in, "Okay. Look, Rose, Tim's your kid. You don't want us to go—we won't go. There's a hundred other things we could do."

* * *

Her dad called her "Rosie Henderson" in Little League. The only girl on the team, Rosie made a rare combination rarer by batting right and throwing left. The only big-league ballplayer like that was Ricky Henderson. Hence the name. She didn't mind it. They were close in those baseball days. He was so devoted to her, and to being together, and playing a sport they both loved. On summer Sundays, the ballpark became their place of worship. He never fit in among the pews of church, a place too stern—he balked at the Teutonic solemnity and distrusted those who would hem him in. Instead, he was in the dugout or clapping his hands at third base, giving her signs. Rosie had a dose of her mother's faith, and would not have minded going to church, but the ball diamond she and her parents shared was a wonderful sanctuary.

Along the way, her parents found the tiny cottage in the woods. Here, her dad discovered a new temple, deep among the trees. He did his obeisance under their canopy, clucking at squirrels, chopping wood, hiking and sailing. The Zehens eventually bought the place, complete with the little red ski boat, the independent-minded water pump, and outdoor biffy.

Rosie loved the cottage, the woods and the lake too, with its warm water and their rustic outboard runabout. She thought fondly of her mother waist-deep in the water, steadying Rosie and her sister, Tess, reminding them to keep the tips of their skis together, as the boat idled away from them. Rosie could still see the tow-rope uncoiling on the top of the water; still feel how she used to ready herself for the roar and the tug on her arms when she shouted, "Hit it!" and the rope went tight.

So much, she wanted her son to share the love of this wild place too. The love for the northern forest and its endless diversity. She wanted to believe the hike to the Narrowing would help grow that love, and the love between the man and the boy too. But she worried that it could just as easily derail the magic of the forest and that Tim would recoil from it, tearful and melodramatic.

Now, with lunch fixed and waiting, Rosie wondered about her father. Direct, impatient and often completely ass-backwards wrong—that was how he had always tried to fix things. His ways might not work with this complex boy, who over-analyzed things until they were frayed and frazzled. Just like she was doing now, she thought.

* * *

The sun was high above and edging towards its westward descent as Matt and Tim enjoyed their hike. Rosie had given her consent, a paper napkin twisted into a thin rope in her hands as she did so. They had just finished the climb up the steep embankment to the train track.

"Shhh, Tim. Listen," Matt said, stopping to silence the noise of his boots on the jagged rock ballast.

"What?" Tim asked Matt, his voice jumping an octave. "Is it a train?"

"No, no, the birds. Chickadees. Listen. They're the most talkative birds in the woods. When they call, 'chick-a-dee', scientists think that means, 'I'm here,' or something like that. But when they sing, 'chick-a-dee-dee-dee-dee,' with lotsa 'dee' sounds, that means 'Look out!' The more 'dees' the greater the danger—like when they spot a hawk."

"Whoa," Tim said, impressed, in his nine-year-old way. "What's *that* call?" he asked after listening for a few seconds, standing still.

"The one that sounds like, 'Hi, sweetie?'"

"Yeah! Hi sweetie, ha!"

"I think it's a mating call. The male chickadee sings 'Hi sweetie!' really loud and clear to let all the lady chickadees know he is in the neighbourhood and is open for business."

"What does that mean? 'Open for business,' birds don't have a business."

"Oh, it's just an expression," Matt said. "Say, do you want to eat our snack now, or after we pass through the Narrowing? We're almost there."

* * *

Matt pulled the hanky from his breast pocket and wiped down his face and his neck, pointing his chin up to get the sweat from the inside of his shirt collar. Being here, doing what he was doing triggered a memory. He recalled his cottage neighbour and friend Kenny Thompson. Kenny was a railway engineer who had

215

hiked the Narrowing with him several times. Matt thought back
to the day a few years ago when Kenny discussed the train and
the demanding terrain.

"I remember coming through here a ton of times," he said
as they rested in the shade at the entrance to the Narrowing. "I'd
have her running smooth, the engine making that nice brum-
brum-brum sound, happy as could be. I'd run her at 35 miles per
hour, maybe edging it up just past 37 if I was behind schedule.
That was a little more than spec for this stretch, but I knew when
to slow it down before the Narrowing here."

He took out a smoke and lit it, waving the match at the sand
fleas that circled his head.

"It was a fair summer day like today, this one time, and we
were running late, and that always put me out of sorts. We had
worked on the brakes in the yard because there was some definite
sluggishness on my previous run."

Matt was interested in any facts about trains and the
Narrowing. It seemed to him such a remarkable spot and the
thing was, no one knew it existed except a few hikers and railroad
people like Kenny. Kenny knew from their many chats how Matt
liked the subject and he played things up a bit as he told the story.

"I tested the brakes on the long downhiller just west of
Minaki and sent a text back to my supervisor, Mike. I'm a Leafs
fan, as you know, and old Mike, he is nuts for the Jets, so I told
him, I says, 'She slowed down just like the Jets in the playoffs!'
Har." Kenny grinned, holding the cigarette between his teeth.

"I still remember his come-back; the smartass says, 'Least
our guys get INTO the playoffs.' Anyway, I stepped the speed
down just a touch, eh. I wanted to keep an eye on things and
take her easy thru the Narrowing, because of the brakes and all."
He pinched the ember from his smoke with licked fingers and

kicked it into the ballast between the ties. The remaining butt went behind his ear for later.

"I mean, late, early—what's the diff? Trouble is, I loved the job and I always felt it was on me to arrive right on time so all the guys at the Symington Yards in Winnipeg or wherever, all down the line, were not put out. I wanted to be dead-on. That day, our three-hour delay for the brake check was pissing me off, big time. Not my fault, but still we were gonna go through the Narrowing at about one in the afternoon, not ten in the morning."

"I get it. Do your best, right? Like how your sister-in-law makes those spectacular feasts for us. Barbeque turkey with all the fixings on July 1."

"Exactly. Pride of a job well done, all that crap, eh? Plus, people get used to the trains being at certain places at certain times—hikers and blueberry pickers, whatever. It is important. Anyway, we're just humming along and it's my favourite part of the run, because of our cottage being nearby and whatnot, and I have this tree book—"

"Yeah," Matt said nodding. He'd seen it many times.

"So, I pull it out like usual and I'm looking at it and spotting the different trees—firs, tamarack, and spruce and whatnot. Well, I suppose I got kind of carried away and all of a sudden, here we are—" he looked up the tracks to the east. "We're just barrelling down into the Narrowing. Right up there where that big dead poplar is at the top of the slope." He stared blankly into the distance for a moment, shaking his head and recalling the moment.

"It's downhill, pretty steep grade, too. I look up, and damned if there's not a couple of people walking the track, way up ahead, in the Narrowing. I lay on the horn, and I mean big time. They've already heard me coming and good thing. Luckily for them—and me—they were right at the end of the narrow spot, and they jumped down the embankment. They were safe. I braked a little, just to test and slowed down a little like I usually did coming through here. When I was about even with the walkers, I chucked an empty *Pepsi* can at them."

Kenny saw Matt's face and commented. "I know, if I don't want people on the tracks, then what the hell am *I* doing here myself? Well, it's safe if you know the train times and also if you don't waste time when you're in the danger zone." He pointed down the track to the darkened place ahead, in deep shadow despite the brilliant sunshine.

"No room for error in there. You can still see the fur of moose scraped into the rock wall. There's been a bunch that have lost an argument with the front end of a train in the Narrowing. No room to get out of the way, 'specially for a big animal. You and I would prolly manage, I think, but I wouldn't want to try it."

* * *

Matt checked his watch, then squinted east for a last long look.

"Two-fifteen, Slim Tim! Let's hustle our butts down through here and get some blueberries on the far side."

Tim looked back and forth. He held his hands slightly out from his sides and did not move, listening hard. A flight of sparrows lifted up from the ground and scattered into the sky as Tim and Matt entered the Narrowing. Matt and Tim's footfalls on the wood ties sounded with hollow resonance in the closed space. They walked fast and in a few minutes were almost halfway through. Matt could see sweat on Tim's neck. He flexed his shoulders to shed his nervousness and saw that Tim was looking less tense, though he still glanced back every dozen strides or so to check behind them.

"Great day for a—..."

Matt sensed the train before he heard it. It was like there was a physical shift in the air—a faint ripple. He held up a hand. "Listen!" he said, surprising Tim with his gruff tone.

He first checked westward down the track and then spun around. There was the train, cresting the hill and braking hard, white smoke billowing up on either side of the engine. It shimmied on its locked wheels and the trailing cars rammed forward, each one butting the next with a metallic crash. The engineer let loose with a long shriek from the air horn and the howl of the braking wheels was deafening.

"RUN, TIM!" he bellowed.

As they ran, Matt judged the distance they had left to the exit ahead. **It would be close. Tim might make it, but he would be too slow. He was panting hard, slowing already, his bad knee locking up every few strides. His hip felt like a red-hot bolt had been driven into the socket.**

Quick on his feet, Tim pulled away until he sensed Matt was falling behind. Then he turned and begged for him to hurry. His eyes were round as he looked past his grandfather at the oncoming train. Matt snuck a look back. **How had the train already gained so much ground?** The screech of the brakes was growing ever louder. The distance ahead was too great. He knew he would not get clear in time. Tim might have been able to escape, but the boy had waited for him and now they had both missed their chance.

"Lie down!" Matt shouted, grabbing Tim's arm.

"No! Run, Gramps! Just run!"

As Tim said this, Matt screwed his head around to check again. The train was coming up on them fast. The engine seemed unnaturally tall in the canyon. Dust and debris flew up around the shanks of the engine and through the tumult, Matt glimpsed the engineer leaning far out of the cab gesturing urgently. He made a patting motion with his palm held flat.

"Lie down! It'll go right by. We'll be okay. Trust me, Timmy!"

Panting, pleading, praying, Matt sank down beside the row of oily wooden crossties. His arm stretched forward as he held tight to one of Tim's boots and then stretched out on his belly and put his cheek against the chalky track underlayment. "HUG THE WALL!" he screamed above the roar of the onrushing diesel engine. "LIE FLAT! HEAD DOWN!"

He thought of Rosie standing alone on the cottage porch, staring out in the direction of the Narrowing. Matt saw her, his little girl, floating in the placid lake behind the ski boat. He heard her adult voice in his head, overcome with fear over Tim's uncontrollable outbursts. Her love for the boy was desperate and fierce and he shook with anger at himself.

The train was now close enough to read the numbers on its nose. It chattered as it slowed, impossibly loud. Every inch of the trench was noise and motion as the debris cloud engulfed them, stinging their bare legs with sparks and cinders.

* * *

Matt craned his neck, eyes squinting ahead to keep sight of Tim's new hiking boots, the soles dusty green and yellow.

A numbing tingle suddenly tore along from his ass cheek to his shoulder blade, quick as a cobra strike. It stung and he could feel the sick, lurching sensation of being picked up like a sack. He was released in the same instant, left with a burning pain where he had been nicked. He was stunned by how quick the danger had come and gone. The front of the train exited the trench and Matt could sense the wheels slowing beside them. The noise had lessened considerably. In a moment he called to Tim, "It's OKAY!

Lie still, we'll be fine in a few minutes."

"Why did I risk it? Why did I risk it?" Matt whispered to himself like a prayer mantra. "Why?"

* * *

Rosie and Matt sat next to each other on stacking chairs in the clinic corridor. Inside the adjacent office, they could hear the muffled voices of the doctor and Tim. The doctor had wanted to go through things with the boy alone, after completing a full physical exam.

Rosie held her father's hand. He sat awkwardly in the chair, with his scraped bottom lifted delicately off of the curving plywood seat. A bandage on his back made papery crinkling sounds in the quiet hallway.

"I swear, Rosie—" he began again.

Again, she hushed him. It had been three days since the train. She leaned against him, head tilted to rest on his shoulder. "I know—never a train before, all those times. I know, Dad. It's... it's a *non-issue*," she said, choosing the word with care.

The air was still in the narrow corridor. Suddenly, Matt coughed loudly, ending in the sob he had tried to hold in. The noise echoed off the linoleum and painted cinder block walls. A tear streaked his ruddy cheek. "I coulda lost him, Rosie! I could have lost Tim."

"No, no," she said, embracing him. "You knew what to do, you made the right choices. That rail line does not get afternoon traffic. That late train was one in a million. The schedule's been the same for twenty years."

Matt thought back to Kenny's story that day on the track. He could see his friend's familiar face, the white of the snuffed cigarette behind his ear. Could imagine the tin rattle of the *Pepsi* can thrown at the people beside the track. Could feel Kenny's

221

disrespect, his condemnation of the brazen foolishness of the hikers. His disdain for their selfishness.

"It was stupid, honey. I knew better. I blew it. We should have just stopped at the edge of the Narrowing. He would have seen the damn thing, but with no risk." Matt's head hung, and he mumbled his words.

Rosie stroked the back of his hand. "Dad..." she paused, gathering her thoughts. "Without the risk, he would have forgotten the day. Just another hike in the woods. This way, I hate to say it, but he lived through an incredible event with you— unheard of, bizarre. He was brave. He's only nine and he bloody well stayed calm and he made a good decision. Our little Tim trusted you, despite his fear. In fact, I suspect we might cherish this whole experience. Honestly... it's true. All of us, even you. One day, anyway?" She paused a moment as if suddenly unsure. "For now, I am going to focus on that idea. If what happened pulls him through, somehow, I'm for it. The path he was on? It scared me. It still scares me. It was hurting us." She gripped his arm, making him look at her face. "Dad, you guys got out of the way of the train. Now you have to get out of the way of the guilt."

Matthew Zehen rubbed his temples with his fingertips.

"Life's not scripted," Rosie went on, her voice small. "And parents aren't perfect and kids aren't perfect. We all just do our best. You don't have to offer your guilt in exchange for him coping with his fear. Accept it, that's all," Rosie said. "I'm not sure many doctors would have agreed with you, about the tough love and all that. I thought it was crap about him facing his fears, but I know how you think." She paused and allowed herself a deep sigh. "Like, if only Tim could just gut it out... I don't know. It's not that simple, but I know how that feels. Wishing he could just be... just be okay."

Rosie sat up straight in her chair. She motioned with her hand, slicing the air. "We'll go on from here, Dad. We'll listen to the doctors and we'll be brave. All of us. I think that's best."

Just then, Tim emerged with the doctor. They were both smiling and her hand rested on his shoulder. Tim was carrying his ball glove and he looked calm. He looked like a kid itching to get back outside on a nice summer day.

"C'mon, Gramps. Let's go home and play catch," Tim said, his voice light as he trotted down the hall and towards the glass doors and the sunshine beyond. Wincing as he rose, Matt stood and followed, listening to Tim's running footsteps echo in the hallway, "tap-tap, tap-tap."

In the Dim Light Beyond the Fence

"Okay, so Dad and I will meet you at the stadium, Sis. We'll park on that same guy's driveway. Hiebert—yeah, I know, right? It *would* have to be an ex-Manitoba Menno, eh—right in the middle of Van? Dad had his Mennonite radar on... heard the guy talking and said to me, "That guy's from *Jantsied.* Like, Plum Coulee or Winkler. Manitoba, for sure. Wanna bet?"

I glanced at Dad. He sat and smiled as we chatted with Rosie on Bluetooth, her voice clear on the car speakers. The conversation made me think of what a poet from Dad's hometown had said on the CBC one time. The fellow was from Hartplatz. He said he could tell if a man was a Mennonite just by the way he *walked.* Said it was something about the wideness of the legs, as if walking in a ploughed field. I always think of that, a man walking with his legs spread wide, boots finding their way between the furrows even when he was in an airport or a shopping mall. It makes me laugh. But there's a kind of pride in it too; not sure how that works.

It felt good—Dad, Rosie and me all on the phone at the same

225

time, remembering a day at a baseball game in the same place, years ago. Rosie and I commented on how Dad had insisted on finding parking somewhere other than the stadium lot.

"Twenty bucks, Tess? That's crazy!" I recalled him saying to me. "The people who live near the ballpark must sell parking spots on their driveways. Remember when we saw that game in Milwaukee and we parked on some guy's driveway, except it wasn't *really* his driveway and he tricked us out of ten bucks?"

We all remember meeting the Hiebert guy near Nat Bailey Stadium in Vancouver. A minor discovery, but all these "findings"—where two Mennonites encounter and recognize each other—are precious to Dad. To me too. Again, I don't know why.

Nostalgia, I reckon, keeps going down the generational line. Sentimentality, more so, maybe. "Memory is a scar I love to touch, but never trust," as Dad's poet friend wrote. Increasingly so, as a person ages, no doubt. Plus, there is the hilarity of how we all make fun of those times when two Mennonite strangers meet and then they do the time-honoured routine. "The Mennonite Game," Grandma Justy called it. "Your name is Dirks? Where are your people from? Ohhhh, Yarrow. Yes, *of course,* I know where that is... we have *Frindschauft* there." It's hilarious because first we tease our parents for doing it and then *we* do it too!

Beyond the nostalgia, there was a hard edge to all of it for Dad and really, the whole Zehen family. Memories Dad shared with us that were not sentimental. His family's struggles—with alcohol; with the sense of being outcasts in the town the Zehens helped to build; of his deep-set dissatisfaction with the smug hubris of Hartplatz and its arrogant belief in divine destiny. Past shunnings, social stigmatization. Institutional misogyny. All of it, the good and the bad. Dad was so proud of the pacifism, though that was tainted in some ways, but so what? They tried. They surely tried. And the generosity! My God! The MCC and all that. Disaster response... Who can fault that? All these things, so complex, some parts contradicting others. Whether he told us or we picked it up in context or from others, it was a part of him he'd never relinquish.

* * *

Dad listened to Rose and I chat on the hands-free, looking ahead and smiling as I drove. We kibitzed, the three of us and I was reminded of one of my favourite Mennonite stories. It happened when I was on a girl's golf and shopping weekend in Tacoma. There was a small restaurant near our hotel called "Friesen Burgers." Dad started chuckling as I began the story, remembering the punchline.

"Yeah, so I dragged my non-Menno girl friends in there, all excited to talk to these Tacoma Friesens that just *had* to be Mennonites. I was certain that they must have some relationship to Diane Cannon, you know? The actor? Everyone always said her real name was Diane *Friesen!* Oh my! *A celebrity!* And one who was so sexy and had starred in a truly risqué movie—for the time anyway. I was *so* let down to find out that the Tacoma situation was all just a mix-up caused by the sign painters! The restaurant owners were not Friesens at all. They were an older couple named Malcolm who had only a kind of rough idea of what a 'Mennonite' was and who saw the error only after their new sign was up on the roof..."

"Remind me... what was the error?" Rosie said, intrigued.

"The sign was supposed to read, 'Fries 'n Burgers' but the painter misread it and made the sign Friesen's Burgers. The Malcolms said at first they made a fuss, wanting it changed but by then the place was doing good business and everyone called it Friesen's Burgers, so they just left it."

I flicked the blinker to turn down the street where our ball-park parking driveway owner, Mr. Hiebert, formerly of Lowe Farm, Manitoba resided. Wide legs and all.

"The funniest part," I added, grinning at Dad, "was that the Malcolms had obviously told this story before. Many times. I can just see the string of Mennonites from up in Abbotsford and whatnot, who stopped in there and asked, point blank and blunt, 'Where are you Friesens from?'"

"In *Plautdietsch,* yet too!" Rosie exclaimed, her voice making the car speaker crackle. "Oh, Tess, that is a great story. I'm going to remember it this time, I know you've told me that one before. So, anyway, we'll see you guys at the ballpark. I can't wait!"

"Yeah, the Hiebert place is right across the road, right by the public swimming pool. I don't know the street number but it's the one with that massive, weird tree. The Monkey Puzzle tree. We're almost there. See you soon."

* * *

Dad and I were on the concession concourse. We were in line for a sandwich and he was quiet and seemed kind of wistful. Usually, at the ballpark, he'd be revved up, more like a grandkid than a granddad. But tonight, our little guy Hank had his own thing—soccer practice with his Dad—and James said it was a can't-miss. Playoffs. Rosie's family was busy too—their kids were teenagers and had something up every night, it seemed like.

"So, Dad," I said as we waited. "This is a dad-and-daughters outing. Rosie's kids have stuff up too."

"No, no, that's fine," he said. I could hear the Hartplatz pronunciation in the 'no,' the way he drew out the 'o' and it all came out kind of nasal. He didn't have that much of a *Plautdietsch* accent, but he sure owned those long Hartplatz 'o' sounds. "Roooad, I tooold you, I knooow, eh?" James says I do that when

I'm tired or if I've been hangin' with one of my old Hartplatz girlies. Rosie and I do it all the time on the phone, on purpose. "On the phooone, yet too once!" Mom always warns us that if we talk like that too much it'll stick and we won't be able to talk without an accent. "*Oba*, toootally, yet! That's terrible beastly true!" we say in reply, getting her goad. Her gooooad.

So here we are, Dad and I waiting on Rosie, feeling kind of loose and happy, waiting for her and her beaming face to come striding up the concourse, all sophisticated and cool. "Ginger cool," she would joke.

Dad's gaze is soft and he keeps looking around like he was trying to commit all of the details to memory: the sky—"Prussian blue" as he liked to call it—the violet-green sparrows darting above the crowd, the rich aroma of frying food, kids selling programs. "Programs, HERE!" their young voices rang in the crowded space backed by organ music from the big outfield speakers. He struck up a conversation with a beer vendor, providing the poor guy with way too much detail about a Twins game he had attended in the old Metropolitan Stadium in Minnesota. It was in 1981, "before I was born," I chimed in. He told about how Mom and he had seats right behind the plate and the vendor had this giant pin on his shirt that said, "Hey, BEER GUY!"

"Grandpa Zehen spent some time here on the coast, you know," he said to me, sipping on the beer he had bought, handing me mine. "He worked with his brother-in-law in a fishing camp north of Tofino and they would come over to Vancouver to meet up with some cousins from Tsawwassen. They'd meet them in Bellingham, right near the border. You know that sea wall down there, well that strip was the happening place to go, eh? Like a scene from *American Graffiti*— muscle cars and whatnot."

We were nearing the counter and I paid attention to him,

although I knew the story quite well. I was hungry and wanted something to go with the stupidly large beer Dad had bought each of us. I eyed the menu, the savoury sweetness of sizzling beef and frying onions making me need to swallow before I could give the counterman my order.

"He coulda made it, you know. Grandpa Zehen, could have. Coupla inches taller and he'd probably have his name on the Stanley Cup. Original Six days, you know." He said this—a story I knew well—and then pushed a twenty at the counterman and said, "One of those sandwiches for me too... with hockey rings."

The counterman looked up from his cash register with a queer look. Dad's voice trailed off sharply when he said that to the guy. He gave his neck a rub and then clapped his hands and said, "Sorry, sorry! ONION rings, of course. Not hockey rings!" His face reddened and he rubbed his neck again, harder now. We moved off to the side and I put my hand on his arm as he continued to talk about his dad.

"Course then, if Grandpa woulda played for the Wings in Detroit, maybe he doesn't meet Grandma, and then there's no me..."

"That's so true!" 'Sooo truuue,' I said, unconsciously mimicking his speech pattern. It fit like an old ball glove, I had to admit. I hugged him and was surprised to see we were almost eye to eye, where he had always had a couple of inches on me.

Rosie snuck up behind us. "Garlic fries on me!" she yelled, giving Dad a fake punch in the shoulder. We had a big group hug and then the sandwich guy said, "Okay, break it up, this is a family ballpark." Which would have been funny a few years ago, but now it was a bit sad because Dad was a little less of the "former ballplayer" type of a fan. More of an "older gent who might have once played some country hardball," fellow.

"Thanks, girls," Dad said. He looked down then lifted his head, eyes full. "This day, days spent with your Mom, your husbands, and your kids—it all means a lot. You know Hiebert, the driveway guy? We talked last time I came to a game. He missed out on this. Didn't have kids, his wife died young and he never remarried. He sees me as 'having it all' and if I stop feeling sorry for myself, I guess I'd have to agree."

I was surprised by his emotion.

He stopped talking for a minute but Rosie and I could tell he had more to say. "Baseball meant a lot to me as a kid, you know. Something I chose, something I was not half-bad at. I was an average Joe with 'warning track power,' but I loved it. To share a game here, now, with you two..."

He stopped then and the sandwich man, who had been waiting for Dad to finish speaking, coughed and slid a tray across towards me. "You folks enjoy the game." He reached across and gave Dad his change and also a friendly tap on the arm. "Yours is on the tray too. Take care."

Dad waved off the change. "Let's go to the field. They got at least fifteen minutes of batting practice left. We can eat there and watch them."

But we didn't make it out to the field.

Without warning, he slumped, bent at the waist, his hands in front of him on the counter. He began to slide down and a man behind us in the queue grabbed Dad in a bear hug to keep him from falling. With Rosie and my help, the three of us shuffled him towards a wooden table filled with condiments. He was unconscious. Rosie yelled, "Here!" and I used my arm to sweep the table clear and make room for us to slide him on. He lay without moving, lips purplish-blue. His body seemed so small to me, outlined as if in homicide chalk by the cluttered detritus of plastic cutlery and condiment packets.

The man who grabbed dad said he had taken a course and began administering CPR. I could have done it too but I was momentarily stunned. Rosie checked Dad's pulse. I watched, confused and desperately concerned. My father's wrist looked heavy in her hand, unsupported and limp. Liverspotted skin, pale and bloodless. I guessed from her face, as she concentrated on his pulse that things were not good. Sticky white spittle gathered in the corners of his mouth. A crowd encircled us, respectful but curious, whispering, "I don't know," and "I think he's just fainted..."

Rosie reported his pulse as "weak," but he always had a slow beat. The sandwich man spoke up to say that there was always an ambulance at these games, so it wouldn't be long until we got him to the hospital. He added that he had phoned 911 and the ambulance crew should be there any minute from their post just outside the stadium.

The guy doing the CPR looked up at Rosie and me. In a low voice he asked, "Is this man your father?"

"Yes," we said at once.

"Does he have a history of heart problems, has he ever had a heart attack?"

"There is a family history," I said. Rosie nodded and added, "he takes daily low-dose aspirin."

"Okay. Well, the aspirin is going to help. I think he should have some more, but the ambulance crew will deal with that, seeing as they are almost here. They'll have everything he needs." He paused and heaved a breath in and out. "The EMTs, they know the whole emerg drill and have the equipment. They'll get him home."

He bent to his task and then asked, "How old is he?"

"Too young for this," I answered, squeezing Dad's hand. In a few minutes, the emergency crew arrived, led by a tall blonde woman.

'Let's get him home!" she said in a loud voice, with a comforting glance at Rosie and me as she began adjusting the gurney up to table height.

* * *

I remember it now as in a dream. The outfield falling away in endless green except for the white chalk lines climbing the foul poles. Fences so distant only immortals could see them; much less challenge them. The ballpark was fresh mown and the sharp scent made me eager to play.

We pull cleats and bats from the trunk of the old *Meteor* four-door. We head for our bench. The ballpark is even bigger than it looks from the road.

Our team warms up in shallow left. Steel rakes rasp on the base paths accompanied by the rhythmic tink-tink-tink of the long spikes driven in at 60'6". The syncopated smack of warmup tosses, back and forth, and lots of bantering. Loosening mind and body, freeing the soul.

Meadowlark alarm cries join with lawn chair clatter as the crowd comes in. Catcher trotting to the mound with his shin pads clacking. I can smell the sting of lime as they draw out the batter's boxes—righty and lefty poured out of the same brown paper sack. The democracy of baseball, a game that takes an irregular world and makes it diamond perfect.

Kornelsen raps out some fungoes to us. He hits a flat line drive to my right and I round on it like a car taking a corner at speed, picking the ball out of the air on a chest-high bounce. It rests in my glove, freshly smudged from the grass—distinct as lipstick on a man's cheek.

The game begins and I'm up. It's not long before the red stitches are spinning, and my soft liner clears the shortstop's glove and settles in front of the galloping fielder. He one-hops it—a little too casual for my liking—so I make an extra wide turn at first just to piss him off.

When everyone is set, I wander off the bag and stop, the first baseman nattering at me and the locals cat-calling our batter.

The catcher's eyes follow me through his mask as he gauges my lead. His cheek is stretched, bulging. Too much chaw. He looks drunk. As if he heard me, he tilts up his mask and a thin brown stream re-wets a dark spot on the sand. The pitcher, a lanky kid from North Dakota, grips the ball with a hand the colour of boot leather as he looks in for a sign.

"You never know," says a woman in the stands. Her voice is low and raspy but loud in my ears as I take my lead and the pitcher goes into his stretch.

Sure enough, he throws over. I'm back in plenty of time and the first baseman slaps me with a high tag. Bloody trapper: it's like getting hit in the chest with a phone book. Jolts me—more than I would've guessed. I throw him a look, pure stink eye. I'm going to steal second, for sure.

* * *

The gravel in front of our bench is littered with sunflower seed shells. It's like the high tide mark after a storm. First game lost and now we're tied here, top of nine. Everyone is a little bushed. I am unusually tired and ahead of us there's still a long car ride home.

Sun setting, swallows darting, a little kid laughs. There's a car parked behind third base, and a family picnics from a blanket spread near the open trunk. I get a whiff of their cold fried chicken and see long neck bottles of beer sweating in a bucket of ice.

"Like you can..." Kornelsen, coaching at first shouts from

cupped hands—big, meaty carpenter's hands. "Duck on the pond, Matt!" his voice echoes off the whitewashed backstop. Our baserunner takes his lead at third.

I pluck at the starchy grey of my pants until the stiff cloth stands away from my thighs to catch an inside pitch. I'll take a free pass if I can get it.

"Hey, Matt, we're aiming for your head, not your legs," the catcher says to me with a brown-tooth grin.

"Do it, buddy. I'll come all the way around and steal home on you," I say back to him.

"Cut the shit, you guys," the ump says, "I gotta get home."

"Me too," I say with a wry wink at the catcher. He looks just like *Groota Peeta*, my old chum from grade school and I give him a shit-eater grin. "Good to see you, Pete."

And then a funny thing happens. The air goes still and so do the crickets and frogs. It's so quiet it's like my ears are ringing. A cloud the colour of a bruise is edging towards us out of the west and I hear that same woman in the stands say, "Let's get him home." I rap the plate with my bat, twice for luck.

"Ball one," the tired umpire says, clicking his counter. Then he touches the catcher's shoulder because the ball went behind my head. "That's the last one like that," the ump says to him, mad.

I am still puzzling about the lady behind the backstop and I realize I hadn't moved an inch. Just stood there and old Pete must have snagged the pitch right next to my head. But come to think of it, I don't even remember the pitch.

Ump says, "Let's go," and I look out at the field and see they are playing me to bunt.

The big North Dakota kid throws hard but he's fading. Nothing but high fastballs and I take the inside ones, sliding my hand up the barrel to keep that idea in their heads. I foul off the rest, biding my time. The pitcher gets on the rubber and then kicks with his right foot twice—stabbing his toe in the dirt behind him. Kornelsen told me about this signal and I'm ready.

The left fielder and the shortstop both take a couple of lazy steps back and towards the line. I see the change-up coming big as a beach ball and I wait so I can knock it by the meathead third baseman who is still at bunt depth.

"See, I don't want to pull it foul," I say to the lady behind the backstop, but I kind of mumble and I don't know if she heard me.

"Sure. Sure thing. I'm with you," she says. She knows what I mean.

"We're almost there, Matt," a new voice adds, her voice both nearby and far away. I think I get what she means, but how does she know my name?

I stride and take my cut as the ball comes at me, right down Main Street.

Then a coldness rushes up my arm and I feel the rumble from that big thunderhead, just like we're driving over a wooden bridge. I can feel it in the muscles in my back. And then my neck tingles as I connect and it's dead-set solid right up into my chest. It feels so good—the bat slowing for the smallest instant by the impact, then completing its arc. The ball makes the wonderful, stinging sound of a solid hit, jumps into the night air, and then it's floating above the lights, heading for the dimness beyond the fence.

I start to run but stop. I think of my dad and how it felt when the snowmobile I drove smashed into the back of his. That cold, cold day on the trail out by Verwandlung Road. That was also a solid connection, but not a good one and I remember when we made it right, the two of us, after many lost years. Me and him, in the hospital and it's like I can smell that place now. As if I was there now with him.

The earth trembles some more and something nearby rattles as I drop my bat. First base is so far away, and there's Kornelsen jumping up and down and wind-milling his arm.

"Go two, Matt! Go two!" he's screaming as I hit the bag, arms pumping, head down.

* * *

The van pulled in ahead of us, one ambulance among the others now, outside the hospital. Rosie and I had followed them from the stadium. I park my car off to one side, and we hurry to get out and trot over to the back of the ambulance. Just as we get there we're met by an emergency nurse from the hospital. She asks who we were looking for, and we tell her it was our father, Matt Zehen, in the ambulance.

"Okay. Look, just give me a sec with the EMT to get a status report and take care of a few other things, and then we'll go from there. May I ask you to wait just inside? There's an area there with water and washrooms and coffee. I'll come find you as soon as possible. I promise."

"Can't we just peek in to say Hi?" Rosie asked. Her voice trembled.

"Well, not actually. In your Dad's case, we received a call as they were on the way in and we've arranged for some urgent care for him right away. We'll let you see him as soon as we can, alright?" As she said this, two men in grey scrubs hustled up to the van and opened the doors. In a minute, Dad, his face ashen and eyes closed, came out attached to machines by a cluster of tubes and wires.

* * *

The emergency nurse spoke in a hushed tone to the EMT attendant in the ambulance. "Hi, Robyn. I hear this did not go well. I'm sorry."

"Time of death, 19:55," Robyn said.

A wordless question hovered, the nurse not wanting to rush things.

"I've been administering for the last twenty minutes," Robyn said, cleaning up the paddles, coiling the cords. We caught a little traffic. It was peaceful. Those two women—his daughters—are in the waiting room?"

"Yes."

"That's good. I'll just get things together in here. You guys get Mr. Zehen ready inside, and then I'll share my conversation and everything with them before they see him."

"That sounds fine."

Robyn signed the form and folded it neatly, trimming the fold with her fingernails, sharpening the crease as she thought back to the ambulance ride.

"He was unconscious when we picked him up at the ballpark," she said. "His daughters were there with him." She packed instruments into cases but stopped, distracted.

"He regained consciousness during the trip here. He drifted in and out. We talked about the game at *Nat Bailey*. He told me about places, ballgames he remembered, back on the Prairies. I said to him, just before he went into arrest, 'I used to love the smell of my old ball glove when I played softball. The musty leather, you know?' He said he knew… and I believe he did. I feel like we had a connection, because of baseball. It was nice to have that, for him I mean, but it meant something to me too. Then I asked him where he played. And turns out he was from the same small town as my grandparents! Hartplatz, in Manitoba."

Robyn sat motionless. After a moment, she stirred, wiped her tears and resumed tidying the van.

"He asked my name, and when I said Robyn Peters, he just closed his eyes and smiled as though, oh, I don't know... He held my hand so tight. Then he looked at me so sweetly—he looked so happy—and said, 'What's your Grandpa Peters' name? I might have played ball with him. Is it Pete, was he *Groota Peeta*?'" She took a long breath and clasped her hands, fingers entwined.

"And I was about to tell him, no, that Grandpa's name was Walter, but... it was too late. Too late."

The nurse dropped her eyes and reached out to rest her hand on Robyn's. With a small sigh, she took the form from her, unfolded it and counter-signed, her pen scratching in the silence of the ambulance interior; the needle on a record at the end of a song.

Wuatsiel...Glossary

I have tried to make the meanings of most of the *Plautdietsch,* or Low German words in this collection clear by the context in which they appear. However, if that fails and in the interest of communication, here are my interpretations of many of the *Plaut* words and phrases found in "Pinching Zwieback."

Originally an oral language familiar across parts of Europe as a common *lingua franca* of commerce and everyday life, *Plautdietsch* offers a multitude of spellings, usages, pronunciations, and inferences. Words and phrases often remain in the original High German and many other "borrow words" come from Dutch, Yiddish, and Russian/Ukrainian languages. The remarkable Grunthaler Jack Thiessen, a longtime friend of my father-in law Henry Kasper, and an occasional kind literary mentor to me in his later years, dedicated a good part of his sizable energy and IQ to creating an academically and etymologically sound *Wörterbuch.* This dictionary has been my chief resource for spellings and meanings. Where Jack T. left me without an answer, I was able to hook my cart to the caring linguistic knowledge of my friend, neighbour, and former fenestration co-worker Jack Schellenberg. Jack S. contributes the added benefit of a lifetime in Steinbach, Mb and so he represents the specialized locality of "Steinbach *Plautdietsch.*" Memoirist, author, and keen-eyed historian Ralph Friesen helped out with an edit of this glossary and more. My thanks to these skilled, good-humoured polyglots.

Other words, especially those in vogue in *Molotschna* and elsewhere upstream of the Western Canadian Mennonites in my stories, come straight out of diaries, or articles in the historical Mennonite periodical *Preservings* and other historical resources.

In some cases, the words are just as I remember them. I'm not a fluent *Plautdietsch* speaker, but I do have a good portion of my mental capacity indelibly dedicated to a thousand or so slurred *Plautdietsch* words and phrases, mostly ill-pronounced and defined in a way convenient to me. This motley lexicon serves me with pleasure and provides an ongoing connection to my expert *Plautdietsch* mother, Justina ("Jessie") Toews (nee Harder) and the numerous childhood and teenage friends who taught me—under the cover of Low German—all of the rude and vulgar things I would ever need to say. My use of *Plautdietsch* in "Pinching Zwieback" is also an important homage to the rich and expressive language that is, to this day, a living part of Mennonite culture in Canada.

Mennonite *Plautdietsch* is simultaneously beautiful and vulgar, precise and generic, flowing and guttural. The language is like the shelves of *Vogt's Economy Store* in the Steinbach of my youth: you could find anything you needed, from *Fünf Spätzle* to *sechs Maden*—provided you were willing to improvise, here and there. (And then argue endlessly about what it *really should be* later.)

—Mitchell Toews

Aufjefollna: One who has fallen off; a religious backslider.

Bazavluk: The *Bazavluk* River, located in what was in 1873 the *Borozenko* Colony in Southern Russia (now Ukraine).

Borozenko: A Mennonite colony—a grouping of settlements—in Southern Russia. (Also, *Molotschna, Chortitza.*)

Brandaeltester: (High German) A *Darp's* chief administrator of fire insurance.

Brüderthaler: One *Mennoniten Gemeinde,* or Mennonite congregation, of which there were many.

Buckweedoag: Stomach pain day; a stomach ache. (Including, but not restricted to menstrual pain.)

Chortitza: A Mennonite colony—a grouping of settlements—in Southern Russia. (Also, *Borozenko, Molotschna.*)

Darschtijch: Thirsty.

Die Owlah: The old one, God.

Die weld: The world.

Dietschlaund: Germany. An inoffensive D-word that is a commonly used substitute for *Diewel* (Devil)—much as "heck" might switch hit for "Hell." Sometimes shortened to the letter D, as in "*Oba, Deee!*" *Diestel,* the wooden yoke used with a team of oxen or horses, is another less-demonic D-word oath.

A Mennonite farmer with a hammer in one hand and a newly bloodied thumb on the other might curse, *"Diestel, Diewel, Schinda, Bädel!"* or "Yoke, Devil, mule-skinner, scoundrel!" a relatively mild oath.

Ditsied: This side, in reference to the Red River. Two land reserves were ceded to the Mennonite immigrants of 1874, one on either side of the Red River: East and West. Residents referred to their side as *"Ditsied"* or "this side" and the other side as *"Jantsied,"* literally the "other side."

Domma Äsel: dumb-ass.

Darp: village.

Denn: Thin.

Düak: headscarf; a woman's head covering.

Dutch Blitz: A fast-moving card game played in some Mennonite communities. Seen as a benign and permissible form of entertainment; a non-gambling game of chance to which the Devil is not invited.

Eins and *zwei:* (High German, as found in "Without Spot or Wrinkle") *Eins:* one and *zwei*: two.

Forsteidienst: Forest service. Specifically, the alternative, non-military work provided by conscripted Conscientious Objector Mennonites in Russia. This, and other rescinded privileges were precursors to the subsequent diasporas of Mennonites in 1874 and particularly the 1920 wave of refugee-emigrants.

Frindschauft (Frindschoft, Frintschoft): Family, relatives. Kinfolk. Lexicographer Jack Thiessen comments that *Frindschauft* also means "friendship" and that "The dialect knows no other term..." which to me suggests that early *Plautdietsch* speakers regarded kin to be kith and kith to be kin. A function of the consistent isolation from the broader societies in which they resided?

Frü: Wife.

Fünf Spätzle und sechs Maden: (High German) Five noodles and six maggots, from Jack Thiessen's Mennonite Low German Dictionary, *Max Kade Institute.*

Gelassenheit: A noun to describe the state of being when, as an act of faith; one submits to the Lord's will. Serenity.

Gierigkeit: (High German) Greed.

Goondach: Good day. A contraction of *Goodendach.*

Groota Peeta: Big Peter. With many people in the small Mennonite communities sharing similar given names and surnames, additional descriptions were often added to clarify. Big, small, thin, tall, etc.

Hartplatz: A fictitious town in South Eastern Manitoba. The word means, essentially, "hard place" and historically can also refer to cleared, rocky, flat ground where wheat was beaten to separate the ripe grain.

Hohn: Rooster. Known to be noisy at dawn or when arguing about religion.

Hund: Dog.

Hundmeed: Dog-tired.

Jantsied: The other side, in reference to the Red River. Two land reserves were ceded to the Mennonite immigrants of 1874, one on either side of the Red River. East and West. Residents referred to their side as *"Ditsied"* or "this side" and the other side as *"Jantsied,"* literally the "other side." Jack Thiessen notes the occasional use of *Jantsied* as a poetic term for Heaven.

Jauma: As in the phrase, *"Jauma, lied etj saj!"* "Misery, people, I say!" Exasperation. (A lighter reference to Dante's "vale of tears?") Jack Schellenberg points out that it might even be used in a "Can you believe it?" or a "It never rains, but pours!" manner.

Joh: Yes.

Joh-Brooda: Yes-brother; a yes-man. See also: *Schmäahmoazh.*

Jung: Boy.

Kackkunta: Kack is slang for excrement and *Kunta* is a gelding. Used together, as in "The Grittiness of Mango Chiffon," a most unique and memorable slur.

Kanadier: Two major Mennonite migrations took place, Russia to Canada. The earlier group, from 1874, were called *die Kanadier,* or Canadians. Those from the second surge, in 1920, came to be known as *Russländer,* or Russians.

Kopptijch: Headwear, caps, hats, scarves.

Kleine Gemeinde: "The small church" or "small congregation," as it came to be known at its founding in the early 19th century in comparison to the much larger church from which it separated, believing the larger body had become too worldly. In the 1950s it changed its name to The Evangelical Mennonite Conference. —courtesy of Ralph Friesen, Victoria, BC.

The Zehen family and many of the other characters are depicted in the stories as (mostly) *Kleine Gemeinde* members who arrived in Canada during the initial 1874 *Kanadier* surge.

Kleiw die: Scratch yourself. (A rude comment, dismissive and mildly vulgar.)

Kuhscheißende: (Highly evocative High German) Cowshit-filled; strong disdain!

Mejahl (Mejal): Girl.

Meksikaunische: Mexican.

Mennonitische: Mennonite.

Midje: Mosquitoes.

"*Mie hungat, mie schlungat, mie schlackat de Buck!*": From "The

Grittiness of Mango Chiffon," where it is remembered as a cruel taunt aimed at those of lesser economic standing: "I'm hungry, my tummy wants something that's yummy!"

Moazh: Ass, backside.

Molotschna: A Mennonite colony—a grouping of settlements—in Southern Russia. (Also, *Borozenko, Chortitza.*)

Morschijch (morschijch) goot: Very good. Exceptional.

Nay (Nä): No.

Nuscht: Nothing. None.

Oba: A common utterance, to add emphasis or as a stand-alone verbal schwa; meaning "Oh, but!"

Oma/Opa: (High German) Female (*Oma*)/male (*Opa*) grandparents. May be used as a familiar for all or any older individuals.

Peeta (Peta): The given name Peter. Pronounced "Pie-tuh." The common Mennonite surname Peters can be pronounced "Pie-tush."

Plautz (Plauts): Flat pie with fruit topping, baked on a pan. A *Plautz* may also refer to a village square in High German.

Rommbommle: Meander.

Rommdriewe: To wander aimlessly, perhaps for pleasure or to kill time. Thiessen: "to bum around."

Russländer: Two major Mennonite migrations took place, Russia to Canada. Those from the second, in 1920, came to be known as *Russländer,* or Russians. The earlier group, from 1874, were called *die Kanadier,* or Canadians.

Rutsch: To slide, particularly as in "bumper-shining" behind an automobile on an icy street.

Sat die dol, Jung: "Sit yourself down, boy."

Schanzenfelder: (From "Died Rich.") Individuals from the town in Southern Manitoba—Schanzenfeld, south of Winkler—said to produce an inordinate number of tall, skinny people. Hence, any tall, skinny person might be called a *Schanzenfelder.* (This interpretation is from my personal lexicon and may have been influenced by those from Chortitz, Manitoba, where people were not as tall.)

Scheen: Goodliness, loveliness. Sometimes, "refined" or "just so!"

Schinda: Literally, a flayer or mule-skinner. Once a necessary profession, but one without much sway or social esteem. (Certainly lacking in Facebook followers.) By extension, *Schinda* is a mild curse; one to which Jack Thiessen assigns some similarity to the Devil. One of my Steinbach—via Stuartburn and

Borozenko—Toews antecedents was an actual *Schinda,* and also a figurative one as he was shunned from a Mennonite church, took exception and he and his co-shunned wife sued that church in Manitoba court—a historical first. He was also a millwright (without papers), an early colonist and diarist, and later in life, a *Schusta.*

Schmäahmoazh: Greasy ass; a slippery character. (Akin to, *Schwieremoazh* or *Schwiearemoazh:* swerve-ass; unreliable.)

Schmeate: Emotional pain.

Schnoddanäs: Snotnose. A common description of a child, usually a boy. Insulting when applied to an older boy or adult, implying an untoward lack of experience.

Schoenwiese: A Mennonite *Darp* in *Chortitza* colony in Southern Russia in 1873.

Schrüwendreia: Screwdriver.

Schusta: Shoemaker. An occupation particularly well-suited to the loquacious and the opinionated (like my paternal grandfather, who was a shoemaker in Steinbach), whose clientele were forced to sit in stocking feet and wait for footwear repairs to conclude, providing a convenient captive audience for the *Schusta.*

Schwiensch: Swinish, filthy.

Späle: Play, or in the case of "Swimming in the *Bazavluk,*" playacting.

Spott: Pronounced "schputt." Mockery. Frequently playful, but occasionally like *Vaspa,* served cold.
Staut: City.

Steewele: Boots.

Süpa: Drinker or drunkard, the identity of which is often the best-known secret in the *Darp*.

Taunte: Aunt, aunty.

Tjinge: Children.

Tjnippsbrat: "Flick board;" the game of crokinole.

Tütje: A small paper sack, most often associated with a bag of goodies given to children at church on Christmas Eve.

Väavodasch: forefathers, ancestors.

Väl mol dankscheen: Very much thanks.

Vaspa: A traditional, late afternoon light meal, often served cold.

Vedaumpte groote oabeit Steewle: (As found in "Died Rich.") Damned big work (boot)."

"West du first base späle?": "Will you (do you want to) play first base?"

Willa Hund: A wild dog. Unpredictable, possibly dangerous and feared or despised, but perhaps most in need of assistance and comfort.

Winnipegsch: Fancy. Perhaps even ostentatious. Things done "the way it's done in Winnipeg!"

Zehen: (High German) Toes. Pedal digits.

Zwieback: A double bun. Perhaps no other *Plautdietsch* word can be spelled and pronounced in more ways. A cultural icon, I have chosen to spell *Zwieback* the way my parents did at Steinbach Bakery. They sold to local customers from the 1950s through to the 1970s and also to *The Bay* and *Eaton's* in Winnipeg. For simplicity, it was, and is, *Zwieback* and is pronounced with a "swee" sound and a hard "k" at the end.

Dictionary:

"MENNONITE LOW GERMAN DICTIONARY/ MENNONITISCH-PLAUTDIETSCH WöRTERBUCH", ed. Jack Thiessen, *Jantsied**, Max-Kade-Institute for German-American Studies, University of Wisconsin-Madison, Madison 2003.

Notes:

Plautdietsch nouns are capitalized in the German way. German (and other non-English language words) are shown in italics, except in the case of the book title, Pinching Zwieback. Common Mennonite surnames are capitalized, of course, but not italicized.

Some latitude has been exercised in the Glossary. Several words are included that are deemed relevant although they do not appear in the text or even elsewhere in the Glossary. These are bonus words; no extra charge. Consider them *Freiwilliges*— which I would describe as voluntary (and usually spontaneous) contributions at the end of a meeting.

*I have taken the liberty of listing the location for the late John Peter "Jack" Thiessen of Gnadenfeld, Grunthal, Gretna,

Winnipeg, Marburg (Germany), and New Bothwell, etc., as the poetically-inspired, *"Jantsied"* which I believe he would have agreed to. —Mitchell Toews

Acknowledgments

Where to start? Possibly with the novel "The Greatest Thing Since Sliced Bread" by Don Robertson. Why? Because this story, which I read as a young boy, stayed with me my whole life. The book about an explosion of fuel storage tanks in Cleveland, Ohio is recalled every time I pass by the site of the *Ert Peters Texaco Bulk Station* (now long gone, but once a symbol of impressive industrial might for younger me) in Steinbach, Manitoba. Mr. Peters' tall, silver fuel tanks used to remind me of the thrilling Robertson classic every time I was near the corner of Kroeker and Main. For 60 years and counting, I continue to be drawn back into that lovely novel. From this experience, I learned first hand the magical, enduring power of the written word.

"Pinching Zwieback" is my own attempt to outlast and outlive and offer an elegy to my life in Steinbach and places like it. It's dedicated to my beautiful children Tere and Megan, and their husbands, Tom and Blair, respectively, and their kids—my endlessly wondrous grandchildren.

Thanks to my Publisher, Matt Joudrey of *At Bay Press*, who, after a referral from Manitoba author Lauren Carter, took a chance on me. To my long-suffering wife Jan, who—in her minimalist and plain-spoken but kind way reminded me to turn the spigot off, every once in a while. Appreciation and respect goes to my superb Pinching Zwieback editors Nina McIntyre and Priyanka Ketkar and my generous and talented writing group, The Write Clicks. To my gracious pre-readers and blurb writers: Zilla Jones of Winnipeg, Ralph Friesen of Victoria (and formerly of Steinbach), and to the *oba scheen* Armin Wiebe of *die Weld*. To my writing heroes—those with sunflower seed remnants (present or ancestral, literal or figurative) in their teeth and also those without.

Thanks, also to the Town of Steinbach, where I grew up and spent more than 50 years, and where Jan and I raised our kids, in constant wonder and (sometimes) confounded observation. Steinbach and its people made me want to be a writer...

Dankscheen to slush-pile screeners, editors, judges and readers from far and wide.

Thanks as well to allies, encouragers, frank reviewers, generous Writers in Residence, and the many Facebookers and Twittering others who read, commented, gave me hope and gave me heck. Thank you all, for all you did. Special mention to my attentive sisters and my cousins (who were my first best friends), Grandma Toews, Irene from Third Street who permitted me use of a story about her lovely mother, Dave & MaryLou, Andrew & Erin, Hans (he of the gas gauge lie detector in "The Peacemongers") & Chris, Jack, Irene & Lisa, the Prosetry folks, the Manitoba Arts Council, the Manitoba Writers' Guild, the Winnipeg Public Library, *Rhubarb Magazine* and those who loved it, *Preservings* and the memory of the irrepressible Delbert Plett. To Kenny in Chilliwack who observed after reading an early story of mine, "Well, it's not awful..." and last, to my beautiful and astonishing parents, Norman "Chuck" and Jessie Toews.

Photo: Janice Toews

MITCHELL TOEWS has placed stories in 113 literary journals, anthologies and contests since 2016. A three-time Pushcart Prize nominee, Mitch was a finalist in the following major contests: The 2021 Writers' Union of Canada's Short Prose Competition for Emerging Writers, the 2022 Humber Literary Review Canada-wide Creative Nonfiction contest, the 2022 J.F. Powers Prize for Short Fiction (U.S.), and the 2023 Dave Williamson National Short Story Competition. Mitch and his wife Janice live in their 1950 cabin in Whiteshell Park. Please visit the author at Mitchellaneous.com.

OUR AT BAY PRESS
ARTISTIC COMMUNITY:

Publisher - **Matt Joudrey**
Managing Editor - **Alana Brooker**
Substantive Editor - **Nina McIntyre**
Copy Editor - **Priyanka Ketkar**
Proof Editor - **Danni Deguire**
Graphic Designer - **Matt Stevens**
Layout - **Matt Stevens and Matt Joudrey**
Publicity and Marketing - **Sierra Peca**

Thanks for purchasing this book and for supporting authors and artists. As a token of gratitude, please scan the QR code for exclusive content from this title.